Ratgirl, Song
ISBN 978-1-6...
ALL RIGHTS RESERVED
Ratgirl, Song of the Viper Copyright 2013
Gayle C. Krause
Cover Art by Fiona Jayde

This book may not be reproduced or used in whole or in part by any existing means without written permission from the publisher. Contact Noble Romance Publishing, LLC at PO Box 467423, Atlanta, GA 31146.

This book is a work of fiction and any resemblance to persons, living or dead, or actual events is purely coincidental. The characters are products of the author's imagination and used fictitiously.

BLURB:

Sixteen-year-old streetwise orphan Jax Stone is an expert at surviving in a dangerous city, where the rich have fled to the New Continent and the deadly daytime sun forces the middle class and the poor to live in sewer tunnels. But she and the other homeless must be wary of rats —the furry ones underground that steal their food and invade their shelter, and the human ones above-ground who steal their children and threaten their lives. When Jax discovers her singing has a hypnotic effect on rats and children, she uses her gift, outwitting the tyrannical mayor, to lead her brother and all the children in the dying city to safety with the help of a ragtag band of friends and a handsome stranger, who holds the secret to her past.

Dedication:
To my husband, Alyn, my chief critic and staunchest supporter.

RATGIRL
Song of the Viper
by Gayle C. Krause

"We are orphans. We use our brains and our bodies to survive. But the only things that thrive in Metro City are the rats, and not all of them are rodents."

Jax Stone

Chapter One

Whoever said the teen years were the best of a girl's life didn't come from Metro City. Hell, they can't imagine what it's like to be me, living in a sewer tunnel by day, and foraging the forest for food or scavenging through abandoned mansions at night. Anything I find that I can't use to survive this hellhole, I trade for money.

And then, there's the Megamark Guards who patrol this dying city. I avoid them at all cost. One never knows when they'll turn on an innocent person. I've seen them beat up the homeless on a wager, or for sheer entertainment. No, it's not an easy life.

We used to live in brick houses and modern apartments, but the sun's savage rays turned our lives upside down. It took a while to get used to sleeping in the day, but night, as dangerous as it is, is the only time we can venture to the surface to seek food or trade our services.

Between the vindictive Guards and the deadly daytime sun, I spend half my time surviving, and the other half planning how to. If this is the best part of my life, I might as well be dead. Only one thing keeps me alive . . . .

Shoved from behind, I topple to the potholed street, protecting the leather-bound book in my arms, and crash into a woman, with two children.

Instinctively, she grabs the closest child, but the other smashes to the curb beside me. Her auburn hair splays across the sidewalk, rivaling the red stream oozing from her forehead. Her threadbare hat lies crushed beneath her arm, next to my book. Street dust blows through its fluttering pages.

The child gazes up at me with tearful amber eyes, but doesn't cry, like she knows she must be tough to survive in this nightmare of a city.

I can tell she's dazed. "I-I'm sorry." I glance over my shoulder. "A Megamark Guard pushed me."

I try to wipe the blood from her face with the sleeve of my filthy cargo coat, but her mother whisks the child up in her arms.

"Please don't!" She doesn't sound angry, just scared. "I'll take her to the Subway Chapel. St. Sally will tend to her wound." She murmurs to the other child. "Hold on to my skirt and stay close to the buildings."

They disappear into the swarm of shabby night people.

I rub my bloody wrists on my jacket, and bend to pick up the book.

A threatening voice above me shouts, "I'll take that."

I freeze. A glance to my left reveals three Guards continuing their reign of terror down the street. They travel in pairs, so the fourth one must be behind me.

"What?" I jump up, ready to run, but he grabs my arm and spins me around.

He's not much older than I am. That can be good and bad. Good, because he doesn't know my tricks, and I can outwit him. Bad, because he's younger than the paunch-bellied assholes who hide behind the authority of the blue Megamark uniform. That means he can run faster.

Think fast, Jax. Either he gets your mother's book or you trade it for ingredients you need for Andy's birthday surprise. Hell! It's a no-brainer.

"Here, take it!" I pretend to hand him the book, which blocks his view of my feet.

One swift kick to his crotch, and he doubles over, gasping.

I run like hell. I'm halfway down the block when he yells, "Get the bitch!"

I glance back.

The others charge my way.

"Shit!" *I can outrun one, but three? I hope they don't know the hidey-holes I do.* I charge down the street, dodging the ragged inhabitants left in Metro City. Burdened by fear and hunger, few look up to see me coming.

I careen between them and the shattered crates littering the sidewalk, making a sharp right past a crumbling brick building into Scallywag Alley.

Rats dart in every direction, disturbed by the loud slapping of the Megamarks' boots on the cracked macadam behind me.

I cut right, without slowing, through a row of upturned dumpsters sitting like giant carcasses, stripped of their skin, behind an abandoned restaurant. I shoot straight up the block until the gated sewer pipe leading to the underground tunnels comes into view. The book's weight slows me down. With stuttering steps, I search for a place to stash it.

"I can come back after I lose them," I mutter. When I stop, I realize the sounds of multiple footsteps have vanished. I risk a glance behind.

One Megamark still follows me.

I push the metal gate forward with the book and slip into the curved pipe, slamming the gate behind me. The concrete block, set there by the sewer people, is perfect to jam it closed.

"Damn you, picker," he shouts. His arms flail through the iron bars. "Watch your back. You don't attack one of the Guards and get away with it."

My lips stretch into a self-affirming smirk. I splash through the stagnant water, forcing rats to scurry behind piles of crumpled plastic water bottles and food wrappers. I call over my shoulder, "Looks like I just did."

* * * * *

I exit the tunnels and make my way back to the old train station, keeping a watchful eye for the Megamark Guards. I weave between bodies in the street, careful not to step on the dead. Their cloying stench hangs in the air. Others are dead drunk, but either way, both kinds escaped this hellhole that used to be our city.

I peel the top layer of skin on my lip between my teeth, as I concentrate on finding Hoffmann. Rough-edged fingernails bite into my clenched palms, causing them to bleed more, because I go out of my way to avoid the drug dealers who slink on every corner. I hate them more than I hate the rats.

Nothing much scares me, but they do. They're planted in Metro City, as unyielding as the old trees. *I* can't make them go away. The Guards, as bad as they are, follow the Mayor's orders. These guys prey on the desperate. I'd like to find out which scumbag supplied the heroin that killed my mother.

If I could gather them all up in one fell swoop, I'd dump them in the toxic river.

At least that would stop them from tempting young boys into delivering their illicit drugs for a promised meal. Andy will never run the streets as long as I'm alive.

I pass vendors selling smoked sausages. The sickening sweet smell of char-roasted meat slathered with imitation barbeque sauce wafts through the air. Its aroma tempts the taste buds, unless one realizes the meat is rat.

The train station is only one block away. I glance up at the Guardian Angel post atop my old apartment building. I'll be safe there soon. First, I need to find Hoffmann.

I swing back and follow the dull glow of light bulbs that dimly illuminate the abandoned railway station. The homeless stand in line hoping for a chance to trade whatever family heirloom they might have left, for food.

"Hey, Jax."

I turn toward the shout.

Rafe and his gang, the Altar Boys, creep along the tracks picking up whatever food fell out of the crates unloaded for Culpepper and his City Council. It frosts my ass that fat bastard, who calls himself a Mayor, and his phony cronies get to eat wholesome food while we're lucky if we eat at all. He's nothing but a murderous tyrant. I can't waste my energy on him now. I have more important things to do here.

I wave back as I spy Hoffmann arguing with Cowboy.

The Air Caravan, packed with food from Antarctica, must have pulled into the old train station right on schedule, two hours before sunset. I'm not familiar with the caravan pilot's name, but I've dubbed him Cowboy because he wears an old-fashioned cowboy hat, like the kind I'd seen in Nonna's old magazines.

Otto Hoffmann's ability to barter is legendary. I study his tactics, as I sit cross-legged on top of a tall, abandoned rectangle that has had the wired glass panels ripped from its metal frame. I remember Nonna once telling me they called it a telephone booth. Now, it stands on the platform, a rusty relic from another time.

I try to keep my eyes on Hoffmann. He's why I came. I caress mother's book, cradled under my coat, knowing it will be the last time I feel its grandeur. When everything went digital in 2040, printed books became obsolete. Now, hardbacks are worth more than jewels, and this one was mother's favorite.

    I know Hoffmann will end up trading it to Cowboy for three times what he'll pay me. I've watched him do it with other items I scavenged from the mansions on East Knob Hill, but I need more than money from him tonight. While I wait until he finishes my eyes wander . . . to Cowboy.

    I study his every move. He's an expert in knowing what is of value in the pile of shit the street people bring to him, in hopes of a few fresh vegetables or a slab of meat not tainted with maggots or green slime, but it's more than that.

    What color lies under those extreme eye protection goggles? I wonder if his lashes are long and dark like the curls peeking below the brim of his hat. His clean-shaven face is a stark contrast to the scraggily-whiskered men of Metro City. So is his body. Where most males here are gaunt, Cowboy's T-shirt stretches like a second skin across his well-defined chest. He must spend his time in Antarctica in the gym, because he's ripped. Not like Rafe, who is the most athletic person I know. Cowboy looks like he's made of sculpted stone.

    I force air through my puckered lips. My loud whistle gets Hoffman's attention.

    He turns to see me perched on the telephone booth's metal skeleton and nods, but he's not the only one.

    Cowboy drops his goggles to his neck, and his stare locks onto mine.

My face grows hot, and not from the residual heat rising from the brick platform.

Oh, my God! My lips are puckered. I hope he doesn't think I'm blowing him a kiss!

I drop my gaze and scramble down to meet Hoffmann near the abandoned ticket counter, opening my jacket just enough for him to spot the book tucked under my arm.

His eyes bug. He escorts me to his office, the dark side of the old train station.

* * * * *

I swing back around and enter the alley to my apartment building, one block over from Main Street. Hiding in the shadows, I hug the building. Rafe camouflaged the back entrance, which no one has discovered. It appears all boarded up, like the rest of the buildings in Metro City; his street smarts protect us.

I crouch behind a recently burned-out car, where the stink of melted plastic hovers like a dense cloud. Then, I burst from my hiding spot, unfasten the fake face over the back trapdoor, and slip into the building's basement. Though it's dark inside, I know every inch of these stairwells. I spent my whole life in this building.

At four, I played *Who's Got The Button?* with the kids from the next-door apartment, advancing up the second floor steps with each correct guess.

Fourth floor reminds me of the time I raced my mother's old Slinky to the bottom of the stairs when I was seven.

Now, as I reach the sixth floor, my thoughts fill with what used to be my life. Our apartment was on this floor. My bedroom was my safe haven. I spent hours there, reading electronic books, playing cyber games and practicing my electric piano amid pink gingham curtains and ruffled bed skirts. I took my academics on the computer, but I needed a real instrument to play my music. And my mother was the best music teacher in Metro City. Sometimes she'd accompany me on her antique violin.

I reach the attic stairwell leading to the roof. Strains of Andy's laughter ring out.

Cheinstein sits in the Guardian Angel spot, a crooked baseball cap on his black, shiny hair, as out of place as I would be in high heels. He'd be more at home in a white lab coat, but that would make hiding from Culpepper and his Megamark Army impossible. If that bastard Mayor knew Cheinstein was still in Metro City, he'd lock him to a Bunsen burner and a rack of test tubes. It's best for all of us he appears to be like every other homeless street kid. He holds the binoculars I scavenged from an abandoned mansion on the east side.

Andy sits by his side, playing with a miniature toy, dump truck.

"Hey you," I say. "Where did you get that?"

Andy jumps up, runs across the flat rooftop, and throws his arms around me. Backing away, his usually mischievous eyes grow hard as blue diamonds when he spots the blood on my arm, but he doesn't panic. Like a little man, wise beyond his four-almost-five years, he asks, "Are you okay, Jax?"

"I'm fine, Andy." I wrap him in my arms, being careful not to get blood on his denim jacket. "You don't need to worry about me."

I can tell by his squint he doesn't believe me.

"Really, Andy. I'm fine."

His grimace slowly disappears until dimples shine on either side of his smile. "Okay."

He picks up the toy truck, and I pat his platinum curls.

I walk toward the Guardian Angel perch, and Cheinstein turns. "I saw the whole shoving thing. Those lousy Megamarks are plain mean. I almost called Rafe, but when you jumped up and ran I knew you were okay."

"I wouldn't have even been on Main Street when they came by if I didn't need to find Hoffmann. Sometimes he's where you least expect him."

"Did you get everything you needed?" Cheinstein's dark almond eyes roll toward Andy, preoccupied with the miniature truck.

"Thanks for asking. I did." I take the binoculars from Cheinstein. "Here, it's my turn to stand watch."

"You sure you're okay?"

"Yep." I focus the binoculars on the street below, then turn back as Cheinstein leaves.

"All right, then, I'm off. Later, little dude." He gives Andy the secret handshake they made up. Cheinstein is great with Andy, like an older brother. "I've got an experiment that's calling my name. See you guys tomorrow."

He ambles toward the roof door that leads back down through the building.

"Thanks for the truck, Beni."

Cheinstein smiles, gives Andy a thumbs-up, and then plunges into the dark stairwell.

I lift the binoculars to my eyes, focusing on the street below. "Where did Cheinstein find that truck?"

"He said it belonged to him when he was little. He found it in his father's desk drawer in the museum's office. He said I could have it."

"Good. Here, I've got something for you, too." I pull thick cylinders of yellow chalk from my coat pocket. Some are broken because of my fall. "I found these underneath corrugated iron pieces that had fallen off the bank windows. They must have slipped out of a carpenter's pocket when they boarded up the building. I thought you might like to draw with them."

"Thanks, Jax." He kisses my cheek and kneels down next to me, drawing on the sun-bleached cement roof. "You're the best sister."

I scan the street below, where I smashed into the little girl. I hope she's okay. I'll never forget her eyes. For a child, they were full of despair.

I take a deep breath, ignoring the stench from the Elan River on the south side of Metro City. Somehow, some way, I'm going to get Andy out of here, and we'll never look back. I don't want him to lose his childhood in this hellhole. They all do.

"Hey, Jax, look what I'm drawing." Andy points toward the concrete slab near my feet where he draws three stick figures, a perfect picture of his family. Not like the family I grew up with, but it's the only one he's ever known, a family of orphans.

The tall one, Astoria, has curlicues for hair and she wears a triangle skirt. The one in the pants and boots is me. Next to me stands a square with wheels, a shopping cart. Andy's the small guy in the middle, with his hands connected to ours.

"Good job, Andy." I wink. "I especially like my boots."

He jumps up. "I'm done drawing. Now, can I have a turn, Jax? P-l-e-a-s-e! Let me look."

His thin finger pokes my shoulder.

"Not yet, Andy. I need to keep an eye out for Astoria. I'll let you use them when she's home safe." I search for her tattered streamer fastened to the corner streetlight.

Tied in a bow, it means Astoria has a customer. Dangling bowless from a knot, it means she's wandering the streets looking for one. And if it's gone, Astoria has finished her appointments and is headed home — to the sewers.

Andy pokes me again. "Can you find me a pair of my own the next time you go picking?"

I turn. Andy's innocent blue eyes shine hopeful for such a tiny favor. It isn't fair he should be in a world where children fight rats for food or snuggle in dirty rags they call beds.

"I can't promise I'll find a pair like these. After five years, the other pickers already scavenged most everything of any value, but I'll try. Maybe Cheinstein has an extra pair of big binoculars, in the museum, he'll let you have."

"You think so?" Andy's eyes grow wide. "Can I go ask him now?"

"No. He'll be at your birthday dinner, tomorrow. You can ask him then. Now, do me a favor and go down and play in the apartment."

"But there's nothing to do there," he whines. Then, a mischievous glint sneaks into his eyes. "Can I look at the pictures in your special book?"

"It's too hard for you to get it out of its hiding place. Tell you what. Before we leave tonight, I'll get the book and we can bring it home. I'll read a story to you at bedtime. We can look at the pictures, together." I sweep him up in my arms, as if my embrace can protect his innocence. "Deal?"

Andy squeezes me in a fierce hug and then wriggles free, bouncing on his feet.

"Deal." He bounds toward the rooftop door that leads to the sixth-floor apartment. "I'll wait for you on the pretty rug."

It never ceases to amaze me how Andy gets excited over the simplest things. But then again, he has nothing to compare his happiness to.

With Andy's departure, I'm left alone on the roof to eat the cup of cold stew Cheinstein saved for me for dinner. It's more like brown water with bits of boiled chipmunk floating in it, flavored with spruce needles.

The stars twinkle above me, as if I should be in a happily-ever-after world, a place where life is normal, like it used to be. That would be awesome. Unrealistic as hell, but awesome, just the same.

My mind wanders to an old song Nonna used to sing to me when I was a child, something about a world over the rainbow. Glancing out over a dark Metro City, silhouetted by even darker skies, I recall the words. After swallowing the last mouthful of stew, I sing Nonna's rainbow song softly. It's wishful thinking.

I turn to place the empty cup on the roof and flinch. Two dozen rats crouch behind me, with cocked heads and beady eyes. They stare at me as if they're contemplating whether they should attack. The leader lurches toward me, and the rest follow.

Chapter Two

"Stupid rats!" I jump at them and they scurry away. The damn rodents are everywhere. With three-fourths of the population gone in the mass exodus to the New Continent, there are now more rats than people here. Someday, I don't know when or how, I'm going to take Andy away from this rat-infested hellhole. Antarctica may as well be that world over the rainbow because it's so far away. They say crops grow plentiful and children actually play outside in the warm daytime sun.

"Keep dreaming, Jax," I mutter.

I'd love to play catch with Andy in the park, but that will never happen here. Too many minutes in the sun, and third degree burns sear our skin. Any longer length of time, and our organs cook.

A deep sigh escapes my lips. Mourning things that never will be, I check the antique watch my grandmother gave me when I was seven. It hangs around my neck, hidden beneath my stained T-shirt.

Dawn will break soon. Astoria's work should be ending. I don't know how she does it, subjecting herself every night to strangers. At seventeen, she's the youngest nightwalker in Metro City. She's in demand especially with the Megamark Guards. They know they can approach her for sexual favors, because her skirt marks her as a prostitute. Any female who does not practice the trade wears pants.

Astoria may be only one year older than I am, but she's as desperate as she is beautiful. Nightwalking is her only means of survival.

I observe other nightwalkers barter their favors, and muscle-bound brutes sell protection from the Megamarks. Farther down the street, where the electricity has been cut off for years, old men stand around fire pits burning wood from the abandoned buildings, more to see each other than to keep warm.

I scan the decrepit cityscape below. My gaze falls upon the Air Caravan parked at the train station. In the dim glow, Cowboy still meets with the homeless. A stirring in my gut makes me want to touch him. I wonder if his arms, sculpted with muscle, are as hard as they look, but I force my eyes back to Astoria's ribbon.

From now on, I'm going to trade my finds myself. The others do. I just need to be all business. No room for daydreaming. That's over the rainbow territory. I have to put it in perspective. Bartering directly with him, I'll get the higher price, and I can add it to Andy's hope jar. Once we get enough money to book passage to Antarctica, we're out of here.

"Yeah, Jax," I mumble, "and it won't hurt that maybe you'll actually get to talk to Cowboy."

I spot Astoria untying the streamer.

She tucks it into her skirt pocket and heads toward the park at the edge of the city. She passes soldiers who harass the vendors.

One watches her saunter down the street. He nods her way, in a polite greeting. *This is something new. A soldier being nice to a nightwalker, in public?*

The other soldiers ignore her, too busy chasing vagrants from stoops and street corners. One poor vendor spreads his arms out on the ground, a bootheel in his back, while soldiers help themselves to his hot kettle corn. When they're through, they knock down his garbage can stove, sending his cast-iron cauldron clanging into the street and spewing cherished popped corn to the dirty pavement.

The rats will feast before the deadly sun peeks over the horizon.

Bile stings the back of my throat. The soldiers have enough to eat. They don't need to steal the street people's meager treat.

Astoria turns the corner safely, and I loosen my stranglehold on the binoculars. Tucking them into my jacket, I cross the roof to inspect the acorn bread dough rising under an old dishtowel. It lays on a piece of slate, heated by the day's sun. I punch it down, then roll it into a square with a water-filled wine bottle. I think of Nonna and her words of wisdom.

"Jax, you need to rely on yourself. The coming years will be a test of survival, and those who aren't prepared will suffer. I may not be around to protect you, but I can ensure you won't starve. You see these acorns?" She held up a handful that had fallen from a gnarled oak near her cottage at the lake. "They make a palatable, protein-enriched bread. Not many know the secrets of the oak. Soak them for several days until the tannins leach out. Change the water each day, until it turns from black to clear. Then dry them and grind them into flour. If you follow my advice, you'll be fine. While others depend on the Corporation for food, you look to the forest to sustain you."

When the city dwellers scrabble over roadkill or moldy cheese, Andy and I head to the park to gather acorns, black locust flowers, and wild chokecherries. Almost everything I need to keep us alive grows sparingly above the sewer we call home.

No one else I know in Metro City is aware food comes from the old oaks that line the park entrance, although it won't be long before the trees stop producing. We've got to be gone before that happens.

"Thank you, Nonna," I whisper.

Once I flatten the dough, I search my pockets for two teabag-sized packets. One contains the scarce spice, cinnamon, and the other a scant amount of brown sugar. I drove a hard bargain with Hoffmann, trading my mother's copy of *Gone With the Wind* for the yeast, spice, and sugar. I even convinced him to include a packet of raisins, and to convince the Barter King to throw in something extra, I must be pretty persuasive myself.

    I made the right decision, selling something Mother cherished to make Andy happy. If she were living, she would have done the same. After all, she'd sold herself into a life of prostitution just to keep Andy and me alive.

    I sprinkle the sweet ingredients on the meager flour paste, roll the dough, then slide it into the solar oven Cheinstein made from mirrors I scavenged. I smile. *What would we do without him? He's more than a genius. He can turn scraps of obsolete machines into viable tools to help us survive.*

    I bound down the steps after Andy, confident the sun will bake the bread. It will be warm and crusty by tomorrow night, in time for Andy's birthday feast. That is, if sweetened paste dried by the intense sun, wild onions, and overly chlorinated water can be called a feast.

    The apartment door stands ajar, but it doesn't matter. Someone stole the lock years ago. The whole building is abandoned, just like most of the others in downtown Metro City. Some have fallen into such disrepair they literally crumble to the street. Huge piles of plaster and worn bricks block sidewalks. Other buildings, tagged with gang graffiti, have holes torn in the walls where thieves pilfered the copper piping. The whole city looks like a war zone and in a way, it is. The poor are fighting to survive.

    This was my home, where I'd lived with my mother before the nightmare began. I find comfort being in a place where I once knew love. It holds no special bond for Andy, but he's safe here when I'm on Guardian Angel Duty.

Andy kneels on the stained and ripped Oriental rug, now half of what it used to be because Rafe needed a bed he could move quickly from place to place. As leader of the Altar Boys, he's an expert at dodging the Megamark Guards.

The tea light on the floor next to Andy casts his shadow, huge and ominous, on the bare, cracked plaster wall, as he plays with something.

The floor groans beneath my boot, where Rafe patched the rotted board with a flattened piece of tin.

Turning, Andy asks, "Please? Can I keep him?"

"Who?" I search for a stray cat or a starving puppy left alone after its master died in the savage streets.

Andy slowly scoots to one side.

A white rat with a black face and pink ears begs before him, a forepaw waving in the air.

Andy shares his last piece of dried olive bread with it.

"Shoo, get out of here." I stomp my foot and shake my fingers toward the long-tailed rodent.

The rat jerks its head at the sound. Its eyes widen, one red and one black, and it turns in the opposite direction, hesitant to leave its promised treat.

"Don't hurt him," cries Andy. "He's my friend."

"Rats are not your friends!" I cross my arms.

"This rat is different, Jax. He even has a name," says Andy. "I call him Squeakers, because he squeaks when he talks to me."

"Don't be silly. He squeaks because that's what rats do before they bite you."

"Squeakers won't bite me. Watch."

My breath catches in my throat.

Andy places his finger near the rat's twitching nose.

"Don't!" I jump to protect him.

Squeakers scurries to a dark corner, beneath an empty bookcase.

"You scared him away."

"Good, 'cause you're not supposed to play with rats." I stand with my hands on my hips. "They're our enemy. They compete with us for what scraps of food we find in the streets and whatever hidey-holes we use to shelter us from the sun."

"There's no one else to play with, and besides, he follows me wherever I go. He's my pet. Look, I'll show you something, but you have to promise you won't scare him again."

I bite down on my lip to keep calm.

Andy sings the lullaby I sing to him each morning. I cross my arms. Each finger flexes, itching to capture the unpredictable rat.

Little by little, Squeakers creeps from his hiding place and perches on his hindquarters, sitting up to beg like a dog. Andy rewards him with a bread crust.

"Now, roll over, Squeakers." He moves his hand in a circular motion.

I can't help but chuckle. The stupid rat rolls over on its back and then jumps up on its feet. Andy promptly gives him the last of the olive bread.

I shove my hands into my pockets, and pace the floor. My gut tightens. I hate to deny him. He asks for so little.

"Okay, you can keep him, but you must promise me you'll feed him scraps you find, not food I give to *you* to eat."

"How will I get him home?" Andy tilts his head. His scrunched platinum eyebrows are barely visible in the candlelight, but his voice reveals his excitement.

"Wait here. I'll be right back." I light an emergency candle I keep in the corner of the empty bookcase and carry it into a bedroom at the back of the apartment. The broken bed frame lays in pieces on the floor. Someone has taken the dresser, and with Rafe's help, I'd moved the mattress into our sewer tunnel so Andy and I could have a comfortable place to sleep.

Tucked in the shadows of the closet, back beyond sight of the open door, stands a trunk. It isn't very big, but it holds my most prized treasures. They're safe here, since no one can roam through the building in the intense heat of the day, and we're here every night.

I kneel before the trunk and place the candle on the floor. Once again, I pull out my chain with Nonna's watch. A skeleton key dangles next to it. I open the locked chest. The pleasant aroma of cedar tickles my nose.

Inside are testimonials to my life—a framed photograph of me, my mother, and my Nonna at her cottage in the country, and a locket my mother gave me when I was five. One side holds her picture, the other, a picture of Nonna. A silver disc of songs and a geisha fan from *Madame Butterfly* are the only tokens I have from my father. I close my eyes and clutch the fan to my chest.

He'd sent them before he died in a plane crash, flying from Australia to Japan on a world tour of *Carmen*. By then, Culpepper had already taken over Metro City and he confiscated or destroyed any form of computer or electronic device. I never got to hear my father sing, but Mother often told me stories about him. Though they never married, she named me after him, the famous, opera-singing Emilio Vito Jacaruso, thus the name Jax. They'd met at the European Music Conservatory before most of the planet became hell.

No one knows who Andy's father is. My mother never talked about her early days as a nightwalker, but I'm sure he was one of her customers. My guess would be Anderson is his last name, because that's Andy's first name. We both use my mother's surname, Stone.

I hear Andy coaxing the rat out from its hiding place, and my thoughts return to Squeakers, as much as I hate rats.

I lovingly place my geisha fan back into the trunk and remove a gilded cage that looks like a Japanese teahouse. It once held Nonna's sweet-singing canaries. It would make a perfect home for Squeakers.

Before I relock the chest, I remove Nonna's special book. Inside is a dried, yellow rose from her grave. Memories blossom each time I touch the petals. Nonna read me a different story each night as we snuggled under the hand-sewn butterfly quilt she made for my bed at her cottage, but that's not the reason I cherish it.

There are no books in Metro City anymore. Culpepper, and the Corporation, destroyed them all when they took over five years ago. Books, and everything else they could get their hands on. No Internet. No phone service. No schools and no churches. Anything that would bring the people information is forbidden.

When Mother lost her teaching job, Nonna said to her, "Of course the scoundrel closed the schools. It's easier to control the ignorant. Join with me, daughter. My friends and I will see him gone."

I clench my teeth at the thought of the Corporation's leader, Sylvanis A. Culpepper, self-appointed Mayor and dictator. My hatred for him will eat me alive if I don't let it go. I've learned to control the feeling since Mother died. It doesn't pay to strike out against Culpepper. Anyone who does ends up dead, or worse.

I suck in a deep breath and dart back to Andy.

"If you can get him into this, it can be his house." I force my smile into a wary grin.

"Yay!" Andy jumps up. His sudden movement sends Squeakers scurrying to the bookcase again.

I pass the shattered mirror, hanging lopsided on the wall, adjacent to the bookcase, as I help him find his pet rat. I can't help but notice how my appearance has changed. The healthy glow of my tanned skin has paled. I release my tight ponytail and my dried blonde hair hangs to my waist like dull wisps of jagged straw that surround my stone-chiseled face, harder and stronger than a few years ago. But my amber eyes reflect determination six-fold from the six jagged mirror pieces.

I will not let Sylvanis Culpepper and his league of City Council assholes defeat me. Andy and Astoria depend on me to survive. In some ways, so do Cheinstein and Rafe.

"Got him." Andy's triumph echoes through the empty apartment, breaking my thoughts. I snap back to attention, stuff Nonna's book into my backpack, then grab Andy's hand. With claws wrapped around a brass wire, Squeakers clings to the side of the birdcage swinging in Andy's other hand.

We make our way down the stairs from the sixth floor to the boarded basement door. I lift the bolt that secures the door from the inside, then push it forward so Andy can sneak out. I duck through the same opening and slip the camouflaged door back into place. Rafe has disguised all of the entrances we use; my old apartment building, Cheinstein's museum, Astoria's pleasure parlor, and of course, the part of the sewer tunnels Andy, Astoria, and I call home.

As soon as we're in the alley, we notice the street crowds have thinned. The pink dawn creeps over the horizon like a silent killer. Already, heat waves ripple through the air. Vendors close down their carts. The homeless and poor disappear to wherever they hide during the day.

Andy, Squeakers, and I sneak home through Municipal Park.

Six feet from our manhole cover, I hear its familiar grating sound, as it slides open.

"Hide." My voice is a worried whisper. I point to a scrub oak bush strangled by a wild grapevine.

Andy doesn't need a second warning. He's known danger his whole life and recognizes it in my tone. He and Squeakers dart behind the bush.

I jump behind a large oak tree on the other side of the path where I have a perfect view of the dark figure exiting our home.

Chapter Three

I place my finger on my lips for silence.

Andy knows he should stay put. He hunches lower, hiding in the bush's camouflage.

The trespasser, dressed all in black from his hoodie to his boots, starts down the bicycle path toward the river.

I step from behind the tree.

"Hey, buddy." One hand is on my hunting knife, the other on my hip. "What business do you have at this end of the city?"

It's past daybreak. The electric grid is powering down after running on half capacity for three hours, the daily allotment Culpepper allows the city each night. The dim glow of the sputtering streetlight a few feet away stretches my shadow across the path to the lopsided manhole cover, making me appear larger than I am.

The intruder stops in his tracks and spins around. "Jax?"

I relax my shoulders.

"Rafe? What are you doing here? And why are you dressed all in black?" I amble toward him. "It's okay, Andy. You can come out. It's only Rafe."

Rafe stands, hands shoved deep in his pockets. The faint sparkle of a silver earring reflects against his dark skin.

Awkward tension changes the tone in his voice.

"Um, I, ah, visited with Astoria." He leans toward me to explain further. "I walked her part way home. Ya know. I wanted to see if she needed anything before the sun rose."

My arching eyebrows ask more than my question. "And did she?"

"Nope. She's all right." Rafe's eyes focus on his combat boots. "The Boys and I had a busy night, tagging. That's why the black."

He unties his tight skullcap. Its indentation in his wiry dark curls is apparent. "Harder for the damn military to spot us. At least when the people see the oak leaf, they know there's help to be found." He waves goodbye. "I'll see you guys tomorrow. Hey, check out my work over on Park Avenue."

"Yeah, Rafe. You're a real Picasso." I tease him in spite of the fact that he *is* a good artist; always has been, ever since we fought over the green paint in Day School when we were four.

"'Bye, Rafe," shouts Andy, waving. "Don't forget my birthday."

"Not a chance, dudenik." Rafe takes off. He stops mid-stride and glances over his shoulder. "Oh, by the way, I installed something new at your doorway." His chin lifts. "Ya know, for protection. Hope you like it." He walks two steps more and yells back, "Tori does."

"Who's Tori?" asks Andy, his face a puzzled grimace.

"I think it's Rafe's nickname for Astoria." I slide the manhole cover wide enough for Andy to slip through. "Why don't you ask her?"

Andy climbs down the iron rungs beneath the cover while I manipulate it closed with the help of a crowbar secreted on the ledge. We tiptoe through the concrete tunnel, past bodies wrapped in assorted blankets and sleeping bags, trying not to disturb them.

A small number of homeless venture this far, to the edge of the city, and I've come to consider them neighbors, nomadic as they may be. A mangy dog sniffs my feet, probably hoping for food.

We live where two sewer tunnels merge. It was the place where the water from the south side of town met the drains from the east side, when the plumbing in the houses above street-level worked. Now, it's just miles and miles of worn brick tunnels. Here, the main sewer structure is reinforced with several concrete arches in a row.

Pride and accomplishment filled me as our home, behind the arches, took shape. Rafe and the Altar Boys helped me cover two of the three arches with tattered, plastic tarps, more for privacy than security. We attached rusted gates from the cemetery behind the tarps for that. In the middle arch, we installed a makeshift wooden door, made from the top section of a park picnic table. We fronted it with a barred grill, once a wrought iron gate from an East Knob driveway.

Cinderblock steps rise to the door because the tunnel space is higher than the sewer floors, a good thing if the toxic Elan River slips past the brick retaining wall along its southern banks during a severe thunderstorm.

Global warming has brought numerous hurricanes, and more often than not, the sewer floors are wet and mucky. But not ours.

A flickering light glows behind the blue plastic windows, casting strange, dancing reflections on the concrete supports outside our door. Astoria is already home, but I wonder why a dog's water bowl sits on the bottom stair. *Did some patron pay her with a puppy? We don't need another mouth to feed.*

I step over the bowl to tap the door through the barred grill with the secret signal. A vicious-sounding dog barks on other side.

Andy jumps behind me, clutching my legs so tightly he almost knocks me over.

Squeakers clings to the inside of the cage, tilting toward the sewer floor in Andy's clenched grasp.

Wide-eyed, Andy peeks out from behind my thighs. "Why is a big dog in our house?"

The deadbolt clicks, and I shrug. "I don't know." I wonder the same thing.

The secondary wooden bolt slip across its latches and the creaky door opens.

I expect a growling Doberman to charge us. Instead, we're greeted by Astoria, her dark eyes shining and her long, black ringlets jostling each other over the patched satin wedding dress she wears for business, the dress she'll never wear for real.

Candlelight behind her gleams on the worn red brick tunnel of our humble dwelling, the bricks' façade eroded by the constant flow of water from years past.

The comforting smell of coffee greets us, too. Andy's taut muscles relax and he marches up the steps. "Where did the big dog go?"

"Yes, where did it go?" I remove Nonna's book from my knapsack and place it on the torn leather desk chair I'd scavenged from one of the businesses downtown.

Astoria's laugh fills the tunnel.

"It's not real." She removes the dented coffeepot from the small brazier in the center of the room, as she points to a mini-megaphone attached to the crude bookshelf near the door.

I inspect the wires streaming to the top shelf where a box flashes a yellow light.

"Rafe asked Cheinstein make this for us," says Astoria. "It's a motion-detector electronic dog powered by solar packs. It will deter trespassers when we're not here."

"And alert us when we are." I throw my knapsack on Astoria's boudoir bench, and plop myself in the pillow-filled hammock that passes as our couch. "Good idea."

"Rafe's always thinking of ways to keep us safe," says Astoria. She hands me a chipped cup of coffee.

"Yes, he is." I can't hide my knowing grin as I swing on the hammock. It's Astoria Rafe cares most about. His life's goal is to protect her. He's loved her since grade school, even though she's one year older.

"Mmm, the coffee smells yummy, Tori," says Andy.

Astoria turns. Her full lips fall open. The sudden flush of her cheeks highlights the red in the multi-colored tattoo that runs down her right arm. "Who told you to call me that?"

"Nobody. Rafe calls you that so I'll call you that, too." Andy's lips break into a grin. "I like it."

"Okay, then. Do you want coffee? I've added crushed hazelnuts to yesterday's grinds."

"Yes, please." Andy rushes to his wobbly chair at the round table in the center of the brick room, hauling his legs up under him. The discarded wire-rope construction spool makes a perfect dining table. He looks to both sides, under the patched scrap tablecloth Astoria made, and then places Squeaker's cage on the floor beside his chair.

Across the room, a scented candle burns in the socket of the Victorian prism lamp from an abandoned hotel. Its light reflects off the patchwork curtain Astoria sewed to cover the ugly blue plastic and metal bars. She'd inherited her abuela's sewing skills, and her sense of color gives the tunnel a homey feeling.

Books fill three old, wooden peach crates, stacked atop each other. Some books belonged to my mother, and some I'd taken from the abandoned library.

"Hey, I saw one of the soldiers gawking at you tonight. His gaze followed you down the street."

Again, color rises in Astoria's cheeks.

"It was Alder." Suddenly, she spins like a schoolgirl, giddy.

This explains the twinkle in her eye. "And? What makes him so special?"

"He's paid me every night for the past two weeks. And, well," she rolls her eyes Andy's way. "We mainly just talk."

"What else do you do?" asks Andy, blowing on his coffee to cool it down.

Astoria glances at me, wide-eyed, as if to say, *what shall I tell him?*

"We . . . . We play games." She stares at the cup she poured for herself so she won't have to face Andy's searching eyes.

"Like the games I play with Cheinstein?" Andy buries his nose in the oversized cup. He slurps his coffee.

"Something like that," I sputter. "Let's go. Time for bed." I set my mug down on the table, and gather Andy up in my arms.

"Let mine cool," I say over my shoulder. "I'll drink it after Andy is asleep."

A dressing screen, made of pieces of quilts I'd found in a church basement, walls off the far corner of the cavernous tunnel room. The ladies of the church quilted every Wednesday, and this one was left, still stretched on the frame, when Culpepper closed the church. It reminds me of Nonna's cozy quilts, like the butterfly one that hangs from the pipes behind my mattress to hide the calcium-crusted brick wall.

Our makeshift bed, raised on abandoned construction palettes, is high and sturdy. A stool sits next to my side and a thick, three-wicked, Christmas candle gives plenty of light for bedtime reading.

After the story, Andy pores over Nonna's special book. He especially likes the picture of the boy climbing the giant's beanstalk.

"I'm not afraid of the giant," he declares. "I'm not afraid of anything." He tightens his small muscles, showing his defiance to all things evil.

I smile. *A boy after my own heart. It must be in our blood.*

"That's enough bravery for this morning," I whisper, stroking his curls. "Come on. Time to close your eyes."

Andy kisses me, and snuggles down to sleep embracing the book. His face rests on my lap.

I sing him Nonna's bedtime lullaby.

"*Close your sleepy eyes. Come rest your weary head.*

You will be safe in your comfy, cozy bed.
I will protect you. Sleep without a care,
and know by my love that I always will be there."

His soft, even breaths suggest he's asleep before I reach the last verse. But Andy's breathing is not the only thing I hear.

Scuffling and soft thuds reverberate in the tunnel, on the other side of the tarp, and scraping sounds rustle in the pipe above my head.

A quick glance at Squeakers, sealed in his birdcage, confirms the noise isn't coming from him, although he's sitting up and listening, too. I usually encounter rats at twilight when I wander through abandoned houses looking for valuables I can trade for money or goods. They scratch and twitter. This has to be a rat! The damn rats are everywhere. Some say they've even witnessed the bigger ones fight with starving dogs over a scrap of food. Others blame the rats for killing the feral cats that stalk them. But the worst news is, they've taken to attacking helpless babies as they sleep. Though there are not that many babies in Metro City, leave it to the rats to find them.

Word on the street is, rats bit Culpepper's own child. And an army of rats overran his wife as she tried to protect the baby. Astoria heard they died from rat bites, but no one knew for sure.

Rodents must know they don't stand a chance around me. I chase any rat that crosses my path, and if they're bold enough or stupid enough to come back, I smash them in the street beneath cinderblocks left scattered from collapsed buildings. But this rat isn't in the street. He's in our home. Well, technically, we're in his.

Sharp teeth gnaw through the copper patch on the sewer pipe above and a furry body squeezes through the narrow opening. He perches on the lip of the tunnel wall, sitting up like Squeakers, listening to me sing, as if he can understand my words. I can't move to attack him because Andy's head is in my lap.

The black rat stares at me with beady dark eyes, seemingly mesmerized by my song. When I stop singing, he sits there like he's waiting for another.

My gaze is drawn to Andy, sleeping peacefully, his head on my lap. Then I glance back at the caged rat. So far, Squeakers has been the model prisoner, er, pet, but if he so much as nips at Andy's finger, he's dead meat.

I'm not taking any chances. I can't have that black rat creeping down to bite Andy as he sleeps. I maneuver out from under Andy's head. Nonna's storybook thuds to the floor.

Andy stirs, but he rolls over, still asleep.

I cover him with the sheet Astoria patched and stoop to pick up the book, ironically open to a page with a child saying bedtime prayers. I remember the last time I read that page. My tearstains are still visible. I slump to the floor, cradling the book. Eyes closed, I rest my forehead on the book's spine. Tears well again. I'll never forget the sinking feeling that coursed through me the night we found Nonna, six years ago . . . .

I press my hand to my stomach to push away the nausea that sweeps through my gut at the thought of Nonna's death.

Mother and I hiked by moonlight to visit her. By the time we got there, the sky sparkled like diamonds, but Nonna didn't answer the cottage door. Thinking she was napping, I dashed inside to wake her, but she wasn't in her bed.

We found her in the garden, slumped over a basket of radishes, black dirt still clinging to their shriveled skins.

Mother, stoic and steely-eyed, gently laid Nonna on the ground between the garden furrows.

"She must have had a heart attack," was the only thing she said, even though red, bumpy rat bites covered Nonna's swollen arms.

By the time we finished burying her, the sun appeared over the horizon. Mother transplanted a yellow rose bush onto Nonna's grave. Teary-eyed, I read this poem:

"Now I lay me down to sleep.
I pray the Lord my soul to keep.
If I should die before I wake,
I pray the Lord my soul to take."

Astoria's voice at the dressing screen brings reality crashing down on my sadness. "Your coffee is getting cold. Is Andy asleep?"

I quickly wipe my eyes and hide my face from Astoria. "I'll be there in a minute."

I inspect the pipe, where the rat had been.

He's gone.

I make a reminder to look for another scrap of copper on my next picking expedition, to plug the hole. I turn, tuck the book under Andy's pillow, and join Astoria in the center of the room.

"I can tell you were crying." She hands me my coffee. "Do you want to talk? You know it's okay to cry. You don't have to be tough in front of me."

She hugs me and rubs my back in tiny circles, like Nonna used to when I was sad. Since Astoria is taller than I am, my face fits perfectly on her shoulder. Her cheap perfume comforts me. At least it's something I can count on every day, as strong and steady as her friendship.

We sit at the table and my story pours out. "I just realized something about my grandmother's death I was too young to understand then. I always thought the rats killed her, but something my mother said was odd. So was her behavior. She hadn't even paid attention to the rat bites."

Astoria cocks her head. "You think it was something else?"

"Or someone else." I sit up, recalling memories I'd long since buried, along with Nonna. "She was dead in her garden at the lake a long time before we found her. I asked my mother where Nonna's friends were. She didn't answer me, like she didn't hear me. All she said was, we'll leave a note for Thaddeus and Daphne. But they were Nonna's best friends. They had tea with her every Friday night. Why didn't they find her?"

Astoria sips her coffee. "Maybe they were away."

"Or maybe they were dead, too. Now, as I think of it, we didn't have time to go find Thaddeus, even though his cabin was close by. We barely had enough time to make it to the cave before the sun blasted down on us."

"What cave?" Astoria's head tilts. "I thought you were at the lake."

"After we buried Nonna, we started back to Metro City, but mother's gaze settled on the pink sky in the east. She said we'd never make it back, so she grabbed my hand and pulled me toward the mountain at the end of the lake, behind Nonna's cottage. She said she used to play there as a child."

    I draw a rough sketch on the tabletop with Andy's chalk. "She said it was once lush with oak trees and towering pines, but even six years ago, global warming already took its toll. The growing daytime heat was too much for their root system on the dry mountainside, because everything ran down to the lake.

    "Nonna and her friends planted trees from a tropical climate, hoping they would have a better chance to survive, and some did. So when I climbed with my mother, instead of tall oaks, small olive trees stretched like windblown hands across the cliff side. The sun was rising higher, and we were only halfway up the mountain. Just past the olive trees, the sun's full heat blasted us, burning our skin. Sweat trickled down our faces and under our arms, and my heart felt like it was about to explode."

    Astoria shifts in her chair, clearly uncomfortable. "It sounds horrendous."

    I grasp my coffee cup, tension building in my fingers. "Each step became harder, each breath more shallow. Mother pushed me from behind until the mouth of the cave was in sight. Then, with one last effort, we tumbled into the cool darkness. We never saw Nonna's friends again."

    "Maybe they went to Antarctica, like everybody else."

    "Or maybe they were given something to make them all die of a heart attack, too. No one questioned when all of the Ecos died within weeks of each other, all of supposed heart attacks."

"You mean the Earth lovers? Your grandmother was one of those environmentalists?" Astoria's eyebrow arches. She whispers, "I don't think they *all* died."

I squint, tilting my head. "How do you know that?"

"Rafe told me St. Sally used to be an Eco, and she came back to the city to help the poor grow roof gardens and recycle water. She lived with the poor and became one of them."

I sip my warm coffee. "Instead of her getting them out of their desperation, they sucked her into it."

"Rafe says her heroin habit is making her mad, but she's the closest thing the street orphans have to a mother."

I think back to my run-in with the little girl. "I had an accident today with a child, and her mother took her to St. Sally to care for her wound."

"That's because she was a nurse and a nun before she came to Metro City." Astoria swallows a mouthful of coffee. "Why would someone so intelligent allow herself to become a heroin addict?"

I suck in a deep breath and stop myself from glaring at my best friend. *How could she say that? Her, of all people!*

After Culpepper closed down the schools, my mother fell into the nightwalker trade. Astoria knew my mother had no choice. She had two young mouths to feed, and she lasted only three years before a heroin needle ended her hell. Andy was two; I was fourteen. "We all have to do what we have to do to survive. Maybe it makes her life easier to bear."

In an instant, Astoria's eyes drop. She stutters a soft-spoken apology. "I-I'm sorry. I wasn't thinking."

I'd met Astoria through my mother. She was Astoria's street mother, always protecting her, thanking God it wasn't me she had to protect from the vultures who preyed on young girls. Astoria and I bonded over our shared loss and adopted each other as family.

By now, my hazelnut coffee is lukewarm, but I savor the taste. "We've got to find a way out of here or we'll all end up dead like my mother and grandmother, or at the very least, like St. Sally."

"We're doing okay with what I earn at the pleasure parlor and the money you get from Hoffmann."

"I just told Andy tonight, the picking is getting harder. When the richies fled Metro City, I used to find antiques, jewelry, and old books, but no matter where I looked, the rats beat me to the food. I'd find rat's nests in kitchen cupboards and abandoned closets. One was even in a mink coat on the East side."

"That's the swanky side of town. Surely, things are still left in their carriage houses they never thought to take with them."

I shake my head, as I gulp cold coffee. "I've searched through most of the abandoned houses up there. Hoffmann's taken everything I offer him. The other person who's interested in what I find is Cheinstein, and then only to invent things we all can use. It's getting tough out there."

"Well, I don't want to alarm you, but it's about to get tougher. Culpepper's kid's death, last week, sent him over the edge. He's crazy. Word on the street is, he's decreed Metro City's vermin must be destroyed, but St. Sally says he's not just talking about rats."

Astoria's narrow eyes betray her fear.

I bolt upright in my chair, clenching my cup, as if it were Culpepper's neck. "What do you mean? What does St. Sally know?"

Chapter Four

Andy is the first one up in the late afternoon.

"Happy Birthday to me," he sings. He feeds Squeakers a piece of rotten apple.

"Yes, Happy Birthday to you, Anderson Stone." I smile at his effervescence. I pull a small bundle from my cargo pocket as water boils on the old refrigerator grill in the fire bowl for breakfast mush. "It's hard to believe you're five already."

Andy's eyes grow wide. "What is it? What is it?"

"It's one of your birthday presents. I thought I'd give it to you now." I set the burlap-covered gift before him. "You'll get others tonight at your party."

Andy rips off the jute and unwraps the crude cloth.

"This is a timepiece like yours, Jax!" Unable to sit still, he turns the man's antique mechanical watch over in his palm until he finds the button that pops the cover open.

"What kind of numbers are these?" He traces one with his fingertip. "I've never seen these before."

The Roman numerals stand out against the round, white face of the pocket watch. Inside the cover, is a faded photograph of a smiling woman with a rose behind her ear. The pink rose highlights her blonde hair and rosy lips.

Andy's finger wanders to the photograph. "Who is this pretty lady?"

"Our mother. I've kept her picture in my locket all these years. Now, I'm giving it to you, so you can always know how pretty she was. It fits perfectly into that old watch, and Cheinstein can help you learn the numerals. It's very old, but it works without energy. You just have to wind it."

"Thanks, Jax." He hugs me tight. "You really are the best big sister."

"And you're the best little brother. Now, I've got to get out there and see what I can find. You listen to Astoria. I'll meet you later, on the roof." I stoop to hug him, and somehow I don't want to let go. He feels so fragile. I'm all he has left to protect him from this vile world. "Be good, little guy, and maybe I'll find you a special treat."

"Okay, Jax," he says with a toothy grin. "I'll be extra good."

I tousle Andy's blond curls, and leave him swinging in the hammock looking at the pictures in Nonna's book. I dare to start my search while the sun is still in the sky. Two hours of exposure a day is what the scientists said we could tolerate, and then only at dawn or dusk. Today, I'll push that limit. If I seek sporadic shelter from the intense rays, I might stretch the twilight hours' allotment into three.

"Later," I say. I don my extreme sunglass eye protection and sunscreen gloves. I'm lucky Astoria and I work different parts of the night. I could never leave him, unless he's with someone I trust. As if the rats and starvation aren't bad enough, I must insure he stays hidden from the Child Solicitors who wander the South Side of Metro City daily looking for healthy children to buy or steal. The members of Culpepper's City Council have no qualms purchasing a healthy child, since most of them have been rendered sterile from the electronics they used incessantly as children.

I open our creaky door to step over a half dozen sleeping kids. Their parents lie a few feet away, but the children always sleep at our doorstep.

I leap, landing a bit too close to a little girl's ear. She opens her eyes, and stares up at me.

"You sing pretty." She smiles sheepishly.

I smile back.

She rolls over to snuggle with her brother. A brown glass bottle rolls out of the rags she uses for a bed. I pick it up to tuck into her bedroll. My throat tightens when I see the label. It's Noova. *What? How did she get it? What is she? Seven?* My tight grip on the bottle turns my fingertips white. *How could they have given it to her?* I charge through the main sewer tunnel trying to rationalize why a seven-year-old would take the birth control serum Culpepper's laboratories designed to disintegrate a woman's eggs.

The serum is mandatory for the lower-socioeconomic girls when they reach fifteen. It insures no bastards from the nightwalkers will populate his city. Astoria took it, but that little girl can't know the implications. I've heard some young girls are spoon-fed the syrup by their mothers in the guise of medicine.

I clench my jaw in an effort not to grieve for the little one. She couldn't possibly be sexually active. Then my brain flicks off into a black area I'd never considered and I cringe. *Is she a victim of those disgusting perverts out there selling the drugs? Does her mother think this is protecting her?*

None of the children is safe, not even from the mothers who care for them. But I have no mother to deceive me, and I've no intention of needing such a potion. I run faster.

When I reach the street, my anger explodes like hot lava. I heave the brown container against the crumbling building that was once the Metro City Bank. The sound of the smashing Noova bottle echoes in the empty street. Tiny shards scatter in all directions, broken, like our lives. The splatter of what's left of the devastating substance instantly evaporates in the hot sun. Too bad the sun can't destroy Culpepper the same way.

Intense heat penetrates my clothing, as I stare at the reason a young life has been ruined. Begrudgingly, I realize I can't do anything about the girl. I need to focus on keeping Andy safe, and that means I need to get moving.

First stop, the abandoned sporting goods store downtown. The front windows are boarded up and the second-story windows are smashed.

They gape like wounds in the sun-bleached façade. I inspect the first-floor windows facing the back alley. Other pickers have already been here. The boards on one of the windows hang askew. I haul myself up to the windowsill and squeeze through. Rickety stairs with chipped paint and rusted handrails lead to a second floor. Some steps are missing, but not all. I jump over the hollow spaces in the middle, and make my way upstairs.

    Cobwebs dangle from the ceiling. Abandoned bird nests crumble to the wooden plank floor from the rafters. Thick dust covers empty shelves and display cases. I jiggle the door of a loose trophy case and yank it open. A small silver coach's whistle lies in a pile of dust in the bottom corner.

    Andy would like this, but it will draw too much attention to him. I'll see if Hofmann wants it, or maybe I'll trade it to Cowboy myself. They must have sport teams on the New Continent.

    The rest of the vast room is empty except for broken chairs, crumbled paper, and bits of foam padding. The door that secured a manager's office, in the far corner, has been ripped from its hinges. The only thing remaining in the small room is an old metal desk.

    I'm pumped now and leap over an exposed hole in the floor with the power of a leopard. Three rats scamper from beneath the plaster debris and scurry for cover under the desk, where empty file folders spilled across the floor.

    I search through them. Nothing is left worth anything to Hoffmann. The long, thin drawer in the desk's center doesn't budge. I slip my knife into the space between the drawer and the desktop, pressuring the latch that keeps it locked. The other pickers must have been on a Smash and Grab raid, because it would take finesse to ease this lock open. But if it's locked, that means something valuable is inside. After several attempts, I spring the drawer free with a quick twist.

Jackpot! In the far corner is a pack of cigarettes. *These will bring a good price.* I stuff them into my coat and continue my search. Underneath a book of receipts is a blue-bound legal document. It appears to be a will. A few dried-up ink cartridges for an obsolete printer flounder near the front.

I ease my hands under loose papers. My nimble fingers settle on a smooth, round disc with a hole the size of my finger in the center. I recognize it as a musical antiquity, like the kind in my treasure box that holds my father's voice. I'm anxious to discover if a music machine accompanies it. I'd love to actually hear my father sing.

I speed up my search, and find a small circular plastic case that pops open like a steamed clamshell. Earbuds connect to very thin wires protruding from the back. I insert the silver disc, close the case, and push the button labeled with an arrow pointing to the right.

The disk spins inside. I insert the earpieces, and pleasant music pours into my ears. Something about it is familiar. I recall Nonna singing a similar song when she worked in her flower garden. I don't know the verse, but I do recognize the chorus. I sing along with the repetitive music, as I work on the left side drawers.

"And the green grass grows all around, all around.

The green grass grows all around."

Loosening the drawers, I find paper clips, colored markers that smell faintly like lemon and grape, and a bound ledger with columns of numbers. I kneel on the floor, singing, as I leaf through the pages. I hadn't seen these numbers since the schools closed.

The disk stalls in the middle of a verse, and the music ceases. I stop singing, but to my surprise, other noises filter through the earpieces. Scuffling, scraping, and squeaking behind me.

I turn. My eyes grow wide, and I back into the desk, gasping.

Hundreds of rats line the empty shelves and the paper-strewn floor. Even baby rats poke their heads from gouged foam in the disintegrated wrestling mat against the far wall. They squat along broken chair legs and up in dangling broken light fixtures. A wall of clicking, chewing fur with smooth, long tails surrounds me.

Hundreds of beady black eyes watch me.

My panic swallows me up. I try to scream, but the air from my lungs passes through my throat like a hiss. Certain the rats will pounce, I clap my hands and jump like a crazy monkey on a trampoline. They scatter into holes they have chewed through plaster walls.

I wipe beaded sweat from my upper lip with my sleeve and toss a stapler and box of staples into my canvas bag. *I'm out of here!* I glance out an empty window. The sun is lowering. The building shadows should be long. Time to go. The words of the song still skip through my mind. I pick up the refrain, singing to counter my fear, and tuck the number ledger under my arm. I could use it to teach Andy numbers.

I bound down the stairs, singing, and when I reach the first floor, I glance back.

Rats, six abreast, line each step behind me. They rush toward me and I scream. This time, a piercing, high-pitched cry escapes my lips. I run toward the open window at the back of the store where a dozen or more children fight to get in.

"Get out of the way," I yell. "Rats behind me."

Wide-eyed, they scatter, just in time for me to jump to the sidewalk below.

I pull my cart from the rusted metal facade of the adjacent building, shove my findings into it, and dart across the alley. Turning back, I see the children pressed against the brick building next to the open window, where hundreds of rats jump out next to them.

The rats land on their feet and scatter throughout the dusty streets, some toward the center of town, some to the park, but most head for the Elan.

My breath catches in my throat. The thought of all those rats scuttling over me if I fell makes my flesh crawl. *Get out of here, Jax.* I scramble away, as fast as I can.

Admiration shines in the children's eyes. They must think I'm brave to be in a building with all those rats. I nod, and then push my dented shopping cart toward East Knob Hill, staying close to the abandoned buildings. For some reason, the Megamarks aren't patrolling yet.

I push the rat episode from my mind and concentrate on a picking plan. *Where would be the best place to look for the binoculars Andy so desperately wants? The banker's mansion is a good bet.* I've found jewels there before, even though most of them were colored paste. They must have taken the real gems with them when they fled to Antarctica. But maybe other things are hidden in that house that will bring money, like clocks, old maps, and leather-bound books. I just need to find them. *Maybe they have binoculars, too?*

I look forward to the joy on Andy's face when he sees what we have in store for him. The sweet acorn bread baked all day in Cheinstein's oven contraption, and Astoria said the rabbit Rafe trapped is solar-roasting in the rusted kettle grill I'd picked up on an abandoned apartment balcony.

* * * * *

After two hours of searching, my cart is only a quarter full. I comb the banker's office and his library, empty of every book. I wander up the winding staircase, past stripped wires, where a crystal chandelier probably hung.

Upstairs, I enter the fancy bedroom, robbed of its elaborate bed. I know this room well. I stole the gold damask curtains for Astoria's pleasure parlor from here. A few broken chairs and a huge, old steamer trunk, like they used on transatlantic ships a century ago, are the only things that remain. The trunk sits next to the stone fireplace, across the room from a smashed floor-to-ceiling window.

Pink rays of sunset shine through the broken glass.

The last time I was here, the trunk was locked, but now the lid is pried off. Items from inside spill out on the parquet floor. Things not valuable to any picker who knows his/her stuff cover the floor: one elbow-length, black satin glove, a torn, silk lady's slip, and crumpled white papers sprinkled everywhere like 3-dimensional snowballs, something I've only seen in Nonna's old, photo albums.

I dig through the trunk, as the sun's rays cast elongated shadows across the floor.

The townspeople should be gathering for Culpepper's meeting. I must hurry.

More crumpled papers lie inside. I smooth one out to reveal original sheet music. Every one of them is penned-notes to an original score.

Whoever lived here was a composer.

Now, the shadowy indentations on the floor make sense. At one time, a baby grand piano stood in this room.

I hum a few bars and step away, not mindful of the stack of old, yellowed newspapers piled between the chest and the fireplace. I step on a broken compact case and fall forward with an unbalanced step. My foot hits the newspapers, and they slide to the floor like a deck of splayed cards.

I hurriedly push them back in their space and my hand jostles one of the fireplace stones. *It's loose!*

I stop pushing paper and start pulling the old fire-starters. Squeezing myself between the trunk and the side of the fireplace, I jiggle the stone back and forth, until it slides from the wall.

I hold my breath. My pulse speeds up. *Maybe something of value still hides in this old place?*

Behind the stone is a small space filled with a red fabric bundle. I reach in, pull it out, and examine it on the bedroom floor.

It's a lady's floor-length, satin robe. It looks antiquated, by its style, with padded shoulders, and a large rhinestone button that secures the fitted waist.

Nonna used to have magazines with pictures of ancient movie stars, and this looks like one of their glamorous robes. It probably wouldn't hold up well under the rough hands of the caravan traders, but Astoria might like it.

Something to make her happy.

A muslin-wrapped package lay hidden within the thick shoulder padding. I open it to reveal a bejeweled, opera-length cigarette holder and a brass pair of opera glasses with a long, ruby-encrusted handle.

My heart skips a beat. I'm immediately transported to a great opera house in a major city I can only imagine. The glittering theatergoers flocking to hear my father couldn't have been more glamorous than the scene in my head.

The closest I got to seeing him was to watch him interviewed on the Internet before Culpepper shut it down. I cradle the opera glasses near my heart.

"I'll give Andy my mini-binoculars for his birthday and I'll keep these," I say. "They'll work perfectly well to keep an eye on Astoria from the apartment rooftop, and I'll trade the jeweled cigarette holder to Cowboy." *I wonder if he's ever seen anything like this?*

I rewrap the items in the muslin and turn the satin robe inside out to protect the material from the rusted shopping cart. Culpepper's meeting will be starting. As the sun drops below the horizon, I head back to the Courthouse Square in the center of Metro City.

* * * * *

Culpepper cremated his family two days ago. Alder told Astoria Culpepper wasn't grieving. He was angry; beyond-words angry. Tonight, he would decree every rat in Metro City be destroyed. It's not like he can just produce another heir. Most of the women left in Metro City are either sterile, have been ordered by Culpepper to take the Noova Serum, or have taken it willingly.

I make my way through the ragged crowd.

Rafe is easy to see, standing on the base of a courthouse pillar to the right of the makeshift stage the soldiers set up for Culpepper's speech.

Strains of grumbling and whispered curses surround me. An uneasy quiver radiates through the mass of homeless street-dwellers, a chilling reminder of the time when Culpepper first announced his own appointment as Mayor.

I'd been holding mother's hand; the mob pulsed like a living multi-headed monster towering above me, protesting Culpepper's rule.

At one point, the crowd strained toward the stage where Culpepper made his announcement, and a man fell into me. I was separated from mother, and it was hard for her to swing back to get me, her belly so swollen with Andy.

Then the crowd surged forward, protesting the loss of democratic rule in the community and Culpepper's self-appointment and I was lost in the mob thinking, how did he go from being the Chief of Police to dictator of the whole city?

People could worship on their own and parents could teach their children at home, but they couldn't produce food. Culpepper purposely closed all access to the supermarkets. Nonna was right. He was up to something. Hungry people were too weak to fight.

I feel a sense of déjà vu, as tension again fills the air like an invisible electrical charge. Just one ill-advised touch, and the crowd will spark into a riot. *He's taken our freedom, our food, and our homes. What can he possibly take from us now?*

The sun's final orange rays shine on Culpepper like an accusatory spotlight before it sinks beneath the distant mountains.

I reach the pillar, as Culpepper takes the stage, and am surprised to see Astoria with Rafe. "Where's Andy?"

"I left him with Cheinstein," she whispers. "They're on the roof keeping an eye on Rafe's grilled rabbit. It should be done in time for Andy's birthday celebration."

Sylvanis Culpepper turns on the microphone. The loudspeakers squeal.

"Many of you are aware of the personal tragedy I've suffered this week."

"Why should you be any different from the rest of us?" I mutter.

"I've called this meeting to declare war on the vermin of the city."

The hapless crowd cheers. Tattered sleeves rise from patched jackets. Moth-eaten shawls twirl above heads tangled with knots, but thriving with lice. And they stink. Most of the people in the crowd have worn, wrinkled faces and sunken eyes. Even the children have dark circles under their eyes.

"It's about time, Culpepper," shouts Old Man Peabody. I recognize him. He was the postman who saved my father's fan and disc from the bonfire that blazed behind the Post Office when Culpepper took over, and smuggled the precious keepsakes to me through my mother.

"It took the no-good rodents to slip into *your* bed for you to take action!"

St. Sally of the Subway howls next to Old Man Peabody, her toothless smile all gums.

"You tell that bastard, Peabody. Too bad the rats didn't get *him*. Lord knows there's enough meat on him to feed the city's entire rat population."

Raucous cheers break out again, and the swarm surges forward, banging into each other. *So much for the spark.* I cling to the pillar next to Rafe and Astoria, as Megamarks push their way through the unruly crowd, dragging the loudest protesters away or slamming them to the ground to shut them up. Still the unruly throng protests.

Officers squeeze around Culpepper.

"Tighten security," shouts the commander.

Culpepper clears his throat and quickly amends his statement.

"Let it be understood. I am not only speaking of the four-legged variety."

An invisible blanket smothers the crowd's boisterous collective voice. The shoving stops. Their protests die in their throats.

"I want the hookers, the drug dealers, the thugs, and the robbers eliminated from Metro City."

"Hear, hear." A few of his supporters and their wives, seated on the courthouse balcony behind him, applaud.

"Fat chance that's going to happen," spits Rafe. "Doesn't he realize that's who is left in this city?"

"Are you kidding me?" Astoria's brow crinkles at Rafe's words. "He's a fat cat!" She spits on the ground. "What does he know, cradled in his oversized featherbed? The drunken soldiers talk about his rich meats and delicate fruits, everything we die for, all delivered to his plate while he sits in that air-conditioned mansion."

My impatient exhale sounds like a snort. "Well, we eat meat and vegetables."

"Yeah," hisses Rafe. "When I trap a chipmunk or a flying squirrel." His face tightens into a frown. "We're lucky if we each get a taste. Most of what we eat is because you know how to forage and we eat better than most of these suckers."

Astoria stares at Culpepper, and then interrupts our conversation. "Did you know his dead wife was only sixteen?"

"Get out!" I scoff. "The guy has got to be fifty."

"It's true. Alder says her parents promised her to him at fourteen, before she was able to receive Noova. Her parents were paid well."

The little girl outside my door fills my thoughts. Was her mother trying to insure she not be chosen like a breeding mare?

"Alder says Culpepper already has his men scouting the young female children for a *pure* girl to be his next wife."

"Well, he's got slim pickins' in these parts." Rafe laughs. "Almost every girl here has spread her legs for food or money or both. He'll never find anyone unless he starts looking for a girl Andy's age."

Again, the little girl comes to mind. I swallow my sarcasm, hoping it will appease the knots in my belly. I drop my gaze, first to my hunting boots, then to my jeans and my cargo coat. If that's true, they'll definitely overlook the nightwalkers. Though I've never been with a man, maybe I should start wearing a dress.

Sylvanis Culpepper continues. "My Council and I discussed this situation at length and we've decided we shall offer fifty thousand dollars and passage to the New Continent to anyone who can rid the city of these undesirable elements."

My heart pounds in my chest. *This is my chance, but how?*

Loud boos reverberate through the crowd. One beggar even throws his soleless shoe at the mayor, barely missing his red-flushed scalp. "Well, start with yerself, ya old buzzard," he screeches.

The crowd agrees, jeering the mayor, and shouldering the homeless man into the air.

"You're a vulture, feeding on the poor," shrieks St. Sally, matriarch of the subway homeless. "God bless their souls."

"You're the biggest rat in Metro City," shouts Hoffmann, jumping up on the pillar base opposite Rafe, Astoria, and me.

Two Megamarks with bully sticks reach up to pull him down, but he's quick, for a middle-aged man. He jumps into the unruly crowd heaving forward to shake the courthouse stage scaffolding.

Two homeless men, one with a scruffy beard and the other with a blond ponytail, shimmy up the back of the stage. The screams of the elegantly dressed woman they threaten to throw into the disheartened crowd alert Culpepper.

"Seize them," he yells.

The Megamarks beat the men down, but four more homeless protestors take their place, and one of the councilmen is also threatened.

"Okay. Okay," says Culpepper. His hands wave in the air in an effort to quiet the unruly crowd. "I will pay thirty thousand dollars just to rid the city of those killer rats, and Scalawag Alley, South Port, and Elan Row can remain intact."

"That's better, you old fart," screams a hard-looking nightwalker, whose bosom bulges from her bodice.

"Spread the word. I want these rats gone in a fortnight. If you know of anyone who can accomplish this feat, please see my Captain, or I'll be forced to import an exterminator. Either way, the rats will be gone in two weeks." He turns on his heel and disappears into his safe, air-conditioned mansion.

The crowd scatters, mumbling, each seeking their next meal.

"Okay, then," quips Rafe. "I'll go check my traps. See you in an hour."

Astoria rushes toward the apartment building. "I'll check on the boys."

I yell after her. "I'll be right there after I get my cart."

The day's intense heat melted the tar, and the cart's wheels stick in the cracks and potholes of the dusty streets. As I pass burned-out cars and shattered storefronts on my way to my apartment building, I hear a commotion on the next block. I conceal my cart in the shadows and duck behind a charred burn barrel the homeless men use. No one stands near it now.

Just as I slip into a dark doorway, I see the reason for the turmoil. Culpepper's guards are picking up sleeping vagrants from the steps of abandoned buildings. They still have a good six hours before they must lock themselves away in their safe places. *What is going on? Culpepper lied! He's already started his extermination.*

I return to my cart and dash down the alley, passing broken crates and smashed liquor bottles. I clench my teeth at the sight of a festering dead cat and hold my breath against its putrid smell. A rat probably got it. But the disgust I feel over some dead cat in an alley doesn't compare to the terror that slides into my stomach as I reach the door to my apartment building. Its camouflage is removed, and the door is smashed open.

My panic explodes like a bomb, sending chills and fear to my numbed limbs. I feel like I move in slow motion, yet I race to claw my way through the debris that was once the door. I gasp for air. Images of what could have happened flash before me.

"Oh, God. Andy!"

As I dash up the steps to the roof, my heart beats triple-time. Air pumps through my lungs like a turbine. The roof door at the top of the stairs leans wide open. I reach the roof, and fall to my knees. The sound of my wails, as I pull my hair, sound foreign to me, like I'm listening to someone's lament, but it's mine. "*Nooooo!*"

The birthday table is overturned and the festive tablecloth Astoria sewed together from fabric pieces is reduced to torn scraps. The cracked pottery bowl that held Cheinstein's boiled rice lay smashed on the concrete rooftop. Dozens of rats lick at the soft kernels.

Andy is nowhere in sight. Neither is Cheinstein.

Chapter Five

"Andy?" I scream. "*Answer* me. Are you here?" I wrap my arms around myself to stop shaking, but my fingertips are ice cold against my hot skin. I can't stop my lips from trembling.

"Andy." Terror strangles my voice. It's not as loud as it should be. I dart in every direction and none, moving in circles, not knowing where to look first.

"Where are you?"

My voice cracks into a choked squeak. *I should never have left him.*

My voice is singing Happy Birthday over and over, hidden somewhere in this devastation, on the recording device Cheinstein jury-rigged from scavenged parts.

Only bones are left of the rabbit we grilled for Andy's feast. Rats, brazenly positioned on every roof surface, have turned over the solar oven. Not one crumb of Andy's sweet birthday bread is left.

I crumple to the ground and pound my fists against the concrete roof, refusing to blink. My belligerent stare meets the hungry rats' beady eyes. *How could child hunters have taken Andy? He's never alone. I took every precaution. I left him with Astoria, just a few hours ago.* She said he was with Cheinstein. I've used him to baby-sit before, but he's still a kid, himself. If the hulky kidnappers found their way up here, there's no way he could have stood up to them. *That's the only explanation. Someone must have known the boys would be alone. Culpepper! While he had us all riled up over his new edict, his goons must have taken Andy.*

"Son of a bitch!" The realization comes too late.

I throw shards of pottery at the furry saber-toothed rodents along the ledge. Sheer luck knocks one to the street below, but another takes his place in the grunting vermin line.

Another quick, terrified scan of the rat-infested roof reveals movement at the sound of my voice.

"Oh God, please let it be him." I bolt to the far corner, near the crumbling chimney.

A bloody hand sticks out from underneath a rat-covered canvas tarp.

Andy! My pulse pounds. I reach to pull him out, but my frazzled brain is working overtime. The hand is too big to be Andy's.

With adrenaline-added strength, I pull the body to the center of the roof. Rats scurry at the disturbance. Some scuttle across the rooftop. Others dive down gutter pipes, as I flip the body over. The blood-soaked face is unrecognizable except for the black eyebrows.

"Oh my God, Beni, can you hear me?"

Cheinstein stirs. I grab a half-empty water jug and dunk one of the fabric scraps in it to cleanse his face. Just as I touch the rag to his brow, a scream rings out behind me.

Cheinstein's head bleeds in my lap, as I turn.

Astoria is as colorless as the sun-bleached concrete roof. Her eyes are squeezed shut against the horror and her fists punch the air.

"Astoria, stop." My voice gains strength. "Where's Andy?"

She falls to her knees, rocking, arms clenched around her waist. Her face is puffy and her eyes are red from crying.

"Be still," I say to Cheinstein. "I'll be right back." I gently place his head on the jumbled fabric mess. His eyes twitch in pain.

"Astoria!" I run to her and pull her to a standing position by her armpits. "Astoria! I need you. Cheinstein needs you. Get a grip."

Holding her head steady, I stare into her teary eyes. "Astoria."

"I'm sorry," she mutters. "I'm sorry. I'm sorry." She still cradles herself and rocks back and forth, tears flowing, snot dribbling down her lips.

"Sorry for what? What did you do with Andy?"

"Nothing, I swear," she blubbers. "I just stopped a few moments to see Alder."

"Why?" I can no longer hold in my anger. It blasts out of my mouth like a speeding bullet. "How could you stop to see a no-good Megamark instead of coming straight here to check on the boys?"

You did this. This is your fault. Just because you needed to stop for a quickie on the way.

Her startled gaze shoots from Cheinstein, bruised and bloody, to my face. She shakes her head in denial. Tears gush again and roll down her cheeks. "I'm sorry. I just wanted to get Andy's birthday gift." She holds out her fist, clenched in terror.

I pry it open to find what were once three foil-wrapped chocolate kisses, now nothing but a brown puddle of goo in her palm.

"Alder said he would get them for me before the party. He stole them from Culpepper's desk. I didn't think five minutes more would make a difference. I'm sorry."

I retreat inward. *Don't be stupid, Jax. She's right. Five minutes wouldn't have made a difference. This was done while we heckled Culpepper. It was a planned attack, but why?*

Cheinstein moans.

I rush to his side and continue to clean his face. Once the blood is washed off, the deep gash above his right eye is revealed. *Geez! They must have used a plank from the broken table.* One eye is swollen shut. Blood oozes from his ears, and small cuts mark his otherwise smooth complexion.

"Come here." I'm as firm as I can be, without alarming Astoria more. "Help me check him for rat bites."

The memory of Nonna's red, bumpy, rat-bitten arms floods back. I refuse to lose someone else I care about to the rats.

Blood stains Cheinstein's sweatpants, so old the patches are patched. His shirt is bloody, too, and I suspect broken ribs. I check his legs. "Astoria, now."

She stumbles toward us and kneels opposite me.

Cheinstein winces when my fingers touch his ankle, swelling beneath his red-striped sock.

This would go much faster if Astoria helped.

"Hold still, Beni. I've got to wipe the blood from your split lip. Who did this to you?"

His swollen lips slur his words. He reaches toward my jacket and brings me closer to his mouth.

"Andy," he whispers.

"Andy?" I grimace.

He shakes his head and his eyes roll back.

"Astoria, call Rafe." I shove the walkie-talkie from my coat into her clean hand.

"What about this?" She waves her chocolate-smeared one in my face.

I wipe it with a clean scrap, and tuck the folded fabric inside my waistband. Melted or not, Andy will still enjoy it when I find him.

"Tell Rafe to get over here now. And tell him to bring help. We need to get Cheinstein to St. Sally."

I leave Cheinstein, his head swaddled in Astoria's skirt and search for clues. Nothing surfaces. I toss the broken remnants of Andy's party aside, but the sound of my voice heralding Andy's birthday on the taped loop pierces my heart like a knife. I throw the black plastic box against the crumbling chimney. It shatters and the endless song ceases.

Slowly at first, one by one, the rats disappear. Then in pairs, and small groups, until they are all gone. *That's odd. When the singing stops, the rats depart.*

Rafe charges on to the roof, and breaks my thoughts. He looks from me, and the devastation behind me, to Astoria and Cheinstein.

"Three Boys are guarding the stairs," he says. "What the hell happened, buddy?" He kneels in front of Cheinstein. "I hope you karate-chopped the other guy's ass."

Cheinstein tries to smile, but his split lip bleeds again and he passes out.

"He needs to go to St. Sally, now. Rafe, can your guys help Astoria take him to the Subway Station? I need to find Andy."

Rafe's dark eyes widen.

"They took Andy?" He shakes his head. His eyes dart nervously around the roof. "I'm coming with you. You know, this may seem strange but families are mourning lost children in the street tonight, too. I didn't pay much attention, but now, with Andy missing—"

"Culpepper's behind these kidnappings," I spit between clenched teeth. "I know he is. I can feel it in my gut. On my way over here, his guards were already picking up homeless men by the hobo fires. He's cracking down on us, like he said he would, but I can't imagine what he wants with the children."

Rafe's lips press together. His stoic face tightens. I almost see his brain figuring out his next step.

"Maybe he's trying to replace the one he lost."

"Or, after the heckling at the Square, he's using the children as insurance to get us to do *exactly* what *he* wants."

"No. If that rotten bastard is behind this, he planned it long before the heckling today." Rafe peers over the side of the roof.

I join him. The people in the street console each other in small clusters.

"Looks like Andy isn't the only one. Remember, Metro City doesn't have many kids left. Between the exoduses two years ago, and the Noova serum, we probably have only about one hundred to one fifty."

"The old school would be a good place," suggests Astoria. "It's isolated and away from the night traffic and trade."

"It's as good a place as any to start looking, but first I need to get some tools."

"Good, and change into black clothes," says Rafe. "We don't want your blonde hair and light jacket sticking out in the night's shadows."

"And you," I say, turning to Astoria. "No pleasure parlor tonight. I can't be your Guardian Angel if I'm looking for Andy, and Rafe is going to be with me, so just stay with Cheinstein. I'll meet you at St. Sally's. Don't go home tonight, either. It's safety in numbers, now."

Rafe clutches her shoulders and stares lovingly into her eyes. "She's right, Tori."

I'm sure he's hoping she can read what he really wants to say. "I'll meet you in front of the school in twenty minutes, Rafe."

"Gotcha. I'll get the Altar Boys to keep an eye out for anything related to kids. See you in twenty." He stoops to pick up Cheinstein. "Let's go, Tori, he's going to need a familiar face when he wakes up."

* * * * *

Culpepper's decree to banish the city's undesirable element is in full swing. Consumed with getting Andy back, my thoughts propel me forward. I calculate every scenario I can think of, as I sneak back to the tunnel, dashing from burned-out cars to piles of building debris, to the park. I run low and fast, the red satin robe and the disc player I found earlier tucked beneath my elbow.

Obviously, rats aren't the only things on the extermination docket. Culpepper lied again. His rat extermination order is an excuse to rid the town of anybody who isn't connected to his Council, but why?

Screams and the thud of clubs bashing bodies echo from the nearest alley. I reach the block before the Municipal Park, and duck behind an overturned dumpster.

The Megamark Guards beat several homeless men with bully sticks. One of them is Old Man Peabody, the postmaster. The feeble guy never hurt a soul. His spectacles lie broken on the ground. His ragged muffler slides from his shoulder, as they roughly drag him past a busted streetlight to a prisoner cart with two black horses harnessed to the front.

"Help," he cries out.

Others already locked inside protest through a tiny barred window.

"You sons of bitches," shouts one.

"Don't trust that no-good bastard Culpepper," yells another.

"Today it's us. Tomorrow it's you. Have pity, man."

"You're no different than us," shouts Mr. Peabody, "except for your three squares a day."

The wagon rolls down the street, with the Guards clinging to the sides, obviously bound for the courthouse.

What fate could Culpepper possibly have planned for us?

When the wagon turns the corner, I dash out into the street to retrieve the broken glasses and scarf. If I don't find Old Man Peabody again, at least the scarf will keep Andy's neck warm at night. *Andy!* Fresh anger pulses through me. I peer through the smashed lenses.

"Fucking assholes. Culpepper will pay for this."

The coast is clear and I run the rest of the way to the sewer tunnel. Either the nomads found another safe haven, or the Guards have already been through here. But, in the distance, a dog barks. I sense relief. *Maybe they just moved to another part of the tunnel?* Yet, as I get closer to home, I realize the bark has a repeating cadence.

My heart jumps into my throat, when I turn the corner. Even in the dim tunnel, the vandalization of my home is obvious. The blue tarps are slashed, but the grilled door still stands. Clearly, the repeated bark of Cheinstein's electronic dog echoes through the sewer tunnel.

The bars behind one of the arches are bent. That's how they got in. The room is trashed, like the birthday party. *What were they looking for?* Scattered pages from my paperback books are strewn across the room, as if a tornado tore them from their bindings. The fruity almond odor in the room reveals smoldering pages in the embers of the fire bowl. My mother's hardbound books are gone.

Nonna's quilt, ripped from the wall, lay in a wadded ball on the floor. I rub its softness against my cheek, trying to protect Nonna's tenderness, fighting the nausea that sweeps through me. My thoughts flood back to the last time it lay crumpled on a floor — the night we buried Nonna.

We'd cleansed her body in mint-infused water and swathed her, first in cotton, monogrammed sheets she'd received as a wedding gift years before, and then in one of her pretty quilts, like this one.

Mom used the garden shovel and I used the claw to dig Nonna's grave behind her beloved cottage.

My mother's words ring in my ear, as clear as if she just said them.

"Goodbye, mother." She brushed the fresh dirt from her palm, and squeezed her hands together, as if she could strangle her grief. Breaking a rose blossom from the bush, she tucked it into her bosom, and bent close to the grave.

"It's his fault, Mama," she murmured.

Fiercely, with gritted teeth and clenched jaw, I inspect the upended mattress, slashed on one side.

"You rat bastard!" It's up to me, now. He's taken everything from me. My mother. My grandmother. And, now, my brother.

I can't let him get away with it.

"I won't let you down, Mom. Or you, Nonna."

I search for Nonna's book. It's not here. A grieving ache shoots through me, so powerful, it fuels my determination. I'll kill that fat ass, Culpepper.

The dull thud of my foot kicking the overturned mattress echoes off the tunnel walls, like the anger that rumbles through my veins, spurring me on. I yank the loose bricks out of the wall, behind my bed. Normally, the quilt covers them, but the Megamarks hadn't even noticed the bricked hole in the wall, where I keep my valuables. I pull out a portable spotlight charged with a solar pack, and a screwdriver, and throw them on the mattress. I search for black clothes.

I find Astoria's long-sleeved black shirt. My jeans are so dirty they'll pass as black. I wrap my long braid around my head and force a man's black stocking cap over it until no blonde shows. I check my watch.

Twelve minutes passed.

I shove Nonna's quilt, the satin robe, the spectacles, and the disc player in the hole in the wall, and close it up again. Since Astoria has my walkie-talkie, I grab hers and dash out to meet Rafe.

People lament openly in the streets over captured children and husbands. The terrified woman, whose daughter I collided with earlier, wails on the corner of Main Street.

"I'll see him dead," she screams.

Her friends console her. It seems her husband attempted to prevent the Guard from kidnapping her twins and they took him, too. Watching her anguish as I pass by, I realize now I know her. She used to own the grocery store my mother took me to when I was a child. Green is her name, and her life is shattered like mine. Her sobs intensify my resolve.

I run faster, as my mother's words haunt me. "I'll see him dead or die trying."

I'd wondered why she whispered to the grave. Perhaps she didn't want me to hear. But I did. And now, it makes sense. Running, I gaze at the starlit sky and send a silent message to mother. *I'll get him back.*

But my promise is cut short. I trip over a dead nightwalker slumped against a fire hydrant, needle marks in her arm. Another realization comes so swiftly, my clenched stomach squeezes the air from my lungs. I roll to a stop near the woman's body.

Mom, did he kill you, too?

A group of angry parents arm themselves with shovels and clubs, obviously with the same intention as mine.

Ten minutes later, Rafe's signal, a whippoorwill call, sounds three times. I approach the school. We meet on the football field in the shadows of the broken bleachers.

"Cheinstein's delivered to St. Sally. She says he'll be okay. Astoria is with him, and my guys are patrolling our perimeter."

"Rafe, other families are doing the same thing we are. Too bad we can't coordinate with them. A whole bunch of us would be better than an army of two."

Rafe's confident headshake tells me I'm wrong.

"No, I don't think so. They'll be useless against the Megamarks. We've got stealth on our side. We're going to infiltrate the building. They're going to protest at the front door. Who do you think will succeed?"

Rafe thrives on this. He's cool and collected and I trust him completely. I also don't have any other choice. We make our way to the dark, empty school. It's obvious the children aren't there.

"They must have them at the White Labs," says Rafe.

My heart sinks. "You don't think—"

"No. No. It's just that it's got a lot more room for all the kids they took. Sally says five boys are missing from the Subway station, and the little brothers of two of Altar Boys are gone."

"They took Mrs. Green's husband and her twin daughters."

Rafe cocks his head. His eyes narrow. "So, they're taking all the kids, not just the boys."

I nod. "It seems that way."

"It's a good thing Cheinstein wears old, shit clothes, and the baseball hat I gave him," says Rafe, as he races toward Town Square.

I'm right behind him when he calls over his shoulder. "If they knew who he was, they'd have taken him, too."

Chapter Six

"Why do you say that?' I run to catch up.

"He can do a lot of things Culpepper would kill for." Rafe leads us toward the massive White Lab building behind Culpepper's opulent, climate-controlled mansion.

73

While I keep pace with Rafe, my mind wanders to the steadfast, even-tempered kid who treats Andy like a little brother. If he'd gone to public school, he'd be a grade behind Rafe and me. But Beni Li is brilliant, thus my nickname for him, *Ch* for his Chinese heritage and *Einstein* for all the super-genius inventions he creates from the pieces of blown-up machines or obsolete technology I find strewn in alleyways or in pot-holed parking lots.

"He had more information crammed into that superconductor cranium of his by the time he was twelve than any of the teachers we knew."

Rafe agrees. "He's got a brain that won't quit. There's nothing the dude doesn't know, and if he doesn't know it, he figures it out. He even made a cool technology game for Andy's birthday present, but I guess he'll never get to play it now."

I stop dead in my tracks. "What do you mean?"

Rafe turns.

I stand frozen. My shaking hand covers my gaping mouth.

"What?" He races back to me. "I didn't mean that. I just meant it's probably smashed with all the other birthday stuff on the roof."

I breathe again. My helplessness is playing tricks with my mind. *Andy is fine. He's got to be.*

Our pace quickens. We pass two shattered storefronts, and fragments of glass crunch beneath our boots.

"Cheinstein's mother taught him a crapload of things," says Rafe.

We turn the corner of the alley. The back of the White Labs comes into sight. Rafe doesn't take his eyes off it.

"It's crazy how much Cheinstein knows. It's almost like mechanical drawings were his picture books. You should see the stuff he hoards in the museum basement."

Rafe turns away from studying the White Lab for a moment. "Have you ever seen his fish tank?"

"If Astoria isn't around, I take Andy to stay with him when I go picking. He always finds something in that place to keep Andy amused, but I've never seen his aquarium." I swallow hard. *I always felt Andy was safe with Cheinstein.* But that was when they were in the cellar of Metro City's abandoned National History Museum, twenty feet below the ground.

"If I was that smart at fifteen, I sure as hell wouldn't be running St. Sally's errands. I'd have been on the first air train out of here."

Rafe's words break my self-inflicted depression. "Yep. Culpepper would kill to get his hands on Cheinstein."

Rafe uses his hand as a measuring tool, guesstimating the height of the building.

"Actually, he kinda already did," I say. "That's why Beni's an orphan. Mrs. Li was Culpepper's Head Scientist and he coerced her into testing the air-control suit before her design was ready. He wanted to start marketing it to other sun-ravaged cities. When she refused, Culpepper threatened to put Beni in the suit to test it out. She had no choice.

"Even though she had a PhD. in Biogenetic Science, nothing in her studies taught her how to deal with an asshole tyrant. She died helplessly in the scorching heat."

"But they said that was an accident."

"Nothing is an accident in Metro City, Rafe. Do you think all of these missing children are an accident? This citywide kidnapping was well thought out, I'm sure. I wish I knew what that fat rat was up to. If he harms one hair on Andy's head, I will personally *kill* him."

"You don't have to worry about that." Rafe nods toward me, and then the building. "We're about to kidnap Andy back."

He puts on a burst of speed and dashes toward the brick wall that surrounds the White Lab.

I follow close behind.

The building used to be alarmed, but Culpepper can't spare the electrical power, now.

Besides, no one is stupid enough to attempt to get into the labs. Chances are, they'd never get out. But Andy's in there, and I'm getting *him* out.

We scale the brick wall and settle in its shadow on the perimeter of Culpepper's executive estate.

His mansion, attached to the White Lab, stands stately and sedate in a city otherwise dying. A horse-drawn black wagon, much like the one that hauled Old Man Peabody away, pulls through the delivery gates, and up to the back entrance.

Ten children are dragged out, crying.

My mouth opens, but no words come out. I swallow hard against my dry throat, watching the kids being shoved through the back doors. They disappear into the voluminous building.

I find my voice. "Andy must be in there."

"No doubt," answers Rafe. Neither of us takes our eyes off the building.

I jump up to race to the door before it closes.

Rafe grabs my arm and pulls me back. "No, not that way."

I follow his gaze. Parents storm the main entrance, the only side of the building exposed to the street. They wave picks and shovels, clubs and sticks, but all are beaten back by the Megamark Guards.

"They're not going to let you or anybody else in *any* entrance. They're probably all monitored." With a quick headshake he continues. "No. We have to find a way in they're not expecting. Wait here."

He leaps forward.

"And keep your walkie-talkie on."

I click the button on the plastic transmitter at my waist.

"Watch where I go, then trace my steps as soon as I call you." He darts out from our hiding place, expertly disappearing into the night shadows. It's not until a tiny red laser flashes near the base of the building that I see he's there. He jumps from the ground, grabs the sill of a corner first-floor window, and then climbs to the protruding ledge above it. Inching his way to a metal fire escape, he hugs the building, as another black wagon arrives, emptying more somber children.

Once they enter the building, Rafe dashes to the roof and disappears from sight.

After what seems like an eternity, but is really ten minutes, a crackling voice from my walkie-talkie startles me.

"Come in, Geisha Girl." Rafe's voice is a husky whisper.

"Ten-four, Alpha Male."

"Coast is clear. Air ducts are our way in."

"Got it."

"I'll wait here for you. Be careful."

I pull my black knit cap farther down on my head and move out with confidence, tucking my walkie-talkie back into my belt.

I tiptoe from the wall to the back parking lot, as if that's going to make my presence more of a secret. Ducking behind a parked vehicle, clearly one of the cars from the massive air caravan that brings Culpepper's staples from Antarctica, I scan the lot for my next hiding place when my walkie-talkie signals a call.

"Come in, Alpha Male. Come in."

I recognize Cheinstein's voice. St. Sally must be a miracle worker.

"Ten four, Dragon."

"Abort mission. I repeat. Abort mission."

I push down so hard on my talk button, pain shoots through my finger. "Why? Do you have Andy?"

"Negative, Geisha Girl. Emergency here!"

"Come again, Dragon," says Rafe. "What emergency?"

"Miss America has lost her crown. I repeat Miss America has lost her crown."

That could only mean the Megamark Guards have infiltrated Astoria's pleasure parlor. I hope they aren't dragging her away like Old Peabody.

"What are her coordinates?" asks Rafe, a hitch in his voice.

"The Miss America stage. It's on fire. Hurry!"

"Where's Miss America?" My voice trembles. I imagine Cheinstein's response before he says it.

"She's inside."

"Copy that." My eyes squeeze shut against the image of Astoria trapped in a burning building. I feel like the fire burns inside my gut.

My brother and my best friend need me. I'm paralyzed. The sound of my hammering heartbeat roars in my ears. I open my eyes.

Another group of children is being herded by the kidnappers into the building.

I make my decision.

They can't hurt all of these kids at the same time, and they're not in a life-threatening situation, at least, not yet. The Guards are still bringing them in. I can only guess what Rafe is feeling as Cheinstein's words sink in. Astoria's pleasure parlor is on fire and she's in it.

Damn it! I told her not to go out tonight.

I dart back to the cover of the brick wall. Within minutes, Rafe is at my side. "We have to go back."

"I know. I've already decided. Let's go. The faster we save Astoria, the faster we can come back to get Andy."

We retrace our steps from Culpepper's estate back toward the center of town, being careful to hide from the Megamark Guards canvassing the streets. Already we smell pungent smoke, and the night sky glows.

We sprint down the alley to the middle of Main.

The collection wagon is parked outside Astoria's pleasure parlor.

It isn't really a parlor, but a vacant storefront that escaped destruction. Rafe reinforced the windows with scraps of plywood from the outside. Astoria said she'd decorated the inside with whatever furniture she retrieved from her own home or traded her feminine charms for.

I'd never been inside. We agreed. Astoria didn't want me seeing where she conducted her business. Since my mother spent her last years as a nightwalker, Astoria thought it might tarnish my mother's memory. Tonight, that changes.

Rafe and I sneak closer to the building. We hear yelling.

"Get out of here, before it's too late, Alder. We have our orders and we don't need you getting caught with one of the whores."

"I won't leave her." Alder's deep voice sounds caring. "She's not like the rest."

"How would you know, boy? You're still wet behind the ears."

A scuffle ensues. The front door opens.

Smoke billows into the dimly lit street. A half-dressed boy is thrown out. He looks to be about eighteen. His shirt, boots, and jacket fly out after him. He still wears the pants of the guard, but his hairless chest is bare. The door slams behind him, leaving Astoria in her parlor with the guard patrol.

    He bangs on the door, screaming.

    "Don't hurt her." His pleas go unanswered.

    Suddenly, Astoria's scream echoes from the building into the empty street. The boy they called Alder pounds on the door.

    "Astoria," he shrieks. "Astoria."

    The four soldiers storm out of the building, whisk him up, and throw him in the collection wagon. He screams her name, as the wagon disappears down the street.

    I creep close to the front door and listen.

    Rafe charges to the hidden back door.

    I pull on the handle. The door is locked or jammed. Either way, it won't budge. I hear nothing inside. *Have they killed her?* Again, my adrenaline kicks in. I pound the door so hard, the wall shakes. I have to save her. The thought of my mother's horrible death spurs me on.

    I dash to the back entrance to join Rafe. By the time I get there, he's nowhere in sight. He must have gone for reinforcements. I try to pull the nailed boards off with my bare hands. Splinters pierce my fingers, and my fingernails break, but still, I can't rip off the boards. The Guards have purposely trapped her inside. Smoke seeps out from underneath the jammed door.

    Moments later, Rafe is at my side with a crowbar. He wedges the boards off enough for me to slip inside.

    I make my way through billowing smoke, covering my mouth with Old Man Peabody's muffler. Smoke stings my eyes. Fire blocks my attempt to reach Astoria in the front room of the store. For the first time, I see what had been Astoria's pretty little haven. The gold damask curtains I'd stolen from the mansion on the hill line the fake window wall with Rafe's plywood beneath them. Flames rise through it all.

"Astoria," I yell, through the muffler.

She doesn't answer, but clearly I hear Rafe stripping the boards off the back door. By the time he stands next to me, the room is a fiery inferno.

"She's not here," I cry, shouting louder than the crackling flames.

"She's got to be. Did you check the bed?"

We sidestep a flaming curtain that hangs from the pedestal poster bed, sequestering the occupant in silent secrecy.

I rip it aside quickly, ignoring the burns to my hand. Astoria's left wrist is handcuffed to the carved headboard. Her head hangs limply to her chest, and thick, black curls hide her face.

Is she dead? My thoughts race as fast as my heart.

I pull her hair up and jump backward, bumping into Rafe. My eyes automatically squeeze shut against the horror before me. Blood drips from Astoria's right eye.

I gather my courage and look again. A piece of colored glass, part of the busted stained glass lampshade from bedside table, protrudes from her eye.

"The lamp must have exploded." Rafe struggles with his crowbar, splintering the fancy wooden headboard.

"Grab one of those window coverings," he yells. "The ones at the far end, not touched by the fire."

Coughing, he trashes the headboard to free Astoria's hand while I yank a panel of the golden damask curtains to the floor.

"I've got it," I cry.

"Good, lay it on the bed." Rafe gathers Astoria's limp body in his arms. He kisses her hair, and cradles her gently, yet, he's desperate to get her out of this raging inferno.

No sooner do I throw the curtain at the foot of the bed than Rafe lays her on it and wraps her up like a mummy. He rolls her until her entire body is covered. Then, he heaves her over his shoulder, and rushes to the ravaged back door.

I hold it open for him.

Rafe looks both ways, and then hightails it down the street. He follows the shadows for cover.

Astoria's limp body bounces with each step he takes.

The intense heat, behind me, pours into the alley. Sparks singe my skin. As soon as Rafe clears the corner, I breathe a sigh of relief. If anyone knows how to stay safe in this hellhole, it's Rafe. He'll take Astoria to St. Sally for first aid.

A satisfied smirk spreads across my face. We cheated Culpepper out of one more death.

A loud boom sounds behind me. A quick glimpse back reveals the rafters of the old building are falling in. I run before the force of the implosion catches me.

Headed in the opposite direction Rafe took, I step out into the dark. The blazing fire makes it impossible to hide in the shadows, now. I lunge forward, away from the flames spitting towards me, but as I do, a large net collapses on top of me, and is cinched tight, stealing my breath.

Chapter Seven

I struggle. The net tightens. The more I move, the more it constricts. A grinding mechanical arm attached to one of the Megamark trucks hauls me up. Fear doesn't possess me; Andy does. *What will happen to him if I'm jailed, or worse? Culpepper's scientists might use him as a guinea pig for some lethal experiment, like Cheinstein's mother.*

My grasp on the suffocating netting tightens until it feels like my veins will pop. With my arms squashed tightly against my chest, I can't move. The knotted net presses into my sweat-streaked face, jammed up against the rough rope.

I slant a glance in the direction where Rafe and Astoria disappeared. The best I can hope for is that Rafe will continue our mission to get Andy back and Astoria will recover to care for him. My only chance is to plan for the moment the guards loosen my rope prison. The knife in my boot will set me free.

The arm swings over an open truck and drops me inside. I scramble from the slackened netting, but it's too late. My feet catch in the ropes, as a mechanical cover slides shut above my head. No way can I climb the walls to escape.

The loud motor spits as it turns over. This is no horse-drawn wagon. The truck rumbles down the street, and I'm sure it's headed toward the Council Building.

Will I be a prisoner, like Old Man Peabody and the homeless they hauled off the church steps?

It stops abruptly, and a side door opens. One of the guards yanks me out.

I trip, and crash to the street. Looking up, my eyes grow wide. I shake my head, denying what I see. I fight back the urge to scream. I was correct to presume the truck took me to the Council building. I'd assumed the jails would be filled with the homeless and rebelling parents of kidnapped children, but I can't reconcile the scene before me with reality.

Vagrants are shackled to old parking meters that line the pot-holed street in front of the Mayor's mansion. The last parking meter stands empty.

My shoulders curl toward my chest. I fight the anger rising in my throat. Andy is my sole concern. He gives me the strength I need. I'm not about to be french-fried by the savage sun. *What a cruel way to die! If I have anything to say about it, Culpepper will pay dearly for this insane torture.*

With deeper breaths, I focus on the Megamark Guard in front of me through narrowed eyes, and push off the ground. I spring forward to strike, closing my arms around his knees, and pull.

His feet fly in the air and his entire weight falls against the guard next to him. They both collapse. In that split second, I take off, running faster than I've ever run before.

Their clomping boots behind me spur me on. They're almost on me. I make an impromptu decision to dart through a narrow passageway between two buildings. Scuffling and curses echo through the night, and at some level, I'm aware they're too big to follow me into the opening, but I don't stop running until I'm well within the shelter of Municipal Park. It's about as far away from the courthouse anyone can get without actually diving into the toxic Elan River.

    I crouch behind a gated area that allows me an excellent view of Main Street. Surrounded by dead and dying scrub oaks, I regroup. I need a plan, and I must make sure Astoria's all right. But, I need to get Andy, and I can't do it without Rafe.

    A large rat scurries past me.

    I stare at him from behind the rusted bars that once marked the boundary of the children's playground. I feel trapped, like an animal in a cage. If the Megamark Guards find me, I'm dead meat, just like the rats I kill that get in my way. *I must have done something to piss off Culpepper. Why is he targeting me?*

    I cling to the bars of the gate, like Squeakers did when Andy brought him home. *Squeakers! Andy was so sure he could do anything a dog could do.*

    I jump from my hiding place and dash toward our sewer, startling a few of the park nomads who run away at the sound of my feet hitting the bike path. As I slide the cover over, Megamark Guards advance from the other side of the park.

    I'm thankful for Rafe's warning about wearing black, and fly down the rungs, touching the sewer floor in record time. I charge down the empty tunnel to our abandoned brick room. No hint of the usual sewer nomads is visible, except for a crumpled, brown, paper bag stuck against the wall with a dark substance. *I hope it's not blood.*

Looking over my shoulder one last time, I again enter through the bent iron bar arch. Immediately, I rush to the corner where our bed used to be to search under the scattered clothing.

Squeakers is not there.

I throw the folding stadium chair across the room. Chattering sounds in the corner, where Astoria's overturned mattress is ripped to shreds. I heave it up. It falls to my right.

The dented, brass birdcage sits beneath the librarian's oak swivel chair and the remains of Astoria's mattress. The cage door is open and Squeakers is nowhere in sight.

"Shit. Where is he?" I storm around the room, madder with each step at the useless destruction. *Why are they so vicious?*

Suddenly, it dawns on me. *If Squeakers is hiding in this rubble, he'll never show his face if I keep stomping around like an angry troll.*

An idea strikes. I tiptoe to the corner of the room to the plastic tub, where I keep Andy's clothing. *If Squeaker's nose is worth that of a hound's, as Andy was so sure it was, he should be able to identify Andy's scent on his T-shirt.*

I pick my way over smashed coffee mugs and the overturned brazier. Dust from bone-white charcoal ash swirls into my nose. I rub my eyes and softly call, "Squeakers. Squeakers, come here."

My attempt to lure him from his hiding place fails.

He must sense my disdain for rats. Then, I remember how he and his black furry friend sat up and paid attention when I sang Andy to sleep. The thought of the roof rats disappearing after I smashed the recording of my voice gives me pause. *Could it be they like music?* I hum a few bars of the lullaby, but Squeakers does not return.

Maybe I need to entice him with food. Andy did feed him bread. I reach into my waistband to retrieve the melted chocolate pieces I pried from Astoria's palm. It has reformed into a hardened mass.

On the floor, I puff Andy's shirt into something resembling the rat nests I found in the mansions. I drop a bit of the chocolate in the center, kneel close to the makeshift nest, and begin to sing.

"*A frog went a courtin'. He did ride. Uh-huh, uh-huh.*

A frog went a courtin'. He did ride, a sword and a pistol by his side. Uh-huh.

He rode up to Miss Ratty's door. Uh-huh, uh-huh.

He rode up to Miss Ratty's door, a place he'd never been before. Uh-huh."

Squeakers peeks out from beneath the toppled peach crates, that once held my books.

I keep singing.

"*He sat Miss Ratty on his knee. Uh-huh, uh-huh.*

He sat Miss Ratty on his knee.

He said, 'Miss Ratty, will you marry me?' Uh-huh."

Squeakers cautiously approaches.

I hold a larger piece of chocolate out to him.

He stares at me with his one red eye and his one black eye, then chatters as if he's talking.

I hold my hand still.

He creeps up to take the chocolate from my fingers.

"So, little guy, you like chocolate. Do you want more?" I watch him.

He watches me.

I don't move.

He does. He crawls right into Andy's shirt.

I imagine he's wondering why he can smell Andy, but he can't see him. Slowly, I pull the shirt from beneath him. He scurries away, then stops to watch me lay it on my arm. On my shoulder, I place another bit of chocolate and continue the song.

"Oh, not without Uncle Rat's consent. Uh-huh, uh-huh.

Not without Uncle Rat's consent.
I could not marry the president. Uh-huh.
Uncle Rat just laughed and shook his side. Uh-huh, uh-huh.
Uncle Rat just laughed and shook his side
to see Miss Ratty as a bride. Uh-huh."

By the second verse. Squeakers scurries up my arm, scoops up the chocolate, and sits, listening to me sing, as he munches.

This time, when I stop singing, he doesn't leave. It seems like he waits for me to begin again. As much as I need him to trust me, I have no idea if he can help me find Andy, and I'm losing valuable time.

I pull Nonna's watch from under my shirt to check the time. 2:00 a.m. — darkness will last only three more hours. I desperately need Squeakers to understand. Slowly, I raise my left hand to my right shoulder, where he perches. I expect him to flee, but he doesn't.

He responds with a soft purr when I pet his head. It's now or never. There's no time to play rat games. I clasp my fingers around him and gently bring him to my lap, still petting and singing. He clings to Andy's shirt, and settles into a comfortable position.

"Oh, no, you don't." The damn rat is going to fall asleep. *At least, he isn't afraid of me. Andy must have worked with him longer than I thought.*

I reach across the corner of the overturned mattress, and lift the dented birdcage.

I bring it toward my lap.

Squeakers looks at me, looks at it, and then drags Andy's T-shirt inside. He sits on his haunches, almost waiting for me to shut the door, like he knows he's on a mission to save his master. I throw in the last bit of chocolate, snap the door shut, and leap to my feet.

In one motion, I grab Squeaker's cage and climb back into the main sewer tunnel.

I make my way to the ladder and gaze up into the night sky. *Would it be less dangerous to travel underground, following the tunnels instead of the streets?*

My decision is made as horses' hooves clomp on the bicycle path, above me.

* * * * *

After slogging through the tunnels in a constant alert state, listening for any undue noise or signal that I may have been followed, I attach

Squeaker's birdcage to my belt with a snap hook, and stare up at the exit to the White Labs. I climb quickly, emerging in the darkness, near the corner of the property. I gaze up to the laboratory roof.

I'm too short to do what Rafe did.

I breathe deep and scan the surroundings for something I can use. My vision lands on the dumpsters and garbage cans that hold toxic waste, at the far end of the parking lot. Toxic or not, they're the best I can hope for.

I pull on gloves, and struggle to lift the lightest one. Carrying it with hurried steps back to the building, I place it underneath the fire escape, and climb on the lid. I still cannot reach the fire escape's bottom rung, but from here, I spot empty produce crates that probably held Culpepper's fresh fruit, piled near the parked shuttle. Two of them should do it.

I stack the crates on top of the can, and precariously climb to the top. The bottom step of the fire escape is within my grasp. I push off my toes, and pull down with all my weight.

The metal releases far enough for me to grab the sides.

I scramble up the stairs to the roof. Packaged air-conditioning units, whose sole purpose is to ventilate the White Lab and Culpepper's mansion, surround me. The bridgeway connecting his mansion to the labs is visible from here. *What are they doing in that lab that he needs to know about, every minute of the day or night?*

I glare at the mansion's windows, every one lit with bright lights. No wonder we get only a measly three hours of electricity. He uses it all.

Another wagon arrives with children.

I crouch to the roof's floor, and choose the air handler closest to me. Quickly, I try to remove the grill. It won't budge. Each minute that passes makes it harder for me to visualize rescuing Andy. I have no idea where they have taken him by now.

I breathe in the cool night air, and release it through clenched teeth, spying another unit with a grill partially pried away. Staying low, I crawl over to it. Screws have been loosened. *Rafe must have done this earlier.*

Being so slight, I easily slip in, but not with my spotlight and solar pack. I leave them on the roof. *I can break through the filters with my knife, but first I need to stop the blower.* It's a good thing there's more than one unit cooling the lab. One disabled unit won't be detected until Andy and I are long gone.

Once I unscrew the protective screen, I face the circulating fan. Even if I time its rotation, no way can I dart through. I need to jam the blades. I kneel back and the birdcage prevents my thighs from resting on my calves. I could use the metal cage to jam the blades, but that means setting Squeakers free before I crawl through.

He's wrapped up in Andy's shirt. If I move fast enough, I can pull Squeakers and the shirt from the cage, and cover him so he takes longer than a few moments to get free. Hopefully, it's the same amount of time I need to pass through the blower.

The blower jams, making an ugly sound.

I jump past the wedged blade, and freeze. Voices echo around me.

"Damn rats must be in the air ducts again."

"Don't worry about them. They'll starve. They always do. Once they get in, they can't get out."

The voices are coming from somewhere down the air duct ahead of me. I don't have much time to contemplate where.

Squeakers escapes from Andy's T-shirt, and scuttles down the dusty stainless steel tunnel.

Stealthily, I follow. Sometimes it pays to be malnourished. I'm small enough to crawl through this industrial-sized air duct with room to spare.

As Squeakers makes a left turn, I realize where the voices come from. A grill that allows the air to flow into the rooms from the HVAC system is ahead on my left and a flashlight is spraying the darkness, through the grill.

Squeakers freezes in the light's beam.

"I told you it was just a dumb rat."

The light disappears, and Squeakers dashes forward.

I follow as fast as I can, trying not to make noise.

"There must be another one," says the first voice. "Probably a buck following the doe. Sounds like he's a big one. You know, I've seen some as big as dogs."

As I pass the grill, I peek into the room. It appears to be a security station, with TV monitors showing all the exits to the building. Guards club another crowd of angry parents, and drive them away from the front door.

The ductwork runs for several hundred feet, but Squeakers plods on like a rat on a mission.

I need to believe he's taking me to Andy.

Tiny LED lights shine on the next two grills, like miniature nightlights, but no lights shine from the rooms below.

Then Squeakers disappears.

"Oh, no!" I whisper, more to myself than to Squeakers. "Please don't slip into some airshaft. I'm counting on you, rat. You'd better be around the corner."

As if he hears me, Squeakers sits, cleaning his whiskers with his paws.

"Okay, rat. I'm not *that* slow."

Here, the tunnel twists and turns, one right after the other, in sharp succession. Left. Left again. Right. Left. Right again, and then another long stretch. Even with the cool air rushing past me, I'm sweaty. Between my nerves and my anticipation of finding Andy, I push on at a rat's pace. Up ahead, light shines into the ductwork from rooms below.

We pass a research room with test tubes and blinking machines hooked up to a major computer. One lone scientist sits logging information in electronic journals.

Children's voices echo from the next room.

My heart leaps, urging me forward. *Maybe Andy is among them?*

The room, sparkling with stainless steel counters and instruments, holds two lines of children, each supervised at various intervals by Megamark Guards. Some joke with them. Others stand rigid, clearly ill at ease in this setting.

At the far end of each line stands a doctor, or a scientist. I can't tell, other than they both wear white lab coats. The children pass by these doctors one at a time, but first the doctors give each child an ice cream cone. So mesmerized by the delicious treat in one hand, they pay no attention to the needle being poked in their other arm.

Are they drugging them? Using them for some horrid experiment, another variation of Noova?

The children seem unfazed by the experience. Maybe the scientists are administering a sedative to calm their fears. None of the kids seems to be afraid. Children are escorted out another door, as the doctors finish with them. I scan both lines for Andy. My hopes fade.

He's not among them.

Squeakers continues without me, scuttling along the long metal tunnel.

I hurry to catch up. It's easy because he's stopped, scratching at the grill before him. By the time I reach him, he's squeezing his body through the vent. I swear rats have elastic skeletons.

My gaze falls from this contortionist rat to the children in the room, and my heart stops beating.

That rat knew exactly where he was going.

Andy and two little girls, who look exactly alike, play a board game, below, in a room that looks like a child's playroom. A gauze pad is taped to one arm of each child. Whatever the doctors administered to the other children, Andy received it, too.

Squeakers chitters and scratches.

One of the girls looks up.

95

"Yikes." She screams and jumps as far away from the air duct grill as she can, cowering against the window behind her.

Andy and her sister look up to see what frightens her.

"Squeakers," says Andy, running to greet his playmate. He pulls his chair closer to the wall, so Squeakers can jump into his arms. "How did you find me?"

"Pets always know how to find their master," I say, "especially one with a good sniffer like Squeakers."

"Jax, how'd you get in the wall?" He cocks his head with the wonder only a child can have.

"Never mind how. I've come to get you out of here."

"Why?" He shakes his head slowly, as if it's the most normal thing for him to be in Culpepper's grip. "I've made two friends."

He turns to the identical girls, who appear to be at least two years older than he is. They both have long, red hair, blue eyes, and smooth white skin, except one has a scab on her forehead.

The one with the scab smiles. She steps closer to Andy and pets Squeakers.

"This is Nyla," says Andy. "She's older than Nellie."

Nellie still cowers near the window.

"By five minutes," says Nyla. "Who are we talking to, Andy?"

"My sister," he replies. "She's the best sister in the whole world. She let me keep Squeakers." A big grin stretches across his face.

Squeakers snuggles against his cheek.

"You have a sister, too?" Nellie takes two steps away from the window. "Does she look like you?"

"Not like you look like Nyla, but we both have blond hair."

"Listen carefully, Andy, I don't have much time." I don't want to scare him, but I need to stress the urgency of the situation. "Be ready for my signal, you know, the one Rafe taught us."

"Yes, I know. But I can't do it back."

"That's okay. You don't need to. Just remember when you hear it, look for me, and be ready to run."

He glances at Nyla, and then back at Nellie.

I give in to his pleading eyes. "All of you. Are you the Green girls?"

"Yes," says Nellie, with an indignant air. "And our Papa is coming for us."

"Well, just in case he doesn't make it here, be ready to go with Andy."

"We will," says Nyla.

"And here." I slip a screwdriver through the grill. "See if you can loosen the vent enough for me to slip you my walkie-talkie."

Nyla, who is taller than Andy, climbs on the chair, takes the screwdriver, then loosens two screws, enough for me to shove the walkie-talkie through, and then she refastens the grill.

"If you need me before I can get to you, use this. Rafe or Cheinstein will answer, if I can't. Somebody will always know where you are."

"But why should we leave?" asks Andy. "Why don't you come be with us here? Mr. C is really nice. He gives us toys and ice cream and—"

The doorknob at the far end of the room jiggles and starts to turn.

"Shh. Don't tell anyone I'm here. And hide the walkie-talkie."

"Okay, Jax," says Andy. "We'll put it with your book. The guard wanted to take it and I wouldn't let him have it."

"Good."

"We won't say a word," says Nyla. She shoves the walkie-talkie and the screwdriver underneath an upholstered chair, in the corner of the room.

The spine of Nonna's book is visible under the chair's skirt.

"Hide Squeakers, too. If they find him here, they'll kill him."

Andy's eyes widen, then he squints, as if he's about to cry.

Nyla darts to the door, and throws herself against it.

It slams shut. "Nellie, open the window," she says.

"Why?" asks Nellie. "The sun is coming up."

"Just do it," says Nyla, a definite authority in her voice.

Nellie immediately obeys her. It's easy to see the power an older sister wields.

Nyla holds the door shut with both hands, leaning all her weight on it. She nods toward the open window. "Drop him out," she says to Andy.

"But he'll get hurt." Andy winces.

"No, he won't," she says. "Rats are like cats. They always land on their feet. Do it, or he'll be rat stew."

Andy feeds Squeakers the last of his ice cream cone, then reaches his arms out the window.

What little I see of the dawn sky glows pink.

The door opens.

Andy releases Squeakers.

In walks Culpepper. "What's going on in here? Why was the door stuck?"

"We were playing hide and seek, and I fell in front of the door," lies Nyla.

"No, we weren't," says Nellie. "We were dropping a rat out the window."

Culpepper's face grows white. "A rat? How did a rat get in here?"

"Through there," says Nellie. She points to the air-conditioning vent. "Andy's sister brought him to visit."

"Damn it!"

Even though those girls appear to be older, that one seems younger than Andy.

"She did?" Anger peppers Culpepper's voice. His fat cheeks grow red, and his nostrils flare, as he climbs on the chair the children used to peer into the vent.

I scoot to one side so he can't see me.

"You're crazy," says Nyla. "It was just a lost rat and Andy was brave enough to catch him and throw him out the window. He saved us."

What a fast thinker that little one is. She reminds me of myself. I smile.

Culpepper's voice is farther away. "Good job, son."

I turn my head back to peer through the grate with one eye, hoping it hides my presence well enough.

"Andy said it was his pet," says Nellie. She steps away from the window and rushes to Culpepper's side. It's clear she seeks his attention.

"Coming from where you live, I understand how you might consider a rat your pet. Do you want a real pet? How about a puppy for each of you? Here." He slides open a wooden panel in the wall, to reveal a computer sitting on a recessed desk. He pushes a few buttons, and the screen comes alive.

"Pick what kind you like. It can be brought from Antarctica with my next shipment."

The children gather around the monitor.

"What is this?" asks Andy.

"It's a computer. I'll show you how it works, but first you must eat. What do you want for supper?"

Nyla asks, "Can I have a peanut butter and jelly sandwich?"

"Scrambled eggs for me, please," says Nellie.

He turns to Andy last. "And what would you like, son?"

"Acorn bread with wild onions, please."

I smile at Andy's request.

"Bread and fried onions," repeats Culpepper. "Would you like steak and cheese with that?"

"What's steak and cheese?" asks Andy.

Culpepper chuckles, but his flinty eyes focus on the air conditioning grill.

Nyla's a natural at taking care of her sister.

Andy should be okay with her until I get him out.

I convince myself to leave after one last peek, but with my rat guide gone, I must find my own way out of this metal labyrinth.

The tunnel runs for what seems like miles, with no grills visible on either side, but soon I smell food. My mouth waters like Pavlov's dogs, and I yearn for something to eat. I must be in the bridgeway from the labs to the mansion.

The next turn reveals a grill opening. My jaw clenches so tightly, it hurts, and I can't stop my fists from shaking. Four chefs race around Culpepper's stainless steel kitchen preparing meats, sauces, and vegetables. *How dare he eat like this every night when the children of the street are starving or forced to eat rat! At least, that's one good thing about Andy being here. He'll eat a whole lot better than he's ever eaten before.*

Crude music wafts through another opening, about fifty feet away. A male voice sings off-key.

As I approach the vent, I'm stopped cold, but not from the frigid air in this duct that turns my fingers and lips blue.

Silk pillows and velvet-flocked wallpaper decorate the plush room, below. White candles in gold filigree candlesticks flicker in the cool air blowing down on them from the vent. Museum-quality paintings hang on the walls. Hell! They probably *are* from the museum. One wall, lined with books, takes my breath away.

Are these all Culpepper's? He must have helped himself to everything. The library's books. The museum's paintings. The church's gold. But it isn't just the opulent room. A man. No. A boy. No, he looks older than Rafe; he lies on the tufted leather couch, apparently waiting for Culpepper to return.

I've never seen a man as beautiful. My mother was beautiful. Astoria is beautiful. But this is a guy . . . and he's beautiful. His T- shirt stretches across his muscular chest, taut and hard. His abdomen is carved like an ancient Italian statue I saw in one of Nonna's art books. His strong jawline emphasizes his perfectly proportioned face. Black hair curls along his brow, and his eyes are so dark they look black.

Oh my God! It's Cowboy. He's singing some song I don't recognize, but he sounds more like a squealing hog.

An elusive feeling blossoms somewhere deep inside me, familiar, yet totally foreign. My heart beats too fast. And then, I see his hat, a black Stetson, like the kind they wore in the old Wild West, laying on the Persian rug next to the couch.

My gaze darts from his hat to his vintage, leather-embossed boots. I recognize their thick, slanted heels and alligator uppers. No wonder I feel like I know him. I study him every time the caravan pulls into Metro City. I've watched him bargain and barter with Hoffmann, his face beneath that giant hat. He's Culpepper's private pilot and purveyor of all things from the New Continent.

"Of course," I murmur to myself. "It makes sense he's here. I hid behind his shuttle in the parking lot."

A quick headshake and I clear him from my vision. *I've got to escape this maze. No time for daydreaming. Clearly, he's Culpepper's man.*

The tunnel seems to end a short distance ahead of me. There must be a way to free myself without having to crawl all the way back to the roof.

I creep a bit farther.

Just as I reach the supposed end, the metal tunnel tilts at a sharp angle.

I can't stop myself from gliding headlong down the shaft, as if it were a slippery playground sliding board.

I land in a totally black space. I can't see my hand in front of my face. I search for my penlight in vain. It must have fallen from my pocket, when I crashed to the floor. My breathing intensifies. The fetid air down here is suffocating. I pull my knees to my chest and wrap my arms around them. My head slumps forward. *Is this it?*

I close my eyes against the inevitable. I've come this far, to end up in a black hole. My bravado dissolves into tears. *Stop! Calm down!* I can't help Andy if I stay trapped here. I gulp the rank air, and force myself to stand.

Tiny bones crush beneath my feet. I feel the small skulls through my worn-out soles. My throat spasms and I retch. I must have fallen into the same oubliette as all those lost rats. I refuse to become a skeleton haunting these walls, although I'd love to haunt the hell out of Culpepper.

My confidence returns with two more steps. I'm getting out of here. I'll search the walls for a plaster slat, then knife my way out, as long as it's not in Culpepper's dining room or bedroom.

Compared to the air-cooled ventilation shaft, this space feels like the back door of Hell.

I stagger forward, feeling my way. Feathery-light cobwebs tickle my face.

Their resident spiders crawl across my forehead.

I'm too busy brushing them away to realize I've come to a dead end. I hug the walls, and when I turn to my left, I feel a gap halfway up the wall. I plunge my fist through the opening, tearing at the loose plaster around the hole, until it's wide enough to squeeze my whole body through.

I drop to the floor again, but this time, a tiny light shines at the end of the tunnel, like a pinprick in a wall of black. Sweat mixed with tears stings my eyes. The stifling air grows hotter. I breathe harder, and plod toward the light. Then, I hear a voice.

Thoughts of who that might be flash across my mind. I turn quickly, backing into a hard wall. The tunnel grows smaller. The light grows brighter. A door opens and I fall headlong into an unknown whiteness, covering my eyes against the blinding light. I land flat on my stomach, and intense heat penetrates my skin. *Have I fallen into the sun itself?*

Repeating flashes of white dots dance before my eyes, throbbing in time with blood pulsing through my veins. I squint to shut out the brilliance.

As I look up, I focus on crystal chandeliers that reflect raging flames. Intense heat surrounds me like fire. I've been delivered from the dark, but the light is no better. My eyes burn.

Someone stands in the center of this inferno room. My eyes adjust to the light. The silhouette of a short, stocky person dressed in an insulated solar suit stands before me. A reflecting visor covers the face, but his raucous laugh echoes over my head.

I collapse in the intense heat.

"Andy." My eyes close. I'm in total darkness.

Chapter Eight

When I come to, powerful, rocklike hands grasp my upper arms and drag me down a long carpeted corridor, Megamarks guards lining each side.

The white walls haven't been painted for years. They're the color of Nonna's chickens' eggs, a speckled pale brown. Straight oak chairs sit against the walls every so often. I twist to the left in an attempt to get free, but my cheek is mashed by a left jab of the armed guard. Pain knifes through my face. Clearly, this isn't the way to escape.

One of the guards opens a door as we approach. I'm tossed into a room and flung to the floor. I hit the carpeting with a thud. Even in the dark, I can tell it's a rich, pile carpet, thick and soft against my bruised face.

The door slams behind me, and a sinister laugh echoes throughout the room. Mocking undertones of amusement scrape raw in my ears. The lights flash on and I blink to shield my eyes. Finally focusing, I take in the gluttonous expensiveness of the room.

Opulent walnut bookshelves, all filled with highly coveted books of yesteryear, cover three walls. Chests stand in piles overflowing with rich tapestries, velvets, and jewels. But what interests me most is the fourth wall, covered with portable power cells, each with a dangling hose to be connected to a white suit for travel outside during the day.

Beni's mother died inventing these suits, and this slob is using them as a commodity to bring him wealth, selling them to other cities around the globe in the same dire straits as Metro City. At that moment, I'm glad the rats killed his wife and child. No man deserves all this. At least, his wealth cannot compensate for his loss.

Sylvanis Culpepper bursts through the door, his bulbous face oozing beads of sweat.

"So what have we here?" he bellows.

I refuse to meet his stare.

He gingerly steps toward me and pulls my head up by my hair. It spills from the elastic that held it securely under my skullcap before I lost it in the slide.

"A girl dressed as a boy. Obviously, you're not of the vermin nightwalkers, are you?"

I spit on his polished shoes. He slaps my cheek with his thick hand, jerking my face to the right. "You look familiar to me, girl. Do I know you?"

"You couldn't possibly know me. I'd never allow myself to be within one hundred feet of your pathetic grossness."

"Spirited, aren't you?" He pulls me to my feet by my hair. I've no means of shielding my vision from his fat, pocked face with grease-filled pores. Standing this close, his disgusting body odor overwhelms me.

He stares into my eyes for a long second. Too long. Then his eyes widen.

"By God, you're the spitting image of your departed mother. That's why I thought I knew you. She served me well." He arches his eyebrow. "Perhaps you can, too, now that she's gone. She never complained, and always did what I requested. I can't say the same for you."

"Guards, call Mrs. Bridgewater. Have her clean this mess up, and care for the girl's bruises. I want her in my room after dinner. It's been a while since I've had me some fresh, young meat."

* * * * *

"Let's go, sweetie. The sooner we clean you up, the more time I have for myself."

Wisps of the older woman's gray hair wriggle from her bun, as she hauls me up by the elbow. Her expression radiates superiority, and she wears each line and wrinkle in her face like a badge of honor. She signals to two younger women, who grasp my arms and guide me out of the room. As we leave, they practically run me into a man wearing a cowboy hat, who walks in at the same moment.

Culpepper's snide comment carries behind me. "Colt, my boy. You're right on time. We might need to postpone our meeting until the morning. Heh, heh. Something's come up, if you catch my drift."

It's no use struggling. These two women must have been subjects in some experiment in the White Lab. Either that, or they eat steroids for breakfast. They are each close to seven feet tall, and built like bulldozers.

Mrs. Bridgewater struts in front of them as if she were the drum major leading a marching band down a football field. Her arms swing with the beat of her own footsteps.

"Set her up in Lab B. I'll be in to relieve you when she's ready," she says.

Lab B? My heartbeat quickens, pounding in my ears.

* * * * *

One strips me of my clothes. The other fills a Grecian marble bathtub with scented water. The first tries to take Nonna's watch from my neck. I fight her, but it's pointless. She buries it in my clothes and takes them from the room.

More heartache. That was the only thing Nonna actually gave me. I've no time to lament my loss. I'm forcefully submerged in the tub. Struggling, I rise to the surface. My hands shoot out of the water and are immediately bound to the sides with leather straps.

Water drips into my eyes. I'm a prisoner in the bathtub.

The Amazon women back off and leave the room. One minute later, Mrs. Bridgewater enters, carrying a sterling silver tray with an ivory comb, a thick-bristled hairbrush, and a steaming cup of liquid, wafting cinnamon and vanilla aromas into the air. The fragrance oddly calms me. It smells like Nonna's house.

"I thought you might take some tea to calm your nerves," says the old woman. She kneels next to the tub and begins shampooing my hair. Mrs. Bridgewater is as gentle as the Cyborgs were rough.

I blink back my confusion.

"You do look like your mother, Jaclyn. She'd be pleased to see how lovely you've become."

My mouth falls open. My voice shakes. "You knew my mother?"

"Hush, darlin'." She lowers her voice. "We can't talk of that. One never knows where the bugs are, or who is listening."

I feel a questioning squint flash across my face. *Both Culpepper and this lady say they knew my mother, but how?*

"I understand it's confusin', sweetie, but know this . . . ." Mrs. Bridgewater leans over me to wash my arm farthest from her, bringing her lips close to my ear. "I'm here to help you, not hurt you. Your mother was like a daughter to me. I couldn't save her, but I'll be damned if I won't do my best to save you from that scum."

Still on her knees, she straightens. "It'll be easiest if you don't resist Culpepper. He'll treat you well, as long as you do what he says."

I stare into Mrs. Bridgewater's watery gray eyes.

She massages coconut shampoo through my hair.

"As soon as we get you cleaned up, he'll be waiting on you. We don't want to disappoint him, now do we, dear?"

She rinses my hair with a pitcher of warm water, and then pulls the tub's plug. The water makes loud sucking gurgles as it swirls down the drain, disguising her whispers.

"When I unshackle you, don't resist. I'll give you further instructions, as I dry your hair."

I tilt my head in her direction. "Mrs. Bridgewater, may I ask you for something?"

"You may ask, darlin', but I—"

"My grandmother's watch—"

"Is perfectly safe." She pulls it from her apron pocket. "You'll be getting' it back when the time is suitin'." *Her words comfort me, but is she telling the truth?*

I dry off. She gives me a white silk chemise, and white slippers, then brushes my long hair, as she maneuvers the hair dryer.

"He's asked that you join him for a meal, and then you are to be delivered to his private quarters. He's scheduled to meet with the shuttle trader, too. His name is Colt. Eat the food. It's all been tested for toxins, and is safe. If nothing else, this night will provide you with a bath and a full meal.

"When the dinner is finished, ask to be excused to use the restroom. Flirt with the beast. Tell him you want to be fresh for him. He can't resist purity. He will call me to escort you, when you stand to leave. Understand?"

She doesn't give me a chance to reply. I lost her at *flirt with the beast*. He turns my stomach, not to mention, I hate him.

"Now, follow me."

"But my brother—"

"Don't you worry about Andy. He's fine. I'm watching over him and the girls, and now, you. It seems I'm a regular nanny, these days." She smiles at her joke, but it looks more like a wan twist of her lips.

My mind reels. I walk tentatively behind this old woman. I don't know her. I don't know if I can trust her. She seems willing to help me, and she says she was friends with both my mother and Nonna, but she could just be saying that. She could be leading me into a death trap. I stumble. *How did my attempt to rescue Andy lead me into the depths of revulsion? Am I doomed to follow my mother's sacrifices for Andy?* The way I see it, I have no choice.

Chapter Nine

Small wall sconces flicker as Mrs. Bridgewater leads me down another claustrophobic hallway. I feel like it's my death walk, but she startles me as we approach a double oak door. She turns to embrace me.

"This is the dining room," she whispers. "Remember, when he asks you to join him in his quarters, smile and ask if you can freshen up a bit. He will be pleased."

My eyes widen at the thought of what will be expected of me. If I were Astoria, it wouldn't be a problem, but then again, Culpepper wouldn't have anything to do with the likes of a nightwalker.

"I'll be waiting for you." Mrs. Bridgewater slips a gold charm into my hand. It's a filigree oak leaf. By the time I figure out where I've seen this before, it's too late to thank her. The double French doors open, and she escorts me in.

Gold candelabras light the dining table, illuminating the fancy crystal goblets and shining china plates. Rich, velvet curtains cover the windows, huge paintings grace the walls, and steaming platters of food line the table, enough to fill fifty bellies, but only three places are set.

Dressed in an ermine-collared smoking jacket, Sylvanis Culpepper sits at the table's head, pompously ostentatious in his gluttony.

"Ah, she's here." He sips his burgundy-colored wine. "Would you mind, Colt?"

I freeze. My eyes meet Cowboy's.

He's much younger-looking up close. He nods, as he crosses the room to hold my chair.

"I can do it myself." I exhale hard as I sit, and pull my chair closer to the table.

"I see that." Colt's eyebrows arch. He backs away. "I'm sure there are many things you can do."

He saunters to his place at the table, exactly opposite me.

I stare at my empty plate. I can't look at him without feeling torn. For months, I've wondered and dreamt about him. Now, to be this close to him, under these disgusting circumstances, I don't want him to see me as a hopeless victim.

"Mrs. Bridgewater," says Culpepper. "Would you mind serving us? The girl first."

I clench the seat of my chair until my knuckles turn white. How dare he call me *the girl*. I have a name, although I'm sure he thinks of me as a possession, not a person.

The puzzling old woman places what appears to be a thick, broiled veal chop smothered in peppery breadcrumbs in one corner of my square plate. Then, a generous scoop of garlic mashed potatoes in another. A vegetable medley of pumpkin, apples, and red onions complete my serving. The sweet gravy smells of maple syrup, and wine. My stomach tightens, as if it can consume the food through my eyes and nose, but I refuse to eat it.

Culpepper helps himself to two of everything. His heaping dish is disgusting. His gluttony accounts for his rotund shape, and the fact that there are few fresh vegetables left to trade for at the Caravan.

My eyes still trained on my plate, I sneak a peek across the table at the trader through lowered lashes.

As if he expects me to glance at him, he smiles.

Thinking of Cowboy bartering with Hoffmann and the others, I wonder how someone so young came to be so powerful in a place like Metro City. He must trade in other cities, as well. *Has he set himself up as Savior to the world?* Hoffmann said Cowboy deals in anything that will turn a profit.

My gaze shoots back to the steaming food on my plate. Their tantalizing aromas wreak havoc with my stomach.

"Eat up, girl," says Culpepper. He sucks the gravy from his veal bone. "I don't want you fainting on me."

He licks each finger in a deliberate motion as he scrutinizes me with his beady eyes, like I'm his delectable dessert.

A knock at the door interrupts his lecherous stare.

"Yes. What is it?" he calls, chugging claret from his goblet.

A Megamark soldier salutes him. "Sir, the street people are trying to free the prisoners."

"Beat them back. The sun will be rising soon. The morons will retreat eventually."

My gut twists. What despicable audacity to call his people morons, and the thought of those he staked to the meters, dying such a horrible death revolts, and sickens me.

"We did, sir," says the guard "But some of them cut the ropes. Two already escaped."

"Must I do everything myself?" he bellows. Wine sloshes out of his goblet and stains the crisp, white tablecloth, as he slams it on the table. He slides back his chair and waddles toward the door.

"I'll deal with this, now." His licentious gaze consumes me, as he leaves. "I'll be busy later, and I don't want to be disturbed."

I would have thrown up on my plate had I eaten anything.

As soon as he's gone, Mrs. Bridgewater is at my side. "Eat. You're going to need your strength."

I gasp. "Do you really think I could allow that filthy pig to touch me? I'll kill him first."

Cowboy drops his silverware, and his elbows press against the table. "Well, aren't we a tough cookie!"

His smirk irritates me. "Who asked you? I can take care of that fat slob before he knows what hit him."

"You won't have to, dear." Mrs. Bridgewater's voice remains calm. She dips my fork into the potatoes and tries to feed me like a grandmother who insists anyone at her table must eat.

"Eat." She emphasizes her words with raised eyebrows. "Don't let a good meal get away."

She shoves the potatoes in my mouth.

"But—"

"For someone who thinks she's so smart, you're not acting like it."

I look up.

Cowboy leans across the table.

"Follow her lead." He nods at Mrs. Bridgewater.

My eyes flash. Meeting his dark ones, something in his face strikes me as honest. He must see my realization, because he winks.

"Eat up," he says, and lowers himself back into his seat. "You'll need your strength if you plan to get out of here alive. The fat bastard will be back soon. If he thinks you're cooperating, your escape will be smoother."

"How do you know what I'm planning to do?" I glance from Mrs. Bridgewater to Cowboy. "Are you telling me—"

He unbuttons his sleeve and rolls it up to his perfectly formed biceps, where a tattoo of oak leaves form a circle.

My mouth drops. "You're an Eco?"

"Shh. And proud of it. Now, Mrs. B. tells me you are, too."

"My grandmother was."

"And she trained you in everything she knew." Mrs. Bridgewater strokes my hair. "Therefore, you're one of us. Though you haven't been initiated into the fraternal order, you are a sister. The charm I gave you earlier should prove to you I'm telling the truth. When you receive your grandmother's watch again, check under the back cover. Anyone who treasures the oak leaf is a member of the fraternal order of Eta Chi Omega."

"Do you understand, Jax?" Cowboy's eyes burn a hole into my heart.

How does he know my name?

"Don't try to be a hero. You're little brother needs you alive."

Culpepper storms back in through a different door.

I focus my attention on my plate, and stuff as much food into my mouth as I can. Anything, to avoid looking at him.

"Stupid vermin. I can't wait for that exterminator. He'll take care of them all, the rats, the nightwalkers, and what's left of those damn Ecos. He chuckles as he pops a stuffed olive into his mouth. "And you, too, my dear, once I'm finished with you. That is, unless you should conceive my child. Then I'll keep you around for a while. Now, eat up."

I breathe deep, ready to spill my sarcastic wit.

Cowboy's raised eyebrow stops me.

In between bites, I coolly reply, "What makes you think I haven't taken Noova?"

"Simple, my dear. Your mother would never have wanted her daughter to be robbed of the love of her own child."

"How would you know what my mother would have wanted? How dare you think you can speak for her?"

Culpepper howls.

"Don't be so naïve, girl." He rises, waddles over to the armoire behind Cowboy, and pulls open the doors.

I gasp.

A violin, so old it might crumble if touched, is encased in glass. The base is worn in the exact same place as my mother's Stradivarius.

The knot in my stomach tightens. There's no denying it's hers. My hands fly to my mouth, and I bite down hard on my lip, to keep tears from forming.

"You all have something to trade." Culpepper leers my way, as he picks his yellow teeth with the end of his steak knife.

I fight the urge to put that knife to better use.

Mrs. Bridgewater places her hand on my shoulder, more for comfort than restraint, but she must feel my muscles tense.

Suddenly, Cowboy jumps up and changes the subject. "So, Syl, about that exterminator? Should I bring him on my next trip?"

"The sooner, the better, Colt. The sooner, the better." He wipes his mouth with his sleeve and steps toward me. "Now, I have more pleasurable things to do than talk business."

Mrs. Bridgewater squeezes my shoulder. That's my cue.

"Um, excuse me, Mr. Culpepper. I'd like to freshen up before we . . . ." I swallow hard, trying to keep down what little food I ate. " . . . get started."

"Very nice. Very nice, dear." His salacious smile turns my stomach. "I shall be waiting with bells on."

Mrs. Bridgewater nudges the small of my back, urging me forward.

Is this where she leads me to a secret door I escape through? I turn to cast a quick glance at Cowboy, but he's already engaged Culpepper in some random matter. It's like I was never there.

"Hurry," whispers Mrs. Bridgewater. "We don't have much time, a small window of opportunity, if that."

She rushes me into a bedroom the size of an apartment. A huge, oversized bed stands against a burgundy- and cream-striped wall, but the other three walls are a sage color.

Odd that a man who hates the Ecos would choose the color of new buds for his bedroom.

Bookshelves line one wall, dwarfing a full size flat-screen TV on the other. Tailored curtains, like the kind from East Knob, hang from triple-paned windows with heat protectors and dark glass to filter out the sun's UV rays.

It's obvious this man has never known the darkness of the sewer or the subway.

Another wall opens into a massive closet, with four caned-inset doors that match the antique caned rocker next to it. I can only guess at the number of silk suits and ostrich shoes this man must own. He has no idea what it's like to live in ragged clothes and filth, never knowing if there will be enough to eat.

I think up ways to deliver justice to this tyrant, as Mrs. Bridgewater takes my hand.

She leads me to the bed and presses Nonna's watch into my palm.

I look up to mouth a *thank you*.

The fierce spark of defiance brightens her old eyes, but my heart pounds in my ears.

I can't bring air into my lungs, as she pulls back the bed sheets. It's then I realize the actual danger I must face in order to help Andy escape.

"Don't worry. It will never happen," she whispers. "But it must look like it will. Come, let me help you remove your chemise."

I stiffen, crossing my arms. "You mean I can't keep it on?"

"No, dear. If you're still clothed when he enters, you may end up getting hurt if he rips it off you. This way, you're in no physical danger."

"But I don't want his lecherous eyes on me."

"Better he get pleasure with his eyes than his hands. Trust me, Jax, I swear on my life. You won't be harmed. I failed miserably with your mother. I shall not fail with you."

She folds my chemise and lays it on the overstuffed striped, silk chair in the corner. Then, she turns back and removes Nonna's watch from my hand, hiding it among the folds of the chemise.

Standing naked, I feel alone and helpless. Like a child. Like Andy. But I embrace the terror. *It's better I suffer disgrace at Culpepper's hand if it will protect Andy.* Suddenly, I empathize with my mother. I, too, can endure suffering for those I love.

"Sit back, dear." Mrs. Bridgewater fluffs the king size feather pillows. "You may cover your nakedness with the sheet. He likes to unwrap his playthings, as if they're a new gift."

She backs toward the door.

I hoist the sheet to my neck.

She places her hands over her heart.

"Trust," she whispers. And then, she's gone.

I sit, shivering in the huge bed, as if I'm ill. Hot with fever. Cold with chills. I can't stop quivering. My stomach rolls in waves of nausea. Before I can feel too sorry for myself, the bedroom door flies open, slamming against the wall, and Culpepper stands in the doorway.

I squeeze my eyes shut, and cover my mouth, as nausea creeps up my parched throat. I hear his heavy breathing. Before he takes one step toward me, the warmth of a bright light heats my skin. I pop my eyes open.

He's pushed a remote button, and the lights dim in the rest of the room, but a spotlight shines on me from the ceiling, like I'm one of his prized possessions, like my mother's violin, or the Renoir that hangs in his dining room.

He stumbles toward the bed with partially dropped pants. He rips off his shirt as he steps out of the pants legs, and they fall to the floor. Popping buttons sound like muted firecrackers. His broad, hairy chest makes him look like a fat gorilla, but the rolls around his middle look like the flab of a cow's udder gorged with milk.

He slithers into the bed, fat belly jiggling, as he slides beneath the sheet.

I grasp the fitted sheet beneath me, clenching it with such ferocity my ragged nails pierce a hole in it. I'm ready to bolt, but Mrs. Bridgewater's warning replays in my mind. "Trust," she said, "Trust."

He pulls the upper sheet corner slowly, revealing my right breast, and then my left, and finally my thin, muscular legs.

Trust! What did the old woman mean? This is too close.

Cold sweat breaks out on my back and chest. My heartbeat thrashes in my ears, and my short breaths increase to near-hyperventilation.

Culpepper misinterprets my heaving chest.

"Ah, good. You're just as excited as I am." A perverted smile stretches across his face.

The smell of his wine-tinged, bad breath disgusts me.

"I can't say your mother was this enthusiastic." He leans toward me with wet puckered lips.

I brace myself for their disgusting touch on my cheek. *I swear, if he touches me, I'm going to vomit in his face.*

An urgent knock at the door stops him. "Not now," he screams. "I'm busy."

"Sir, it's imperative. I hate to disturb your pleasure, but the mob broke through the back entrance, and the lab on Level One is on fire."

"Don't move. I'll be right back." He doesn't even finish talking, as I jump from the bed.

"Oh, no you don't," he yells.

He couldn't catch me if he was in good shape. *Maybe I can run circles around him until he collapses? Maybe I can cause a heart attack?*

"Enter," barks Culpepper.

I'm not counting on the soldier at the door. A young guard with honey-colored hair enters. In that moment of panic, I think I know him, and he's come to rescue me, but my hope is dashed.

"Seize her, and handcuff her to the bed." Culpepper dresses, refusing to leave until his prize is secured.

The soldier chases me around the bed several times. I try to jump over it, but he snags my ankle, and drags me to the headboard, under Culpepper's watchful eye.

Then, Culpepper darts forward, and locks my wrist in silver handcuffs.

"You *will* be here when I get back." His glowering eyes burn. He pinches my cheek, turns, and pulls on his pants. He stomps down the hall shouting orders.

The soldier follows obediently, but hesitates at the door. He sticks his foot in the threshold to prevent it from closing.

A moment later, a man's hand grabs the door's edge. A small exchange of whispers takes place, and the soldier leaves.

The familiar dark silhouette of a man in a cowboy hat enters.

Again, I squeeze my eyes shut. Some naïve, lingering instinct from childhood makes me think, *if I can't see him, he can't see me*. Or maybe I just don't want Cowboy's beautiful, dark eyes to see my body this way, and can't face him when they do.

But he does. *How could he not?*

I struggle to cover myself with the sheet, but I can't reach it. I'm locked to the headboard in all of my skinny, naked glory.

His clean, soapy smell touches my nostrils. I can tell he's close. My eyes flash open.

He hovers over me and unlocks the handcuffs.

I jump to my feet, and scramble for the sheet.

"Let's go." He heads toward the door. "Mrs. B's got clothes for you."

He stops short at the doorway.

Forgetting my embarrassment, in the moment of escaping, I charge into his muscled back, hard and toned.

He doesn't notice.

"Fuck," he says. "We don't have time." He grabs my hand and pulls me toward the closet. Opening the third door, he pushes me in. He jumps in beside me and quietly closes the door, just as Culpepper reenters the room.

"Goddammit," Culpepper bellows. "How the hell did she get out of here?"

"Daphne," he screams, his shrieking voice filled with rage. "Get your ass in here. Where's the bitch?"

I gasp, but Cowboy pushes his finger to my lips. Now, I know why she spoke of Nonna. She was her best friend. I guess St. Sally was right. The old Ecos aren't all gone. How did Mrs. Bridgewater come to work for Culpepper? *Keep your friends close and your enemies closer.*

Mrs. Bridgewater rushes in. Her acting skills are superb. She casts a nervous glance toward the closet.

"I don't know, Mr. Culpepper. I was stationed in the bathroom waiting, as you instructed. The warm bubble bath is drawn."

"Fuck the bath. I want the bitch. I'm finished playing games."

"She couldn't have gotten far." Mrs. Bridgewater wrings the skirt of her dress. Her gaze darts around the room.

I feel Cowboy's sharp intake of breath, as he wraps his arms around me. He tucks my head under his chin.

I think I've stopped breathing.

We peer out of the caning on the closet door.

Culpepper's eyebrows rise. He charges toward us.

Chapter Ten

In that split second, Cowboy pulls me into a bear hug.

Surprised, I savor his closeness and the security of his arms.

"Sir." The young soldier is at the door again.

"What now?" Culpepper spins, throwing his hands in the air. "Did you find her?"

"Sir, we found this down the hall. It must have fallen from the girl's grasp as she escaped." He holds out a woman's antique timepiece on a gold-corded chain. It dangles from his fingertips.

It can't be mine. I watched Mrs. Bridgewater tuck the watch into my white chemise, earlier.

I divert my gaze to the folded, silk gown on the bedroom chair. The faint glimmer of Nonna's watch, enmeshed in the fabric, is obvious under the spotlight.

The one the soldier holds is identical.

Culpepper sweeps it from his fingers, then rushes down the hall.

Mrs. Bridgewater follows behind him.

The soldier hesitates again. "Five minutes. Lower hall. Side door."

Cowboy and I are still locked in an awkward embrace.

"We don't have time to get your clothes. Here, take mine." He backs away, removing his tailored, Western shirt. He throws it at me, as he pries off his boots with his opposite foot, and strips out of his jeans.

In seconds, I'm wearing his clothes.

In the faint light that shines through the caning, he looks every bit as beautiful in his skivvies and cowboy hat as he did fully dressed—until he takes off the hat, and slams it on my head.

"Tuck all that sweet-smelling gold under my hat. It's a ten-gallon. It'll hold all your hair."

"But what about you? What'll you wear?"

He throws one of Culpepper's silk robes over his muscled torso. "You don't think I have other clothes? Quick. Your ticket out of here is waiting on the first floor."

"But—"

"Just walk calmly down the main stairs. Use the map in my back pocket to shield your face. Pretend you're reading it. For a while, they'll think you're me."

"How stupid are they? You're a giant compared to me."

"Stupid!" He shoves me out of the closet, following close behind. "That soldier who just bought us some time will help you out. Now do it."

"But you're six inches taller than I am!"

"You think they're going to notice with a fire raging in the lab?" He pushes me toward the bedroom door.

I turn. "What about Andy and the other kids?"

"Don't worry. They're safe, especially Andy and the twins. Mrs. B is caring for them."

He peers out the door, and then slips into the hall, his bare feet slapping the tile floor like he's in no hurry.

I rush to the chair, grab Nonna's watch, and then remove the map from his back pocket. I slip into the hall with the unfolded map of Antarctica hiding my face.

At the bottom of the stairs, I meet the same tall, honey-haired soldier. His face looks so familiar, but I'm sure it's because I've now seen him three times.

As he unlocks the door in the servants' quarters, his hazel eyes meet mine.

"Here." He offers me reflective sunglasses, like Cowboy's. He dons a pair himself. His wide-brimmed hat shields his face, as we walk to the shuttle. He opens the door, and drops the push-button starter in my hand. "In case Colt doesn't make it out."

"What?" My heart feels like it's beating at the speed of light.

"Wait for him in the driver's seat, but whatever you do, don't take off the hat or glasses. The cameras will see you drive out. This shuttle is protected from the sun and it will get much hotter outside." He fishes for something in his uniform and slips a note into my hand, then turns and strides back to the White lab, entering the same door they took the children through.

I shake my head. I've escaped, but now I've got a new problem. What does he mean, if Cowboy doesn't make it out? I can't drive, though it can't be that hard. It must be like steering my shopping cart. Left is left and right is right. I study the controls behind the steering wheel, and then glance back up at the soldier.

Just as he reaches the door, Cowboy rushes out, dressed in alligator boots, tight jeans, and another big hat, only this one is white. *How many hats does he have?*

"Move over." He climbs into the shuttle. "Where to?"

"The only place I can go. St. Sally's."

The shuttle zooms out of the parking lot, as the sun begins to bake everything in its light.

Nausea grips me again. My nails dig into my palms, as we pass the prisoners staked at the parking meters. They squirm and reel, as the sun blisters their skin. I cover my face with my hands.

"How do you deal with this? I'd like to stake him out on the front lawn of his precious mansion, and let the sun give him a taste of his own medicine, not enough to kill him, just enough to give him third degree burns, so he can suffer."

"Before you go planning revenge, we have to get your brother out. Got any ideas?"

"Actually, I do. Take me to the Third Street Subway."

As Cowboy drives the shuttle toward the subway entrance, I glance down at the paper in my hand. A name is hurriedly scrawled across the front: *Astoria*.

* * * * *

Cowboy steps out of the shuttle and takes a whiff of the air wafting from the subway entrance.

"Holy shit!" He waves his hand in front of his nose. "It smells like an old outhouse in the middle of July."

"A what?" *What is this Fancy Dan talking about?*

"An outhouse. You know, one of those small buildings outside the main living quarters they used for one's personal business, way back when. My grandfather had one behind his mountain cabin in the country."

"Your grandfather lived in the country? So did my grandmother." As an afterthought, I add, "But she had a toilet in her cottage."

"That doesn't change the fact that it reeks down here."

The smell of unwashed clothes, body odors, and smoke mingle with the overpowering stench of human waste.

"This isn't the Grande Texas Hotel, you know." We continue down the stairs to the platform. "Culpepper has stolen our homes and our livelihoods."

Faint light filters down the steps from above and dimly shows a large black rat humping a smaller gray one on the concrete ramp in front of us. I kick them into the blackness beside the platform.

They squeal as they land.

"The sewers aren't something a fancy cowboy like you would understand, but it's the way we live."

"Oh, so now I'm a fancy cowboy? What does that make you, a plain ratgirl?"

"Could be. Especially since I plan to claim the reward for getting rid of the damn things."

"You?" His voice strains. He tries to keep it from rising. "How are you going to do it by yourself? You can't handle getting rid of the rats in this city, or Culpepper. You would have been raped by that sick bastard if Daphne, Alder, and I hadn't stepped in."

I puff out my chest, and straighten my shoulders. "I don't need you to protect me."

"You weren't saying that in the closet. In fact, I got the distinct feeling you liked being protected."

"How could you tell what I liked? You were too busy touching my ass!"

He clears his throat. "Oh, really. I can leave now, you know."

"Nobody's stopping you. I didn't ask you to follow me down here."

Sarcasm laces his answer. "I want to see what great plan you've come up with."

"Just shut up and give me a light. We're getting to the tunnel."

He pauses, and I stop to turn. "You *do* have an instrument with some sort of a light, don't you? First rule of the sewer people— always carry a light. *My* solar penlight is in my jacket."

He chuckles. "That's incinerated by now. No, I don't have a light. I didn't know I'd be spelunking this morning."

I march off in a huff. "Try to keep up, Cowboy. You'll have to follow the sound of my footsteps, then."

I ease myself into the well between the platforms, where the trains used to run. The concrete space is filled with stagnant puddles. No need to worry about the third rail, these days. The power to the subway was the first to get disconnected. I hear Cowboy pass me on the platform above.

"Hey, Cowboy, you don't hunt with those ears, do you?"

He stops short.

"I'm down here. Be careful. It's pretty steep."

The sound of his alligator boots splashing in the foul water brings a smile to my face. I can imagine the expression on his. "We're almost there."

This time he snatches the belt loop of my jeans, dragging me back a few steps.

A dim light flickers ahead, showing a stepladder against the edge of the platform. It's tucked behind a wall of useless lights and track controls.

We climb to the platform floor.

Rafe's artwork covers the once-white tile walls. Mattresses line the back wall beneath the spray art, as if it were a military barracks with one big difference — no starched clean sheets crisply folded at the corners here.

Instead, lice-infected blankets and tattered cushions lay heaped on each mattress.

In the far corner, a blue plastic tarp hangs, to isolate one mattress from the rest.

Smoke billows into the subway tunnel from the other end, where Cheinstein leans on a crutch. He hands wood scraps to a redheaded woman cooking something that resembles meat.

Cracked glass vases hold a dozen flickering candles. Three large ones, in a pie plate, are set on a folding table in the middle of the platform. The rest, shining through tall, ruby red glass, sit upon a crude altar made from stacked concrete blocks, topped with a balsawood door and an embroidered altar cloth. A large crucifix hangs on the wall above it.

The click of Cowboy's heels draws the attention of the subway dwellers.

"Where are we?" asks Cowboy. "In the Church of the Living Dead?"

A woman's strong confident voice answers him.

"You are in St. Sally's of the Subway." She steps out from the shadow behind the blue tarp, pauses, and then rushes forward. "Jax? Is that you?"

"Yes." I turn to introduce Cowboy. "And this is Colt Conrad. He's—"

"I know who he is." St. Sally steps forward and clenches Cowboy in a welcoming embrace. "Colt, how is your grandfather?"

Colt shakes his head. "He's not with us anymore. My dad found him in his rocker, about six years ago. He said he'd died of a heart attack."

Something in Colt's words triggers my memory of Nonna's death. He must have been an Eco, too.

St. Sally continues. "Boy, I miss him and his stupid jokes. He kept Rose, Daphne, and me in stitches, even in the worst of times. We could sure use some of his humor now."

My eyes widen. I stare from St. Sally to Cowboy.

"Don't look so surprised, Jax," says St. Sally. "His grandfather was one of the charter members of Eco."

I nod. "I figured as much."

"Yes, he used to make tea for us every Friday, and your grandmother, Rose, made the scones with fruits from her orchard."

The realization of who Cowboy's grandfather was comes like a spark in the dark. "Don't tell me. He was Thaddeus."

Cowboy's index fingers shoot forward in the air like two pistols. "Bingo."

Cheinstein hobbles out of the shadows.

"Jax," he yells. "Did you find Andy?"

"You're looking much better than the last time I saw you. No, I don't have Andy, but I did speak to him."

"Culpepper has all of the children in different parts of the lab," says Colt.

"And his mansion," I add. "He's got Andy and two little girls in an elegant room in his house. I watched him interact with them. He actually is treating them well. He offered them his food, and showed them how to use the Internet, suggesting he would buy a puppy for each of them."

"Why would he do that?" asks Cheinstein. "It's like they're his guests, not his prisoners."

"You're right. But why? I don't think he'll harm them. He's treating them almost *too* good. I need to get Andy out of there before I put my rat plan into action. One of the little girls he's with, I think her name is Nyla, is very motherly toward Andy. I'm sure he'll be okay, as long as he stays with her until I can get him."

At the mention of the girl's name, the redheaded woman jumps up from the grill. Her eyes fill with tears.

"Nyla? You've seen my Nyla? Is Nellie with her? Did you see my husband, too?"

I focus on the woman's worried face. "Mrs. Green?"

Her lips curve into a half-smile.

"Yes, Nellie is with Nyla."

"And William?"

I stop speaking. *How can I tell this woman, with dark circles under her eyes, and a brow wrinkled with worry, that her husband died an awful death at the meters?* I drop my eyes, and take her trembling hands in mine.

"I'm sorry. He did try valiantly to free the girls, but they beat him and the other parents into retreat.

"Was he killed?" Her eyes pray my answer is no.

I simply nod.

She wails into St. Sally's shoulder.

"How did you escape, then?" asks Cheinstein.

"You would have been proud of her," says Cowboy. "Somehow she got herself into the HVAC unit."

"You crawled through the air conditioning ducts?" Cheinstein looks surprised. "How did you think of that?"

"She didn't." The corner of the blue tarp flips up. Rafe stands beside it. "She followed my plan."

I run to his side.

His eyes are red and swollen from crying, but he tries to hide it by rubbing them, as if the acrid smoke bothers them.

Only one thing would make Rafe cry.

An ache wells in my chest. My voice comes out a low whisper.

"Oh no. Don't tell me . . . ." I cover my mouth with quivering fingers, stopping my own words; I don't dare to complete my thought.

"She's still with us, Jax," says St. Sally, placing her arm around my shoulder. "She's lucky you and Rafe got there when you did."

"May I see her?" I finger the note Alder gave me. *Maybe it would make her feel better?*

"You may," says St. Sally. "But before you go in you should know something."

I narrow my eyes. "What?"

"She doesn't look the same. I couldn't save her eye, and the skin across her cheek needed stitches. Right now, her face is swollen, but in a few days the swelling will go down and we can see more of what the injury entails."

"She's alive, at least." I duck under the tarp.

Astoria is propped up with all the pillows Rafe could find.

Candles burn on each side of her mattress. Wrapped gauze covers the right side of her face. Cloth strips encircle her head. She looks like a child in a mound of scorched marshmallows.

I grasp her hand, and she flinches, but her breathing is steady.

St. Sally stands beside me. "She won't hear you. I sedated her until the worst of the trauma passes. The heroin will lessen her pain."

I turn on St. Sally, my eyes wide. "You didn't—"

"I had no choice. She'd be screaming in agony without it. She won't be the first nightwalker to hide her pain behind the shadow of the drug."

I swallow hard. *Does St. Sally know the circumstances of my mother's death?*

I slip Alder's note into Astoria's hand, and place her other hand over it. I can't take the chance Rafe will find it before she wakes.

As I step back to the platform, St. Sally convenes a meeting. She, Mrs. Green, and Cheinstein sit at the card table. Hoffmann, Rafe, and Colt stand behind them.

Colt holds the fourth chair out for me.

St. Sally speaks. "Colt tells us you have a plan."

Chapter Eleven

Hope shines in their eyes. All except Colt's. His reflect something else. I'm not sure what. Concern, maybe? What do they think I'm planning? I can't change the sun's course or the ravaging rainstorms. Hell, I can't even get my brother back from Culpepper without their help, but I can do one thing. I'm sure of it.

I ease myself into the last chair. "Yes, I have a plan. I'm going to take Culpepper's challenge to rid Metro City of the rats. I plan to take Andy to Antarctica, and pay for my friends' passage with the thirty thousand dollars."

"That's it? That's your plan?" Hoffmann paces behind the group. "When Sally summoned me on the walkie-talkie, I thought it would be more substantial, not just a bunch of orphans trying to escape this hell."

"What did you think I was planning?" My gaze shoots to Colt. *What did he tell them?*

"A way to rid us of the scum that threatens our lives," Hoffmann cries, his hands flailing in the air.

"Culpepper? Believe me, I would if I could, but someone pointed out to me recently that I must prioritize my efforts." Again my gaze lands on Colt.

He nods. "You're right." He inches closer. "Start small. If the rest of you don't mind, I need to hear the plan. The caravan is scheduled to move out any minute and Culpepper thinks I'm already aboard. If there's anything I can do, or anything you need me to bring back for the effort, I need to know, now."

"First, how you plan to rid the city of the rats?" St. Sally also sits forward with her question. "There are thousands of them."

Her spark of interest gives me the confidence to tell them. "I'm going to sing them to the river, where they'll drown."

Cheinstein looks skeptical. "Um, I hate to interrupt your fantasy, Jax, but first of all, singing to rats? And second of all, rats are great swimmers. They can swim for miles. They won't drown."

Rafe jumps to my defense. "Yes, under normal circumstances that's true, but the Elan is a toxic pit of poison, thanks to the runoff from Culpepper's labs. It's a brilliant idea, but I don't understand how you think you can get one rat there, never mind all of them."

"If I prove to you I can get the rats to follow me, will you all help? I can't rid Metro City of Culpepper, but I can eliminate the rats. At least that's one thing that would make your lives better."

"You're going to sing to the rats?" asks St. Sally, still unconvinced. "I don't understand.

"I'll prove it to you. I can call hundreds of rats with my song."

"What song?" asks Colt.

"It doesn't matter. Lullabies. Church hymns. Children's songs. Watch!" I walk to the edge of the subway platform, and face the black pit.

My human audience sits behind me.

Hopefully, my rodent audience will soon cover the tracks in front of me.

I choose a pretty song I remember, from when Nonna took me to church. Loud and clear, I sing out *Ava Maria*. The acoustics of the empty subway carry my voice.

Soon, I hear skittering. I finish the entire song and start again. My human audience is silent, so are the rats.

At the end of the second round, I whisper. "Rafe, bring a light, but don't move too quickly."

Rafe's cautious footsteps sound behind me. He flicks the button.

Beady eyes reflect the sparkle of his penlight.

I look over my shoulder. "Everyone, quietly bring your light."

Colt tiptoes to my side, his cowboy hat pushed to the back of his head. His eyebrows rise. His eyes widen, as he shares a look with me.

"That was beautiful," says Mrs. Green. She also glides softly to the edge.

The others follow.

Soon, multiple lights shine upon the multicolored mass of fur on the tracks.

Hundreds of rats sit upright, mesmerized, as I continue singing.

Colt whispers beside me, "I'll be damned."

His hand on my shoulder sends a tingling sensation through me. I turn.

He's watching me, not the rats.

And then, I stop.

The rats linger, waiting for more song. When I don't sing again, they wander off.

"Are you telling me singing will rid us of those miserable creatures?" asks Hoffmann. "I can sing."

"So can I," says St. Sally. "I was high soprano in St. Theresa's convent. Let me try. If one voice calls that many, maybe a whole chorus will call them faster. We could be stationed throughout Metro City."

By now, the rats have scattered.

St. Sally takes a deep, controlled breath and sings *Adeste Fideles*, a Latin Christmas Carol. She finishes and waves for the lights.

Everyone clicks them on at the same time.

The well is empty.

"So, it's not the singing," says Colt. "It's Jax's voice. It's hypnotic."

"It's beautiful," says Mrs. Green, still crying. "I believe you can do it, Jax, and when Culpepper and the City Council give you the reward money, would you do me a favor? Would you take my girls with you?"

I clear my throat. "Of course, I will. I don't think anyone here would protest me taking two more children with me."

"Well, what about the rest of us?" bursts Hoffmann. "Are we supposed to stay here and rot?"

I'm taken aback by his anger and strike with my own. "You'll do fine, why can't you pay for your own passage? Lord knows you trade my findings for more money than you give me."

"Yes, but after I pay the bribe to the Megamark that patrols the station, I barely have enough to trade for food."

"At three thousand dollars a ticket, Jax can take nine of you with her and Andy," says Colt. "So let's hear how she plans to get into the Council to present herself. If she's successful, then we'll worry about who goes with her. This all has to take place in one week. That's when Culpepper expects me back again."

"I can pose as the exterminator you're bringing from the New Continent."

"How?" asks Colt. "Culpepper would recognize you in a heartbeat, especially after last night."

My face grows hot. I want to forget the near rape, but I'll never forget that bastard's salacious eyes.

"You wouldn't have a chance to get one word out, never mind one note."

"I would if I wore a disguise. I could change my appearance."

"It might work," says Colt. He checks his watch. "Quickly, what will you need from me besides an escort into Culpepper's Council Meeting?"

"After last night's close encounter, I need to change the color of my eyes."

"Okay. I'll bring contacts. What color?"

"Let's make them otherworldly. Purple."

"I can do that. I'll give them to Hoffmann, as part of his trade. I'll also give him the time and place where we shall rendezvous. Good luck, everyone."

"Here, you'll need this to get back to the entrance." I hand him one of the flashlights on the table.

His dark eyes meet mine and he winks. Then, he dons his special UV sunglasses and sunscreen gloves and sprints toward the surface.

"We'll need a place to meet," says Rafe, bringing my attention back to the group. "One not easily found by the Megamarks."

"Our sewer tunnel is trashed," I say. "And the apartment is obviously out of the question."

"They've randomly been targeting different subway stations, too. We're just lucky they haven't gotten to this one yet," says St. Sally.

Cheinstein starts to speak. "We could—"

I clear my throat, warning him with my eyes, and a slight headshake. "We have one week to come up with a solid plan."

"What were you going to say, boy? Do you know a place where we can meet?"

Hoffmann leans toward Cheinstein, rubbing his hands together as if he were about to discover a new hiding place he could infiltrate.

Cheinstein's eyes meet mine. Then, he shoots a glance at Hoffmann. "No. I was going to say we could eat before we decide. The meat is ready."

"We can eat after we decide who'll accompany Jax out of here, if she's successful." says Hoffmann. "If I'm going to play an important role in the exchange of goods for the disguise, I think I should be one of them."

"My first priorities are to my friends. Astoria, Cheinstein, and Rafe will be next after Andy. Nyla and Nellie make six. That leaves three spaces and Mrs. Green should take one of them. The girls have already lost their father."

"So that leaves two spaces," says St. Sally.

"Yes, and you will take one of them. Without you, half of us wouldn't be alive." I nod back toward the blue tarp where Astoria sleeps.

St. Sally stares, openmouthed, over my shoulder.

Cheinstein's eyes widen.

I spin around. Everyone's eyes are drawn to Astoria, clinging to the tarp beside her makeshift hospital bed, the yellow note unfolded in her hand.

Her voice is barely audible, but there's no mistaking what she says. "Alder will take the last spot."

Rafe beats me to Astoria's side.

She crumbles into his arms, dropping Alder's note on the floor.

I tuck it into the jeans I'm wearing and rush to make her comfortable, again propping pillows at her back, as Rafe eases her down to the bed.

Conscious, she struggles to keep her good eye open. She runs her hand along the massive bandage covering the damaged one.

"Is it gone?" she whispers.

"Is what gone?" I answer back.

"Don't play games with me, Jax. My eye. It feels like it's gone."

"She can't answer that, Tori," says Rafe. She wasn't here when St. Sally stitched you up."

Astoria gasps. "Oh, my God. Andy? I remember he was missing. Did you find him?"

I look to Rafe for reassurance.

He strokes Astoria's blood-soaked curls.

Should I tell her?

He nods.

"No. I didn't get him, but I will. We were just discussing my plan."

"Alder says he will guard him with his life. For that, we owe him."

Rafe flinches. He steps away from Astoria's reach, and his gaze shifts to the floor.

"We don't owe that damn Megamark Guard shit." His eyes flash at Astoria. "I would have gotten Andy out of there just fine if Alder hadn't put you in danger."

"Rafe, calm down." I press my hand on his. "We don't know Alder had anything to do with it. From what I saw out front, he tried to protect her."

"Whatever!" He storms out, his bravado or his feelings hurt. Or both.

Astoria moans. "The pain. It's back."

"St. Sally," I call. "Astoria needs you."

St. Sally enters the makeshift room with her drug paraphernalia in her rosary box. She lays the syringe, an antique silver spoon, and a stretchy rubber tube, once used for physical therapy, on the soiled sheet.

I leave before she concocts the mixture she's about to shoot into Astoria's veins. I don't want to be reminded of my mother's demise. I can't bear to watch Astoria follow the same path.

On the other side of the tarp, Rafe tears into the charred meat with such violence, he's either terribly hungry or the meat pays for his jealousy.

Mrs. Green offers me a piece, but I refuse. "You eat it. I ate last night."

"I'll bet you did," says Hoffmann, bristling. "Your belly is full, and you smell like flowers, not piss and B.O. like the rest of us. Doesn't seem as if the Big Man treated you too badly."

I glare at him. "You have no idea what I went through."

"How bad could it have been?"

I want to lash out at his arrogance, but draw in a slow, controlled breath before I answer. "Horrible. Even a nightwalker would have been scared."

"I doubt that. Your little friend, in there, seems pretty cozy with the Guard. I'm sure she wouldn't mind a roll with their boss."

I lunge toward him, my fist cocked and ready.

St. Sally slips between us, and leads Hoffmann a few feet away from the grill with a strategically placed arm around his waist. The flickering embers reflect on their faces, as they speak.

"Hold your tongue."

Hoffmann's voice carries through the empty station. "Why should I?"

"Otto, don't antagonize the girl. Her plan might work. You witnessed the power of her voice, and you have such an important role in this charade. Without you securing the colored lenses from Colt, the plan will never come to fruition. You heard her say Culpepper knows her eyes. I wouldn't worry about whether you take place number eight or number nine. I'm certain you will have one." St. Sally's pacifying voice soothes the cranky pawnbroker.

"What about the nightwalker? Wouldn't Jax honor her friend's request? Would she actually consider a no-good Megamark before one of her own people?"

"I wouldn't worry about that, either, Otto. A week is a long time, especially in this ever-changing city." St. Sally nods toward Rafe, still stewing at Astoria's request. "Culpepper's young gun may not live to see the day Jax attempts to claim the reward."

"Ah." Hoffmann strokes his chin. "I see your point." A smirk stretches across his face and he seems satisfied with St. Sally's implication.

"You go about your business, and I'll take care of mine." She sweeps her hand toward the altar, and Astoria's bed. "When the day arrives, I shall send one of the Altar Boys to fetch you. They'll bring you to our new meeting place, for clearly each passing day brings this hidey-hole closer to being discovered."

Hoffmann's disdain reflects in his gray eyes. He lowers himself to the tracks.

"So long," he yells. "It's a date—one week from today."

He waves, then shuffles along the tracks into the dark subway tunnel headed toward his own sanctuary.

With Hoffmann gone, St. Sally calls Rafe, Mrs. Green, Cheinstein, and me back to the table. She takes my hands in her gnarled fingers.

"Jax, I'm sorry I brought Hoffmann into this, but his participation at the caravan station will not draw attention, and you need those lenses for your disguise. What would you have me do?"

"I need you to nurse Astoria back to health. The sooner she can travel, the sooner we can leave. Rafe will bring her to the museum." I search Cheinstein's face.

His smile brightens. The dark scab on his lip doesn't break.

"I knew you were going to suggest the museum, but the fewer people who know where we are, the better. The museum is the perfect place to finalize the plan. As soon as the sun sets, Rafe and I will meet you at the secret entrance. The three of us will search what's left of the displays for items we can use in our scheme."

"And me?" asks Mrs. Green.

"Your job is to keep Astoria's walkie-talkie on at all times. I told the children to contact us if their situation changes. Right now, they're under the watchful eye of Daphne — Mrs. Bridgewater."

"She's a wonderful person," says St. Sally. "They couldn't be in more loving hands."

"I agree, and that's why the ninth spot should be hers."

"Very well, then," says St. Sally. "No one reveal the chosen nine to Hoffmann. He can be a vindictive son of a bitch."

* * * * *

I curl up on one of the stained mattresses along the wall. Nonna's watch presses against my chest. I can't get comfortable. I check the time and am startled to discover the case rattles, but the hands still keep time, so I ignore the noise.

Exhausted, my brain clicks away on scenarios of how I can get Andy out of Culpepper's clutches. *What should be the next step of my Rat Plan? Is Hoffmann trustworthy?*

Somehow, Cowboy sneaks into my thoughts. I recall his closeness. I remember his warmth. Despite the danger, he was right, I did like being in his arms. I roll over. *What's wrong with me? Now is not the time to be falling for a guy I hardly know.* I squeeze my eyes shut, and after tossing and turning, sleep finally comes.

Several hours later, someone shakes my shoulder. I feel like I've just fallen asleep.

"Jax. Something is happening above," says St. Sally.

I bolt upright. "What?" I scan the platform.

Rafe is geared up, ready for combat. Cheinstein stands next to him, leaning on his crutch. Both are dressed in black.

I rush to their side. "What's going on?"

"A massive thunderstorm," says Rafe. "It's so dark up there you can't even tell it's day. The sun is nowhere in sight, but neither are the Megamarks. The downpour makes visibility almost nil and anyone with half a brain will stay sheltered."

I smile. "Which is why it's the perfect time to make our escape."

"Lightning brightens the entire sky in the distance," says Rafe. "And the storm front is bringing it closer. If we leave now, we can dodge the bursts of light and make it to the museum before the Megamarks start their patrols again."

The crinkle of the plastic tarp behind me draws my attention.

St. Sally pulls it back, and pushes Astoria, seated in a wheelchair, into the middle of the platform. Duct tape secures a plastic bag over her bandages, and St. Sally's old, black nun's veil, covers them both.

Lips clenched, Astoria grips the wheelchair tightly.

My darting glance to Rafe questions why.

"They're going to end up searching here, and she's in no condition to run. No one will expect us to move in a severe thunderstorm. Between the steam rising from the hot asphalt, and the huge drops of rain pelting the ground, you can't see a thing. It's the best we can hope for. Parts of the streets are already washed out. Everything that isn't tied down is headed toward the river. I'll push Tori. You help Cheinstein and clear away anything that might hinder the chair's wheels. You ready?"

"Yes." I tuck my hair beneath Cowboy's black hat.

"Hurry," says Rafe. "The storm is raging, now."

St. Sally approaches me. "I'll check with you when I can. Mrs. Green has already bundled the bandages and tapes. I'll be packing my things."

I give her a wary look. "What things? Your rosary box?"

She ignores my reference to the drug paraphernalia. "You can find us in the catacombs beneath The Immaculate Heart of Mary Church. A few of the street families are already established there. The Altar Boys will be our contact. Rafe knows how to get in touch with me, if you need me."

"Let's go, Jax." Rafe taps his boot impatiently.

Cheinstein has already hobbled halfway up the handicap ramp to the entrance. As I run to help him, St. Sally slaps a crinkled brown paper bag in Astoria's lap. It doesn't take much to guess what's in it.

I smell the rain before we reach the top of the ramp. *Rafe was right.* The downpour looks like a solid gray wall. Black clouds obscure the sun, which is good for us, but the torrential rains are treacherous.

Rafe steps into the alley to check the street.

"Just want to make sure no Megamarks are on patrol in this bitch of a storm," he shouts. He returns, grabs the handles of Astoria's wheelchair, and darts out into the downpour.

Cheinstein and I follow. Cowboy's hat protects my eyes from the onslaught of raindrops, but their driving intensity feels like tiny knives piercing my skin. They furiously bounce across the pavement, and ping off whatever glass windows are left downtown, but they fall so fast, they merge into a free-flowing stream.

The sky is an ever-changing light show of blue flashes and flickering purple sparks.

Cheinstein uses his crutch with such proficiency, his walk becomes a fast hop. At the corner of Third and Main, the massive strength of the storm's water rushes down the street. Gutters at the curb on either side have become small swirling streams carrying everything from cardboard boxes to empty plastic bottles to bits of plaster and wood from the piles of collapsed buildings. As storm waters meet the torrents of rushing water from the adjacent corner, a small river forms, taking everything in its path toward the Elan River.

Rain blasts into Rafe's eyes. "This Goddamn rain is blinding me." As fast as he wipes his eyes, they fill again.

"We have to cross here," he shouts, trying to compete with the thunder above us. "Hold tight to Cheinstein, and watch your own footing."

"Are you ready?" I ask Cheinstein, grasping his waist.

"Yeah. Let's go. The museum is only three blocks from here." Cheinstein doesn't have a hat; the raindrops pelt his face, too.

I swipe his hair back, trying to relieve the rush of rivulets into his eyes, when a scream rings out ahead of me.

Chapter Twelve

Rafe is knee-high in water at the center of the intersection, fighting to free himself from the branches of a gnarled tree, where the streams of debris merge. I can barely make out the tipped wheelchair ahead of us. Astoria is not in it.

My grasp tightens on Cheinstein. "Will you be okay?"

He nods.

I leave him on the sidewalk. "Wait here."

Almost losing my balance, I splash through the oncoming water in the street, determined to reach them. As I approach Rafe, he flings the wheelchair into my hands.

"Shit! Take this!"

I lean my entire weight on the wheelchair, holding it down against the rushing water.

Finally, Rafe frees himself and splashes after Astoria.

The rushing current sweeps her down the street, the paper bag clutched in her arms.

A large piece of wood hits Rafe from behind and knocks him down. Astoria is carried farther away. All I see is St. Sally's bobbing black veil in the onslaught of water.

"Oh my God!" I bite down on my lip to control my fear. I hold my breath; everything seems to move in slow motion, but I concentrate on aiming the wheelchair toward them, dodging shit the current carries, careful not to lose my footing. As I drive forward, not thinking of my own safety, I cut the distance between us.

Rafe abandons trying to run. I can tell by the determination on his face his anger drives him. He plunges into the street turned river and frantically swims toward Astoria.

She desperately clings to a streetlamp pole down the block.

Rafe catches up to her.

We've gone three blocks in the wrong direction, and the construction debris is more abundant here. I dodge old crates, broken wheel barrels, and boards with nails sticking out. When I look up, I'm a few feet from Rafe and Astoria.

He desperately grasps the same pole, his arms wrapped around Astoria from behind, cradling her against the onslaught of debris.

As I reach them, Rafe grabs the wheelchair, while I support Astoria.

She's too weak to stand by herself. Her bandages are soaked, but she still clutches the crumpled bag. *Her pain must be overwhelming to hold on to that bag through all this.*

Rafe eases her into the chair. We both take hold of the handles, our arms crossing in front of each other and steer it toward a lesser current on the sidewalk. The crooked shadow leaning on his crutch, just ahead, is Cheinstein. We struggle the last few yards to reach him.

"Let's make two trips," I shout. "First, Astoria, the same way we brought her here. Then, we'll come back for Cheinstein."

Rafe gives me a thumbs-up.

Cheinstein nods and holds his position, using his rubber-tipped crutch as a support.

Rafe and I use the same double-steering technique to get Astoria across to the opposite corner, where the torrential rains run into the street from a sloping sidewalk.

She's safe parked at the top, clinging to another lamppost, above the rushing torrent.

We slosh back for Cheinstein, and with each of us on a side, we practically carry him through the raging water. Safe on the other side of the street, we stick to the sidewalk until we get to the alley behind the museum.

Cheinstein waits with Astoria, as Rafe and I open the camouflaged entrance, something the Megamarks would never find, thanks to him.

I slip through first, and turn back to assist Cheinstein.

His crutches thud as he hurries to the second disguised door, the entry to his dad's basement laboratory.

Rafe guides Astoria into my hands, and then slips through himself. He whisks her around, and pulls her close. His eyes close, as he wraps her in his arms. "I'm sorry. I was so anxious to get you here I should have been more careful."

"It's fine, Rafe," she says. "We're here now. Everything will be fine."

"Okay. I've got to go back and help St. Sally move," he says. "You have the walkie-talkie?"

"I have three," answers Cheinstein from the lab. "I calibrated a new set the other day."

"Good. Call me if you need me. See you soon, Tori." He runs his hand lovingly along her unbandaged cheek, and then climbs out the exit, securing it as he leaves.

I guide Astoria into the giant basement room. "We need a place where she can lie down."

"She can rest on my cot," says Cheinstein. He nods to the corner where a small folding bed is set in the shadow of one of the pillars that supports the high vaulted ceiling of the museum's work lab. Here, Mr. Li and his team of archeologists rebuilt the massive dinosaurs that were exhibited on the first floor.

Cheinstein turns on the lights. Powered by solar cells, the tubes are first dim, and then grow to a white brightness. He pulls his wet shirt over his head, behind a wall of oak file cabinets.

He returns in dry clothing while Astoria shivers.

"Do you have anything that will fit her? She needs to get out of these clothes."

Cheinstein rummages through the file cabinets. I lean against a large wooden worktable covered with tools and pieces of machines. Some parts are mismatched, some in the process of invention, setting up strange-looking mechanical things that might peel potatoes or fly like remote helicopters. Another, equipped with a black, square box, blinks blue from a small solar cell.

"I have these." He offers me a pair of men's boxer shorts.

I grimace. "I don't think so. You don't have anything else?"

He pulls out every drawer of the oak file cabinet and comes up with a mismatched pair of socks and a hat. He stares at me, wide-eyed, and shrugs.

No wonder he has patches on his patches. The boy has no clothes. *If I ever get out to pick again, I'll find him some.*

He scratches his head, like he's unearthing an idea in that thick, black mop of wet hair.

"You could try one of the displays upstairs, but it's really dark up there. The dinosaurs were dismantled and sold to other museums, and the rest were either looted or broken by the Megamarks before they boarded up the museum, but there might be something left."

Hmm. That accounts for the paintings in Culpepper's home. "Where should I look?"

"First, check to make sure it's still raining. You can't tell whether it's day or night down here. If the sun has returned, you take the chance of dying from the heat on the upstairs floors, and you can't go up at night because you need a light. Culpepper's soldiers will see it glowing through the upper-floor windows."

"I'll be careful. Keep Astoria warm until I get back."

"I'll make coffee," he says. "That's one of the two things my dad kept for late nights. Coffee and rice." He starts an old-fashioned percolator powered by a fully charged solar cell, as I make my way toward the disguised door that leads to the first-floor stairs.

"Be careful when you step to the other side," yells Cheinstein. "Rafe made the door look like a broken mirror and tiny pieces fall on the floor every time it's opened."

"Thanks for the warning." Shattered mirror pieces crunch beneath my boots, as I climb the marble stairs.

The rain hasn't stopped. Its intensity increases, pounding the windows like a giant power washer. Rafe calculated the perfect time for us to get here. By the sound of the thunder, the storm is right over us. Lightning flashes illuminate the first floor of the museum. *I hope he's okay.*

The only things that remain of the displays where the ancient dinosaurs stood are the engraved bronze plates describing the beasts' name and prehistoric era.

I remember coming here with my mother when I was Andy's age. I always begged for a soft pretzel. The snack bar, across from the dinosaur display, used to be filled with people. The posters on the wall fascinated me, while we waited in line. They listed what floors the displays were on.

I step over torn napkins, and two rats scurry across my feet from behind the food counter. *They probably use the napkins to cushion their nest.* I scan the ripped posters, still mounted on the wall.

First Floor – *Dinosaurs Triassic period – Cenozoic Eras*

Second Floor – *Neolithic Cultures 7,000 to 3,000 BCE*

Third Floor – *Medieval Age 400 to 1400*

Fourth Floor – *The Space Race 1957 to 2011*

Fifth Floor – *The Observatory*

Lightning, through the beveled arched windows, illuminates my way up the massive marble staircase. *Something must be left on the mannequins in one of the displays.* Since the Neolithic clothing was nothing more than animal skins, I go straight to the third floor.

The Middle Ages display is ransacked like my sewer tunnel. Shards of colored glass from a stained-glass window depicting The Crusades litter the floor like tiny pieces of rainbow. A bust of an ancient philosopher lies in fragments. Three years of dust and grime penetrate the mannequins' costumes, and a few have holes where rats sought fancy fabrics for their nests.

The Medieval illuminators' pictures hang crooked on one wall, facing depictions of the actual styles of the early Renaissance. Scholars and the wealthy wore red. Peasants wore undyed wools of brown and gray. Above the pictures is a fake balcony. Gnawed ratholes make the papier-mâché and wood balcony look like moldy Swiss cheese. A smashed mannequin of Juliet Capulet hangs over the side. Her wig lies on the floor beneath her, and one arm dangles longer than the other, but she's still dressed in her gown. I need that gown for Astoria.

I push a replica of Henry VIII's Tudor throne beneath the balcony. Climbing to the top of the high back, I balance on tiptoe, reaching for the mannequin's dangling arm. My fingers barely touch the tip of the sleeve, but I stretch to grasp its edge. I jump from the throne to the floor, and the mannequin topples over the edge, bringing the entire rat-eaten balcony with her.

With no time to get out of the way, the most I can do is protect my face with my arms. The mannequin and I are buried beneath plaster of Paris, papier-mâché, wire mesh, and thin slatted wood strips. Coughing, I wriggle from beneath the debris to find another mannequin has fallen on top of me. It's the boy who was supposed to be Romeo. He's dressed in a tight red jacket, with puffy sleeves laced to the armholes, a red velvet laced doublet, and red and yellow velvet breeches. Yellow leggings with bows at his knees complete his outfit, well, almost. Someone stole his shoes.

I sit him on King Henry's throne and quickly undress Juliet. *Astoria needs this dress more than she does.* I strip out of Colt's wet clothing and slip on a servant's tunic.

When I return to the basement, Astoria huddles beneath an old beach towel. Her hands cup a mug of coffee stew. Chunks of stale bread float in the coffee.

"Where did you get the bread?" I ask, hanging Cowboy's clothes over a chair to dry.

"St. Sally packed it in my bag." Astoria nods toward the wet paper bag on the floor next to the cot.

"Here's yours," says Cheinstein.

As I sip steaming coffee, my thoughts wander to Andy. *What is he having for breakfast today?* By the way Culpepper treats him, he's probably slurping up baked cinnamon French toast with fresh strawberries or blueberry waffles with real maple syrup. *What if he never wants to come home?* Pff. *What home? I won't blame him if he chooses to stay where his belly can be filled with wonderful food instead of dandelion greens and pine nuts.*

I take another sip and sit next to Astoria. "How do you feel?"

"I'm tired, but I feel better than I did yesterday. I need to sleep."

"Well, put this on first." I set my coffee on the floor and slip the mannequin's under-dress over Astoria's head. The beaded bodice that goes over it is trickier to get on, and I lace it up for her. I towel her hair dry, now, in tight ringlets. Without that ugly bandage, she could have been Juliet.

"So what's the next part of the plan?" Cheinstein tinkers with his inventions as we speak.

"I need a disguise. Obviously, I can't march into the City Council looking like myself. Culpepper would recognize me with or without clothes. I must convince him I'm the exterminator from the New Continent."

"How about a wig?" asks Astoria.

I wring the rainwater from St. Sally's black nunnery veil and cover my blonde hair with it. "What do you think?"

Astoria nods. "You can't miss those amber eyes."

"It's a good thing Colt is bringing you purple contacts," adds Cheinstein. "Even with dark hair, we can still tell it's you."

"How about no hair?" I ask, jumping up from the cot. I'm excited with the possibility of fooling Culpepper. "And no eyebrows. And weird magnifying eyeglasses that make my purple eyes look bigger than normal."

"You'll look like a freak," says Cheinstein.

"Good. The freakier, the better. What else? A moustache?" I stick a piece of black electrical tape, from the table, on my upper lip. "Or a tattoo down the side of my face."

"Why don't you get a pirate hat with ostrich feathers while you're at it?" Cheinstein laughs. "Maybe he'll think you're Captain Hook."

"Let's make a list of disguise possibilities. Between what you've got here and what I can pick, we should be able to come up with something that will work."

I follow Cheinstein into his father's private office. I assume it will be barren, with a desk, a computer, and a bookshelf, but I stop mid-stride and my mouth falls open.

Cheinstein stoops to pull a museum ledger out of the bottom drawer of a desk, but the giant water tank across the room, filled with green plants on the water's surface, fascinates me. Oversized solar cells, which Cheinstein obviously connected to a solar panel somewhere, powers the lights shining above the tank, and fish, live, non-toxic fish, swim through and below the plants.

"So this is what Rafe meant when he said you had a fish tank. I thought he meant you had a small aquarium, with neons or guppies or something. This is awesome!"

"It's not a fish tank, it's a synergistic combination of aquaculture and hydroponics called aquaponics. It was my mother's experiment. The plants get nutrients from the fish, and the fish get oxygen from the plants. With her Ph.D. in biogenetics, she didn't know if she wanted to be a doctor or a scientist. She dabbled in both areas before Culpepper offered her the Head Scientist position at the White Lab." His gaze goes distant.

I can only imagine he's thinking how his life might be different if she had chosen the medical field instead of science.

I touch his hand in an understanding gesture. I've played the *what if* game many times.

He snaps out of his contemplation to meet my gaze. "It's efficient and eco-friendly. I'm trying to grow lettuce from the super-seeds she developed before she died. And, when the fish get bigger, we can eat them with a salad made from the lettuce."

"But they're goldfish."

"They're carp. My mother's family ate them all the time in China. We can, too."

"Culpepper would flip if he knew you had a self-sustaining food source going on here."

Cheinstein's smile breaks into a grin. "Well, we just won't invite him to our first fish fry."

"Your mom would be so proud of you, continuing her work. Did you help her with anything else?"

"She developed a conscious anesthesia so doctors could converse with their patients during surgery."

I squint, trying to remember what they did when the hospital was open. *My mother had a friend who was operated on, and I think she told me she was conscious.*

"Didn't they already have that?"

"Not really. They used a variation of this idea for brain surgery years ago, but this is for all procedures."

"Amazing! Did she finish it? This could be worth millions. She'd have gotten the Nobel Prize."

His shiny, black hair falls into his eyes, as he shakes his head. "Unfortunately, it required refrigeration when she worked on it. Since we don't have that anymore, I've been analyzing the components to try and break them down from solids into liquids. The fish are my control group. Want to see how it works?"

"Sure." I lean over the large tank.

Cheinstein scoops up two fish and places them in a small glass aquarium filled with water from the main tank. Then, he dissolves a gray powder in the water. Within moments, the fishes' motor skills cease to function. They float next to each other and only their eyes move.

"Are they okay?"

"They're fine. Once the effect wears off, I'll put them back in the main tank."

"So it's like putting them to sleep with their eyes open."

"Yeah. That part works, but I don't know if, in this form, the anesthesia will block the nerves from pain."

"Someday, when we're in the New World, you'll have a chance to find out."

As we turn to leave, the torn front page of *The Metropolitan* falls from Mr. Li's journal. It lies open on the table before me. The headline on the top of the newspaper reads: *Citizens Flee as Corrupt Police Chief Takes Over City!*

"Look. It's dated more than five years ago, when most everyone left the city." My mind wanders to my best friend's tearful goodbye. Tia's dad was one of the biggest investment bankers in town, and he'd paid enough money to take his whole family to Antarctica. At the time, I wished I could hide in Tia's trunk, but that was before Andy was born. *If I managed to sneak into Tia's luggage, who would take care of Andy, now?* I wonder if he misses me, or if Culpepper has filled his belly with sweets and his mind with lies.

Cheinstein breaks my thoughts, as he reads the article aloud.

"'Metro City, October 2, 2506, Lisa Lipton. Bankers, judges, businessmen and their families flocked to the International Airbus terminal today, outbidding each other for seats on the flight that would take them away from what some are calling "Metro City Madness."

"'In an unusual step, Police Chief Sylvanis A. Culpepper has named himself Mayor of Metro City. The city Ethics Committee had no comment, as most of them were bound for the New Continent. They are being replaced by a City Council hand selected by Culpepper.

"'An effort to investigate Culpepper's wrongdoings has failed. The police have become accomplices to the coup. Renamed The Megamark Guards, their actions are now that of a dictator's army.

"'Serious allegations have been made about the Ethics Committee's own conduct resulting in droves of people, with the means, leaving Metro City. Those who stay behind, either by choice or financial circumstances, can only hope Mr. Culpepper will show a benevolent side, as he aims to make Metro City the seat of his empire.

"'This will be the last issue of *The Metropolitan*. Likewise, Mayor Culpepper has shut down Internet access, the libraries, schools, and churches.'"

I huddle over Cheinstein's shoulder as he reads. All thoughts of fish, Culpepper, and costumes vanish when an unexpected voice echoes in the next room.

I dash to the crinkled paper bag on the floor next to Astoria's cot.

"Hello. Hello, is anybody there?" It's a girl's voice. "Andy is crying and he wants to talk to his sister."

Chapter Thirteen

"Andy?" I grasp the walkie-talkie, moving so fast I fumble with the talk button. "Don't cry, Andy. I told you to call if you needed me. Talk to me. I'm here."

The hitch in his small, tentative voice tears at my heart.

"Where are you, Jax? You said you'd come back."

"I'm with Cheinstein and Astoria. I need to find a way to get back into Mr. C's house, where you are."

"Why can't you just come and get me?"

My grip on the walkie-talkie tightens, as my mind pushes into overdrive. "Is he hurting you?"

"No. He's nice to us. I just miss you. I went to sleep for two nights without a story. Can't you come read us a story?"

"Andy, I'm too big to come to Mr. C's house. All of the other kids are little, like you. Can Nyla read to you?"

"She tried, but she can't read very well. And Nellie always wants to stare at the princess in the pumpkin carriage all the time. I keep telling her pumpkins are to eat, not ride in."

I smile through my tear-filled eyes. "Did you look at your favorite picture of the giant?"

"No. Last night, I wanted to see if the man who led the rat parade had one like Squeakers. I miss him, too. Is Squeakers with you?"

"No. He's probably back at the tunnel waiting for you. I'll search for him tonight."

"Good. I don't want him to be lonely without me."

I'm *lonely without you, Andy, never mind your silly rat.* "Andy? Do you have the book, now?"

"Yep. Nyla is looking at the mermaid picture."

"Could you ask her to find the rat parade page again?"

I hear him ask.

"Here it is," she says. "It's right before the mermaid story."

"Andy, what does the man leading the parade wear?"

"He has a red and yellow striped cape and a hat with a big red feather."

"What color are his clothes?"

"He looks like he's got red shorts on over long yellow socks."

Before he even finishes describing the outfit, I know what I'm going to wear. *It's sitting on the mannequin on the third floor.*

"Thanks, Andy. Maybe you and Nyla can make up stories from the pictures?"

Astoria struggles to sit up.

"Is that Andy?" she whispers.

I pat her arm, and nod. I feel the tenseness leave her body, as she slides back down on the cot.

"Okay, Jax," says Andy. "So, are you coming tonight?"

Quivering sobs interrupt his words. At least, talking to me has calmed him a little bit.

I muster false cheer to ease his loneliness. Choked by my own emotions, I struggle to speak.

"Not tonight, sweetie. You'll know when I'm there. Do you remember what I told you? What to listen for?"

"Yes. The bird call I can't do."

"That's right. When you hear the whippoorwill call, get ready to run. Either Rafe or me or one of our friends will be there to get you. Okay?"

"Okay, Jax. Bye."

The walkie-talkie falls silent before I get to tell him I love him. My grip loosens. It drops on the cot, as my brain furiously gives birth to an erratic, new rescue plan.

Astoria again makes an effort to sit. "Is he okay?"

"Yes. He just misses me." I slide next to Astoria and throw my arm around her shoulders. "Now I know why you held on to that bag so tightly."

"You told me Andy would call us on that walkie-talkie. I couldn't lose it."

"You did great, Astoria." I hug her.

She dips her hand into the bag and pulls out the bloodstained gold damask curtain from her pleasure parlor.

Dazed, a questioning smile spreads across my face.

"Why would you want to keep that?"

"The fire destroyed everything else."

"Don't worry. You're going to have a whole new life when we get out of here. All of us are." I squeeze Astoria's hand. "Are you in pain?" *I don't want to suggest the heroin.*

"Sleep heals me," she says, much to my relief. "St. Sally sent me here with a packet of crushed willow bark if I need something to ease my pain. I refused her narcotic. I see what it does, every night. I don't need to end up like your mother."

Good girl!

"So sleep, and I'll try to salvage what I can from the tunnel. Is there anything you specifically want?"

"Abuela's embroidered pillow."

"I'm sure it's still there." I hurriedly dress in Colt's damp clothes. "Andy wants me to look for Squeakers, and I need a few things that were left there, for my plan."

"You're going alone?" asks Cheinstein. "Shouldn't you call Rafe?"

"I'll be careful. It's not far." I pat Astoria's arm. "You rest, and when you wake up, I'll be here."

Astoria slips back down on the cot and closes her eye.

Cheinstein makes a bed for himself, with blankets and towels, underneath the large workroom table.

"If you need me, call. If she needs something medical, call Rafe. I'll be back in a few hours."

As I make my way to the camouflaged entrance leading to the alley, I change my mind.

The rain has stopped and the setting sun casts long rays through the arched windows on the first floor. They light up the marble staircase. I dash to the third floor, instinctively knowing where I left Romeo. I stop short at the wrecked medieval display.

Dozens of rats feast on fallen papier-mâché and small bits of plaster from the balcony. I'm afraid of stepping on one in the dim light. With one deep breath, I charge through them, grab the mannequin, and sing, as I strip his clothes.

When I look up, the rats have stopped eating. Their beady eyes focus on me.

I tuck the red velvet costume under my arm, and continue singing, as I make my way back to the stairs.

"One misty, moisty morning when cloudy was the weather, I met with an old man clothed all in leather.

He was clothed all in leather, with a strap beneath his chin.

Singin' Howdy do? And howdy do? And howdy do again."

As I amble down the staircase, the rats follow, flowing over the steps like a furry waterfall with pink snake tails. I hang Romeo's outfit on a brass wall hook near the secret exit and push open the door. I leave, singing until no more rats exit the museum. Standing in the center of the alley, I'm surrounded by scratching, scurrying rats. I sing my way to the park and have a following of over one hundred.

* * * * *

The streets are almost deserted, but a few homeless children seem to be following behind the rats. The Megamarks must have missed them. I want to tell them to hide but two bedraggled men, drunk or drugged, stagger into the street, distracting me.

Several vendors have set up carts, but the sickening, sweet smell of roasting rats is not obvious tonight. I check the time. Nonna's watch tells me it is eight o'clock, prime trading time. *Where is everyone?* Only drunks and orphans brave the streets.

As I approach the park with my rat brigade, three Megamarks stand around my manhole cover. It seems a coincidence they're posted at my door. I glance back, worried for the children, but they've disappeared. They must have seen them, too.

Silently, I climb the old oak. Perched in its cover, I listen. With no song, the rats scatter.

"Holy shit," yells one of the guards. "Where the hell did all these rats come from?"

The other two turn slowly, their bodies clearly tense. I smile at their unease. *If they only knew.*

"Looks like they're headed to the river," says the second. His voice shakes. He tries to ignore the rats running over his feet. "I can't wait for that rat catcher to get here. Once the rats and vagrants are gone, Culpepper can turn Metro City into a major capital again."

My interest is piqued. *What?*

As the last of the rats pass them, I strain to listen to their conversation.

"I hear the plans are in place. He just needs financial backing. He's hoping to lure the bankers to return," says the third.

"I think he's crazy," says the first. "Would you leave a naturally sustainable city to come back to one that needs to be climate controlled 24/7? Even the nights here are unpredictable. When it rains, they're damp and when it's not raining, it can get pretty damn hot."

"Hey. Culpepper's not suffering, and our barracks are pretty cool. He's harnessing the sun's energy, and that'll never run out."

"Yeah, and now that he has all those kids, he's got a ready-made work force to dig the foundations. He'll give them food. They'll give him their blood and sweat. By the time they are men and women, the new underground city will be built and they can quietly be eliminated, if they don't die from exhaustion first."

That's what he wants all the kids for? Not Andy. Screw my rat plan. I'm getting him out tonight.

"Hey. We've been standing here since the rain stopped and the dampness is soaking into my bones. She's not coming back. Don't know why the old man is making such a big deal about one girl. He can have anyone he wants."

"Yeah, but this one is different. Something about her connection to that little boy he's so fond of."

My ears perk up at the reference to Andy. *How could Culpepper have grown fond of Andy already? He barely knows him.*

"Whatever. She's not here. Let's go."

I waste no time. As they pass from sight, I hurry down the manhole with a new plan bursting in my head. I can't wait three more days for Colt. I've got to get Andy out now.

Floodwater from the streets rushes through the lower sewer section, and makes running difficult. I just dried out from the day's encounter, and now I'm soaked again. Excess rain has puddled at the uneven sections of the tunnel. They're filled with dead animals and upset waste pots. The reek of urine and crap mixed with decaying carcasses is unreal.

I enter the arches the same way as before, and go straight to the wall with the loose bricks. Hurriedly, I throw the red satin robe, Peabody's broken spectacles, and the disc player in Nonna's quilt. Next, I dash across the room to get Astoria's grandmother's pillow. It's damp from the rainwater that seeped through the floor, and it smells sour, but it's not damaged.

I take a sweeping glance across the only home I've known for the past three years. Mother's sheet music, strewn all over the floor, ripped and wet, brings tears to my eyes.

I miss her, and Andy. My chest aches. I blink a lot, to prevent tears from falling.

The wooden bowl, purposely turned upside down by Astoria to keep the pine nuts and hazelnuts from the rats, has not been disturbed. I scrape the handful of nuts into my palm, then funnel them into my pants pocket.

Newfound determination forces me into action. I gather up some loose music sheets, hoping I've taken mother's original compositions, and throw them, and the pillow, into the quilt. I tie it closed with my kerchief, hanging from the water pipes, and make my way back to the manhole cover.

I have one more stop.

* * * * *

The Guards sealed the camouflaged door to the apartment building after their rampage.

If I were a Megamark, or a drug dealer, I'd believe entry was impossible, but I'm slight of frame, and a cellar window is not difficult for me to slip into. *Me and the rats.* I kick the small pane of glass in so I can unlock the window. Forcing it open, I throw my quilt package through, then slip my feet first, twist my body over, and ease myself into the bowels of the apartment building.

My eyes adjust to the darkness, and I'm driven to find the stairs that lead me to our sixth-floor apartment. It's a matter of familiar footing until I'm standing in the center of my old life.

I dash to the closet, remove the trunk, and pull out the geisha fan and the disc of my father's songs.

As I turn to leave, I hear chattering. I expect to see rats, but I'm not expecting Squeakers.

He sits on the Oriental rug, waiting. Waiting to be fed. Waiting for Andy. All I have are the nuts. I offer him one, and he scoots up my arm to eat it on my shoulder.

My head falls back, as I glance skyward.

"Andy will be so happy I found you. Too bad I don't have the birdcage now." I speak to the rat, as if he were a person. "What can I use to carry you?"

I answer my own question, and hurry into the wrecked kitchen.

The black refrigerator, with doors ripped off, stands like an obelisk in the center of the linoleum floor, a monument to my past life. Enormous roaches scuttle from beneath it to the skeletons of the counters, now empty of their drawers, and cupboard doors. I remember them filled with canned goods, and pasta, and the cast iron pans Nonna gave to mother. Flowered canisters used to sit beneath the now-shattered window. As quickly as I remember them, I spot something green and flowered in the back corner of one of the empty cupboards near the floor. It's the flour canister.

Perfect!

The missing knob leaves a hole in the cover. I rip a piece of rusty screen from the broken window, and secure it inside the canister's top so Squeakers can breathe.

He seems to sense my urgency. I pour the handful of nuts into the can and he willingly slips inside. I place him inside my quilt carrier, dash down the stairs and kick out a window from the second-floor apartment that leads to the fire escape. A quick glance below shows a clear escape, but just as I step out, I'm caught in the center of a spotlight. I hear the dreaded words.

"Stop where you are, or I'll shoot."

Chapter Fourteen

The spotlight blinds me—for a moment.

Three Megamarks stand in the street below. One holds a gun, another the spotlight, and the last waits directly beneath me.

At first, I panic. Blood pulses furiously through my veins, encouraging me to flee, but somewhere in my head, I realize this is exactly what can land me back at Culpepper's to rescue Andy. Slowly, I lay down my bundle, and raise my arms.

"I'm coming." My voice sounds calm, even though my heartbeat screams in my ears. "Don't shoot."

The beeping and static of their scanners, and a single shout in the distance, are the only noises that break the stillness of the night. Before I reach the street, the Megamark below me grabs my elbow, yanks me behind the iron steps, and pushes me up against the bricks.

The guard with the light yells, "Can you handle this one, Stern? Taggers are two blocks over. We just got a call from the park patrol. They're spraying that ECO shit all over the library."

"Got it," says the Megamark pressing me to the building. "Send the wagon. I'll keep her cuffed until they get here."

With my face smashed up against the wall, I hear the other soldier call for backup.

"Should be here any minute. We're off, then. After you dispose of this one, meet us on Fourth and Charles."

"Will do," says my captor.

His military mannerisms are efficient, but there's something about his voice I recognize.

As soon as his colleagues round the corner, he turns and unlocks my cuffs. "Go."

I look up into the same defiant, hazel eyes I saw at Culpepper's.

"Alder?"

"Go." He pushes me forward. "The wagon is coming."

"I don't want to go. I want to break Andy out of the mansion."

"What?" He narrows his eyes. "You can't do that alone."

"I'm not alone. I have you."

"Where's Astoria?"

"If I take you to her, will you help me get Andy?"

He glances around, as if weighing his options, then wets his lips and nods with a jerky assent.

"Colt warned me you'd try to pull something like this. What if one of my partners arrested you? You'd be dead when the sun came up."

"But it wasn't them, it was you."

"Yeah, only because I recognized Colt's shirt."

"What?" I snap. "You pay attention to what the freakin' guy wears?" *Colt again. Why does he keep popping up?* "How does Colt know what I'm going to do? He doesn't even know me."

Alder cocks his head toward me. "Obviously he knows you better than you think he does."

"Does he know I'm doing this?" I scale the fire escape. A quick glance back reveals a wide-eyed Alder below me, as rigid as a wooden soldier.

"What are you doing?"

I swoop up the quilt with Squeakers, throw it down to him, and slide down the wrought iron railing.

The clopping of horses' hooves grows louder.

"Hurry up," he says, guiding me down the alley. "They're coming."

As we turn the corner, another Megamark patrol heads our way.

I stop, pulling my arm out of his clench. "Do we have a deal or not?"

"Deal," he says. "Here." He shoves my quilt bundle into my left arm and twists my right arm behind my back. "Act belligerent. It should be easy for you."

"Damn you," I curse, and pretend to twist away from him.

The other patrol comes dangerously close.

"Need help?" they shout.

"Got this one," Alder yells. "There's more a block over. My partners went after them."

The patrol heads down the street toward the taggers.

We break into a run. The museum isn't far.

*****

I drop the quilt on the floor. "Squeakers is in there, Beni. Do you think you can find a cage for him?"

As Cheinstein searches, I sneak Alder out of the darkened doorway, trying to prepare him, and lead him toward the back corner, where Astoria rests on the cot.

"Don't look alarmed when you see her. One whole side of her face is bandaged."

"What the hell are you doing, Jax?" Rafe emerges from the pillar's shadow, a hostile tone in his voice.

"Rafe. I didn't expect you back so soon."

"Soon? I was lucky to get back here at all. An army of Mega Goons was after us. Hell, they got two of the Altar Boys. The Museum is our safe haven, but now you bring this asshole straight to us."

He stares at Alder, standing behind me. Hate burns in his eyes. We both know it's more than because Alder is one of Culpepper's soldiers. Rafe charges across the floor to stop inches from my face. His wild-eyed gaze penetrates my gut.

I smell his fury.

"You crossed the line, Jax!" He storms away from me, shoving Alder as he passes him.

I pivot to face him, stomping away. "It's not what you think, Rafe. He's a friend. He helped me escape from the mansion and he's protecting Andy."

"Right! He looks like he's protecting Andy." Rafe's voice grows loud. "He's a mole sent to befriend you so those fuckers can wipe us all out."

"That's not true." Astoria speaks from the pillar's shadow.

Color drains from Alder's face. Lips trembling, he charges past me, ignoring Rafe's hostility.

"What did they do to you?" He tries to cradle Astoria in his arms, but she twists away, waving him back.

"No. I don't want you to see me like this. Go away Alder. Forget me."

"You heard her," yells Rafe. "She doesn't want to see you, buddy."

"I can't forget you, Astoria. You're all I think about." He reaches for her soft hand, and caresses it between his rough, calloused Megamark palms. "Every moment I'm away from you, I anticipate and plan for the next moment I'll be with you."

I pretend not to hear Alder's innermost thoughts; I sidle back toward Rafe, but his face isn't red from embarrassment.

He glares at Alder.

Astoria's shoulders sag. Though she doesn't meet Alder's gaze, neither does she pull her hand away. Moments pass in silence, and then, there's a hitch in her voice when she answers. "But I'm ugly now."

Rafe charges toward them, and tries to drag Alder away from Astoria.

Alder shakes his shoulder loose, ignoring Rafe. It's like no one is in the room except him and Astoria.

"You can never be ugly to me." Alder's voice is tender. He swoops Astoria in his arms, turning her scarred face to his lips. "I don't care what you look like on the outside. I know you from the inside. Your warmth. Your giving. Your heart. I love you."

She clasps her arms around his neck. Her sobs hide her reply, but I know what it is.

So does Rafe.

I try to distract him, to save his heart from breaking, but there's no need.

He storms out of the cellar, back into the danger of the street.

When I turn around, Astoria and Alder are hand in hand.

I gasp.

Astoria's bandages are gone. In their place, she wears a black eye patch. The stitches along her cheek are still visible, but the swelling has gone down.

My hand flies to my mouth and my vision blurs with unexpected tears.

"What are you gawking at?" she asks.

"Sorry. I was expecting the whole bandage thing." My hesitant smile spreads into a grin. A feeling of confidence seeps into my thoughts. *Astoria is going to be okay.*

"St. Sally said to take it off after two days to let the wound breathe. Air will heal it faster and Cheinstein was very careful removing the gauze and tape. He should be a doctor in the New World."

Cheinstein blushes.

"Where did you get the eye patch?"

"After you left, Cheinstein went up to the maritime display."

Cheinstein laughs. "One of Blackbeard's pirates now has two eyes."

"It fits you well, and hides most of the scar on your cheek." I lay out the contents of my quilt on the worktable next to Squeakers' new home, the small glass aquarium Cheinstein used in his fish experiment. "Hey, Cheinstein, come help me."

I keep him busy with my plans for getting Andy back, but my main reason is to give Alder and Astoria some privacy. After everything is laid out, I call back to Alder. "Are you ready?"

"What are you doing?" Astoria asks. She rushes to my side, still holding Alder's hand.

"Alder's taking me to Culpepper's to get Andy. You and Cheinstein must work on the rat plan while I'm gone." I place the red satin robe next to her gold damask curtain. On a pad from the curator's office, I sketch a diagram of a striped cape. "I need you to make me a red and yellow cape like the curtains you made for the tunnel."

I turn to Cheinstein. "I need you to find some way to amplify my voice. It needs to touch every rat in this city. Every one of them is going to die, except Squeakers.

"Now, I'm going to get Andy, and Alder is going to help me. If I'm not back one hour before sunrise, call Rafe. He'll probably find me shackled to one of the parking meters in front of the courthouse."

"Jax, this is crazy," says Cheinstein.

"I must get Andy out of there."

"Take care of her, Alder." Astoria grabs his arm. "For me?" she whispers.

Alder kisses her forehead.

"I'll do anything for you."

Turning to me he says, "We'll start with a new shirt."

"I don't have time to change. It's almost dawn."

"You'll change unless you want Colt to be implicated in your crazy scheme. If I recognized Colt's shirt, Culpepper will, too."

I glimpse down at the black snap-button shirt. Alder has a point. No one in Metro City wears shirts like these. No one except Cowboy. "Okay, Beni, how about we swap shirts?"

"Sure," says Cheinstein. "That shirt is a lot newer." He throws his worn chambray shirt my way, with its holey elbows, and frayed collar.

I slip a black vest over the shirt and tie my kerchief from the quilt bundle around my neck.

"Give me your hat, too," he says ripping off his baseball cap.

I take his hat but place Cowboy's on the top of Squeaker's cage. "I have a feeling Colt might want this back."

* * * * *

Alder and I make our way back through town. The vendor's market is empty except for a few drunks, who stagger in the street, unaware they should be hiding. Whenever we run into other patrols, I become the loud-mouthed prisoner and Alder becomes the bullying soldier.

"So what do we do when we reach Culpepper's?"

"You bring me in. Say you've been following me since I escaped."

"That's not a good idea. I can't control your safety once you leave my sight. He raged for hours when you got away."

"Look, the first priority is to get Andy. The second is that I get back."

I'm the bait. Astoria and Cheinstein love Andy like a brother and they'll take care of him. So before I show up on Culpepper's doorstep, I need to be sure my distraction is the key to Andy's freedom. I stare into Alder's eyes, and it's obvious he's thinking about Astoria.

He returns my intense gaze and nods. "What do you need from me?"

"You've got to get Andy out."

He hesitates to answer. His voice is overly quiet when he does.

"Even if I could somehow get word to Daphne, and she could get him to the servants' door, who'll pick him up? It won't be you. You realize that!"

"You could take him to the museum. You just need to whistle like a whippoorwill. Cheinstein will let you in."

"But, first I need to get him past the guards. Don't you think they'll notice me taking a kid out, when everyone else is herding them in?"

"I've thought about that a lot. Tell him Jax says he needs to play hide and seek with you. He'll know what that means. He's very good at being quiet."

"And why would he trust me? He doesn't even know who I am."

"Here." I slap my kerchief in his hand. "He'll recognize this. Tell him I want him to wear it so he can be like me. He'll cooperate.

"Then, tell him to crawl into one of the empty vented vegetable crates from the kitchen. Put him on the dolly, and wheel him to the parking lot where the other empty crates are stacked. Anyone who sees you will think you're just adding to the pile waiting for pick up at the next Air Caravan delivery."

"So assuming that works, how's he going to get over the brick wall? Surely, he can't climb."

"No, but he's small enough to squeeze through the space between the locked delivery gates. Once he's outside the wall, he can hide in the same bushes where Rafe and I hid."

"Then I pick him up, and take him to the museum?"

"Exactly."

"Wrong. You're forgetting two major things. One, Cheinstein doesn't trust me, and two, if I get discovered with Andy outside the mansion, I'll be marked a traitor. I won't be able to work from the inside, like Colt."

"Colt? You mentioned him a lot tonight." I narrow my sight and tilt my head. "Do you two know each other?"

"We grew up together. We were best friends, as kids."

"What?" A Megamark and a Fancy Dan city slicker from the New World. "How did that happen?"

He frowns, presses both hands to his hips, and lets me have it. "You act like you're the only one who had it bad. We all have. Some of us, more than others. If Colt's father hadn't smuggled him out of Metro City right after he found his grandfather dead, he never would have left."

He stops to lean against a burned-out car. Alder needs to spill his guts. It's eating him up, and since he's familiar with my life story, I listen to his.

"My life was hell. Colt saw how my father spiraled. He went from a respected accountant to a sales clerk to a handyman to a drunk." He steps away, and then quickly returns. "After the booze became harder to get, drugs were readily available from the street. Soon, he brought no money home. Colt and I were going to run away."

"Everyone in Metro City has a story like that. Mine's almost the same except it was my mother. I never knew my father."

He points his index finger at me. Clearly, his voice shows his agitation. "You don't get it, Jax. If it weren't for Colt, we would have starved. He smuggled vegetables from his grandfather's garden, and sometimes he'd steal a loaf of bread from the bakery."

"I wouldn't have pictured him as Robin Hood." A warm feeling floods me. We talk of Colt, and the memory of his arms around me surges.

Alder continues. "One evening, as we slept, my father sold my newborn baby sister. Members of the City Council were actively seeking babies. My mother, distraught over his actions, withdrew into herself, wouldn't eat, and wasted away to skin and bone.

"My father was lost in drugs. My younger brother was starving. I had to do something, so I joined the Megamark Junior Patrol. The measly stipend put some food on the table, but when the last airbus pulled out, I tried to board my mother and brother. She wouldn't leave without me. When people without tickets stormed the airbus, an outbreak of violence took them both." His tearful voice broke. "She reached out to me. He clung to her leg. They both died." Alder's silent tears flow.

I wrap my arms around him. "I'm sorry. It must have been awful to see your family die."

"Don't you understand? I'm telling you this because I don't want Andy to be like me. If we're not careful, he might see you die in the morning."

"We have to believe that won't happen. If they tie me to the meters, Rafe will get me."

"What if they shoot you instead? Rafe can't help you then, and neither can I."

"Let's go. I'm not changing my mind. I must try."

As we make our way to the mansion, slipping through back allies, and across vacant lots, Alder tries to talk me out of it. He shakes his head.

"Is a life of privilege worse than the life you can give him? Think about it. My fucking father sold my sister and now she lives in comfort. I wouldn't dare take her away from that. I see those kids every day, and I have no idea which one she is. It eats me up."

"But we don't know if Andy will be one of the lucky ones, or if he'll be on the child labor force Culpepper expects to build his new city. I heard the guards talking about it. I'm getting him out of there, and once Colt gets back, we'll put my rat plan into action. By this weekend, we'll be on our way to Antarctica, and you're coming with us."

He stops walking and stares at me. "Don't joke with me. It's not funny."

"Astoria asked me to buy you a ticket." I continue toward the mansion.

Alder falls in step beside me.

"You've got it all figured out."

"It's what I do best. Plan my work and work my plan."

"I hope it works." Alder shakes his head. "For all of us!"

We stop at the corner before Culpepper's mansion. Guards drag street people from the back of the black wagons that swarm the street, then fasten them to the meters, two at a time.

"This isn't good," says Alder. "They're not even taking them before the Council. You'll never get in to see Culpepper."

A Megamark soldier heads our way.

"No. I won't calm down," I scream. I turn to run, and hear the soldier's footsteps behind me.

"Oh, no, you don't," Alder yells. He throws his arms around me like a bear.

"You need any help, buddy?" asks the guard.

"Nope. I've got this one."

I struggle in his arms.

"Hey, is the boss seeing any of these scumbags first?"

"No. He just gave us carte blanche orders. Fry 'em all. The wagons have made three runs tonight. We've swept all of the subway platforms, and the tunnels on the south side. Pretty soon, none of these sewer rats will be left, and the boss's plan can begin."

Alder's grasp tightens as the soldier speaks. I feel his chest billow with a gulp of stinky night air.

"I think he might want to see this one," he says." She's the one who escaped from his bed the other morning."

"Oh, yeah. I heard about that."

My hair tumbles down as the soldier pulls Cheinstein's hat off my head. His fingers, calloused from bully sticks and guns, slide down my cheek. He looks me over.

"You're right. He might want to see her. Too bad this one's got to fry. I'll make way through this mess for you to take her to the door. Then it's up to the old man if he wants to exact his own revenge on her."

He pushes aside vagrants and soldiers alike. "Make way. We've got business for Culpepper. Move it."

In a few short minutes, we stand at Culpepper's front door. Alder says, "Do you want to take her in? I'm going back out to search for more."

"Sure, I'll take her."

My stare meet Alder's.

He backs away. He's off to help me save Andy, although his eyes aren't as confident as mine.

I yell, "Culpepper. God damn you, you bastard!"

I throw myself against the door, screaming. All eyes, both prisoners and soldiers, are trained on me. The other street people start screaming too.

The front door is thrown open.

Culpepper's eyes bulge. "You," he hisses.

I throw my shoulders back and look the fat ass directly in the eye.

"They captured her some time ago, but she struggles so much it took this long to get her back here," said the soldier. "We thought you might want to exact your own revenge, sir."

The hate in his eyes is obvious and his haughty laugh pierces my soul. "I have no need for her now. Cuff her to the meters like the other vermin scum."

My confidence evaporates. *This can't be. This isn't what I planned. I thought I'd at least get to see Andy.* I stutter, "B-But I thought you wanted a child. You were right in assuming I hadn't taken the Noova. I was scared. I'm a virgin, but I'm ready now. I can give you a child."

"I don't need you. I've found my son."

I squint. I'm confused. *Astoria said the rats killed him.* "I thought he died?"

"That was my newborn son. I'm speaking of my eldest son, Anderson."

Chapter Fifteen

The shaking starts in my knees and travels through my entire body until my lips and fingers tremble. My fingers are cold, like I'm dead. I stare at Culpepper but don't see him. Instead, I focus inward to imagine my sweet Andy grown into a mean tyrant.

Beads of sweat trickle down my face, or maybe they are tears. I take in uncontrollable shallow breaths, almost sobbing, as I collapse against the soldier, which makes it easier for him to drag me to the street.

I'm stunned beyond words, but before the door closes, I hear a child in the foyer. "Daddy, come read us a story."

I finally find my voice.

"No!" I scream. The Megamark must think I'm protesting my certain death. Andy being Culpepper's son is worse than death. *My mother allowed this to happen. She knew all along. Did she hope Culpepper would take pity on her and save us? Did he turn his back on her? Or worse?*

Now, I'm about to die. I clench my fists, even though the Megamark's cuffs hold my wrists immobile. I shake my head, refusing to believe this is true, but my worst fear is realized. *Andy will be alone with that monster.*

I should be angry. Angry at her. At Culpepper. And most of all, at myself, for being so stupid, but I'm numb. Did I really think I could sweep right into the mansion and rescue Andy? My plan should have worked. My mother's secret destroyed it.

I desperately search for Alder, but with all the Megamark Guards dressed the same, I can't find him. I writhe as I'm thrown to the curb, squirming to get away. The metal cuffs dig into my wrists, as the Guard yanks my hands to the meter. The click of the lock snapping into place is unusually loud. I turn. The boy sharing my meter wears rosary beads as a necklace. He's one of St. Sally's Altar boys.

People wail. Bodies thrash around me. The Megamark slams a bully stick into the belly of a man with a blond ponytail shackled to the meter next to me. His loud protests stop. He gasps for air.

I arch to view the mansion behind me. Crystal chandeliers sparkle through the tinted windows. I picture Andy in that room listening to a bedtime story from Nonna's book, and I wonder if he'll forget about me. *But it wasn't Andy's voice that called the beast Daddy.*

In a way, Rafe was right. He wasn't looking to replace his dead son. He was searching for his other offspring. *The needle I witnessed in their arms wasn't injecting them. It drew their blood.*

My shallow breaths turn into deep gasps. I finally understand this man's power. *How many women did he sleep with in Metro City?* I try to imagine the number of women involved, but reel at the disgusting thought of sex with that monster. *If he finds and raises all the children he fathered, would he train them to be as diabolical as he is?*

Andy couldn't be mean to an ant. *He can't have inherited his father's demonical genes.* The thought pierces my heart like a knife. My pulse flares. Still, I can only think of getting him out of there.

Piercing shrieks shatter my thoughts. I look up. The Megamarks are few. Most are picking up ropes and bully sticks left on the ground. All up and down both sides of the street, people are tied two and three to a meter, waiting for a torrid death.

I'd give anything to start this over. Alder was right. I didn't plan it to the end. My thinking was irrational. Swayed by my heart. I missed the real reason he kidnapped Andy.

One soldier inspects the couple shackled next to me. Kneeling, he speaks to the pony-tailed man, whose dazed eyes show no sign of understanding his words.

"The boy is with the boss. The vegetables weren't delivered. D says take comfort in tea." Then he jumps up and leaves.

I follow his advance to the courthouse. *Was that a coded message for me?* As he gets to the door, he turns, removes his cap and runs his fingers through his honey-colored hair, then pivots back and enters the safety of the climate-controlled building. A jolt of hope runs through me. I swallow hard and nod. *Andy still has Alder and Mrs. Bridgewater to get him to safety after I'm gone.*

The Guards all seek safety. Not one remains on the street. As I ponder Alder's cryptic words, screams break out down the street. I wiggle enough to see the sun peek across the mountains. The morning rays shine on those in its path. It's still too early for the heat to burn them, but they're screaming because it will. Altar Boy and I will be two of the last to burn, listening and watching our fellow citizens' agony, anticipating what death will feel like.

I squeeze my eyes closed, though I can't shut out the sounds of their fear until the thrashing of my own heartbeat hammers in my ears.

If the sun is already up, either Rafe didn't get Cheinstein's message or he's so pissed at me for taking Alder to Astoria he's chosen to let me fry. I fidget, as I open my eyes and focus on the building's slowly retreating shadow. Soon, the sun will shine its death rays upon us. I slump forward.

"I'm sorry I failed you, Andy." Tears distort my vision. I hang my head in defeat as drops fall upon my knees. I thought I had it all worked out. "I'm sorry."

A subdued voice answers me. "Don't be sorry yet, Jax. We still have rats to roast."

I look up through blurry eyes, not believing my hazy vision. Rafe, wearing reflective sunglasses and a wide-brimmed straw hat, kneels by my side. "Rafe. Oh my God, Rafe!"

"I got your message. Where's Andy?"

"He's still inside with Culpepper." I nod toward the mansion. Rafe's presence pumps energy back into my veins. "You're not pissed at me?"

"I didn't say I wasn't. I know you did it for Tori and Andy."

My muscles loosen and I'm ready to run, but Rafe isn't finished.

"Well, your plan worked great, didn't it?" His words cut.

I glare at him. "Stop busting my ass. Are you going to get me out of here or not?"

"First, I'm freeing him." He pulls a bolt cutter from behind his back and snips the manacles holding the Altar Boy to the meter.

The boy jumps up and another gang member throws him a cutter.

Rafe snips me free, then gives me a cutter, too.

My first thought is to use it to smash Culpepper's windows. I clench and unclench my fists around the cutter, as if swinging the tool like a bat would gain access to Andy. *Now, more than ever, I need to rescue him from the clutches of that vile bastard.* I search for which window would serve best as an entrance, but, someone tugs my elbow.

"Not now, Jax." Rafe pulls me back to the plan.

I breathe deeply, then turn to free the man next to me, and the woman next to him.

Up the street, freed people flee back to their hidey-holes without so much as a peep. Some nod their thanks.

By the time the sun's heat is unbearable, the parking meters stand empty. Rafe and I are long gone, hidden in the bowels of the subway.

* * * * *

Rafe whistles the whippoorwill signal at twilight.

The bar scraping against the heavy door rumbles in the empty alley. Cheinstein opens the door to the secret entrance. We shimmy our way in to find Astoria sitting at an old-fashioned treadle sewing machine.

She stitches red satin and gold damask stripes together. The sound of the needle zipping through fabric in an even cadence brings me to her side.

"You've made a ton of progress on this."

"It gives me something to do besides feel sorry for myself, and if this plan gets Andy back, it's worth it."

I nod at her, and sit at her feet, as she sews. "Yeah, you know I miss his soft scent most of all. I hope after all those potions and lotions in the mansion, he'll smell the same."

"How did you get the machine down here?"

"I brought it down from the Industrial Revolution display," says Rafe. "Cheinstein helped. That's what I was doing when the sun came up."

"Oh, *now* you tell me. You made me think you were going to let me fry!"

"Then who'd make my breakfast?"

I slap him on the arm. "Smartass!"

"Everything here is going according to plan," says Cheinstein. "I'm working on the amplification now, using my father's podium microphone from his lecture room as my base component, but I still need a few modifications to throw your voice in various directions at the same time. Strategically placed solar-powered speakers should work perfectly. The Altar Boys are doing that now."

"So we've got the costume going, and the sound system is in progress. Rafe, any luck in finding a skiff down at the docks? This whole thing depends on us getting our hands on a boat, and you're going to have to row it."

"I haven't been to the river yet, but the old Captain's rowboat should still sit at the pier. I'm sure we can use it. It would have sunk by now, if it had a leak."

"So that leaves my face." I tuck my hair beneath Juliet's long brown wig and turn to Rafe. "What do you think?"

"Your eyes are a dead giveaway, no pun intended. And no one else has high cheekbones like you. Since Culpepper saw you up close, a wig won't do it."

"Then we must do something more drastic. How about a tattooed face and body, like the freaks in the circus or those motorcycles dudes?"

"Who is going to do it? That's an art in itself."

"You could do it. You're a great artist."

"Yeah, if you want me to tag your face! You know, Jax, you come up with some wild ideas. I might be able to paint your face, but I can't tattoo it. That calls for needles and special inks and stuff we just don't have. Not to mention *I can't do it*!

"Wait. Painting my face. You're on to something. If we had face paint or makeup, you could design my face to look like it's tattooed. But where are we going to get makeup?"

"I'm not sure, but I think Mrs. Green was some kind of an actress after Culpepper closed her grocery store. She might have some stashed somewhere."

"Good. When you pick up St. Sally, ask Mrs. Green to bring whatever she has." I pull my hair so tight, my eyebrows arch. "I think I need to do something with this hair too. Shorter, or none at all."

"Yeah, a bald head and a painted face." Rafe laughs.

"And purple eyes," says Astoria. "Don't forget Colt is bringing you contacts."

I grab Old Man Peabody's broken spectacles from the table and prop them on my nose.

"How about magnifying lenses to make those purple eyes look huge?" I turn to Cheinstein. "Could you do that?"

"I can try. My father kept magnifying glasses in his desk."

As Cheinstein rushes to his father's office, a whippoorwill whistle sounds at the door. My eyes meet Astoria's. I'm sure mine are as wide as hers.

"Who the hell is that?" spits Rafe. "We're all here. Maybe St. Sally came early."

He cautiously slides open the bolt.

Two legs in dark blue Megamark uniforms squirm into the opening, followed by two more.

My mouth drops open.

Two Megamark soldiers stand shoulder to shoulder in the museum basement, scanning the room.

"Fuck!" Rafe turns and hits the pillar behind him.

Chapter Sixteen

The wide-brimmed hat hides Alder's hazel eyes, but there's no mistaking the dark eyes of the Megamark next to him.

His intense stare causes my heart to turn cartwheels. Heat rises to my face.

Rafe's rant interrupts my surreal moment. He's practically in Alder's face.

"What the fuck are *you* doing here?" He challenges him like a wolf protecting his territory, but I give Alder no time to answer.

"What's wrong? Is it Andy? I need to know he's okay and that Culpepper didn't take my escape out on him."

"No. Culpepper's pissed, but he's not stupid. He came very close to exchanging some of the children for their parents at the meters to teach the street people a lesson, but then he'd be short that many workers, so instead he's placed a bounty on your head. Patrols are doubled, all looking for you. If you're caught again, he wants you brought straight to him and he'll kill you himself. To be exact, he said, 'That bitch is giving them hope. I'll call another meeting, and publicly kill her myself. No one crosses me and gets away with it. And she's done it twice. I'll pay three thousand dollars for her capture.'"

Colt moves toward me, his jaw clenched. He looks so different in a uniform, more than attractive. Commanding. Dominating. Powerful. A scowl marks his reddened face.

"Why would you ever pull a stunt like that, tonight? The plan was in place. You almost blew it."

The flutter in my heart screeches to a halt, as anger dowses my passion. I glare at him.

"Oh, I need to ask your permission before I try to save my brother? Since when did you become my keeper?"

"I didn't say that." Quickly, he glances away, shaking his head, then shoots me a disgruntled look. "You always twist my words."

"I'm out of here," says Rafe. "This is too much for me."

He charges toward the door.

"Wait," yells Colt. "The plan is moved up. Culpepper sent an email demanding I bring the exterminator early. He has no idea I'm already here. I took an empty shuttle and left the caravan with my co-pilot. He'll be pulling into the station tomorrow at midnight, as scheduled, after he drops off the supplies for Baghdad. We have one day to pull this plan together." He focuses on each of us, one at a time. "Can you do that?"

"What about the real exterminator?" asks Alder.

"I never contacted him. As far as Culpepper knows, the person I bring to the mansion at midnight *is* the exterminator."

Cheinstein returns, holding two magnifying glasses. "I've got to mold the spectacle frames around these lenses, and I'm almost set with the amplification system. I need a few more hours."

I turn to Astoria. Alder stands next to her. She places the unfinished cape on his shoulders. "I need to make a collar and sew the hem. Then, the cape is done."

I glance at Romeo's red velvet breeches and tunic folded on the chair beside her.

"We can do it. I just need the disguise for my face worked out." I spin back toward Rafe. "Everyone needs to be here."

"I'm on it." The plan's urgency diverts his anger away from Alder. "I'll be back as soon as I can, with St. Sally and Mrs. Green."

"Be careful," shouts Alder. "The streets are swarming with Megamarks looking for Jax. Anyone not wearing a uniform is suspect. Here, take mine." He sheds his jacket.

"I don't want your lousy Megamark clothing. I've evaded you assholes for this long. What's a few more hours?" Rafe pulls on his black skullcap and lifts himself through the secret entrance in one motion.

Alder glances at me, eyebrows raised and lips taut. "I hope he's right."

He hesitates, and his eyes go blank, like he's willing Rafe to safety, then he asks, "Is there anything I can do to help? I alerted Mrs. Bridgewater. She has Andy and the twins occupied. She's having their dinners sent to their room every night, and will wait for our signal. When you go back to claim the reward, she'll have Andy ready to go."

"See if Cheinstein needs any help?"

As Alder confers with Cheinstein, and the sewing machine hums along, Colt grabs my elbow.

"I need to talk to you privately."

Once again, a fluttery sensation rolls through my stomach. *What is wrong with me?* I can face that scumbag Culpepper with no qualms, but Colt's touch makes me tremble.

I don't answer, but instead make my way to the first-floor landing. It's dark, but the faint glow of the dim streetlight outside the giant arched window illuminates the marble steps. I'm ready to blast back with whatever insult he lays on me this time.

"Sit." He paces in front of me. His voice has lost its tension.

"I'll stand, thank you."

"Do you have to be so obstinate about everything? Can you just listen, please?"

His dark eyes focus on mine, and he smiles.

I'm not ready for that. His deep dimples shatter what is left of my resistance. I search his face, from his long lashes to his thin lips. Satisfied he's not going to chastise me again, I return my gaze to his lips, as he speaks. Slowly, I lower myself to the step.

"I realize I've only known you for five days, but I feel like I have really known you my whole life."

Squinting, I tilt my heard toward him.

"My grandfather used to talk about you all the time. He said you and your mother sometimes came by when he had tea with your grandmother, and he thought you were . . . what did he used to say? A lovely girl."

I smile. Memories of Thaddeus flash though my head. *He used to play hide and seek with me, and, best of all, he told me stories about the butterflies, and all the animals, now extinct.*

"I didn't care about girls then. I thought I ignored what he told me about you. But I guess I did listen, because this past week, after I met you, all of his stories came back to me. About the nature hikes through the mountains you insisted on taking, and how you were mesmerized by his stories of the flight of the milkweed or dandelion, and how your sparkling amber eyes filled with wonder every time he told you something new."

He rubs the back of his neck. His gaze drops to his alligator boots. Breathing deeply, he pauses, fiddling with the gold buttons on the uniform sleeve, and then he looks into my eyes again.

"But mainly, it's my own thoughts of your sparkling amber eyes. They fill *me* with wonder."

I'm nervous meeting his gaze, but my heart pounds. I'm drawn into his dark eyes, like the night that cloaks the world outside. All I know is that his words make me feel like I've never felt before. I can't stop smiling.

"Look," he says. "I want you to know I've never met anyone like you."

I blink. Suddenly I don't know what to do with my hands. I want to run my fingers through his black hair, disheveled from the Megamark cap. I fidget, shifting my weight too much. Colt pierces the wall around my heart. It simply crumbles, and there's no time to reinforce it. *Even if there was, I don't want to. I've been staring at him for months, and now, he's staring at me.*

"Say something." His cheeks flush in the dim streetlight. "You always have something to say. Your silence makes me feel like a jerk."

For once, my sarcastic tongue fails me, so I simply move toward him, lost in his eyes.

Before I know it, his grip is firm around my waist, and I melt into his arms. My emotions burst like fireworks. I feel his heart beating almost as fast as mine. I cling to him, feeling more alive, and on fire. He tucks my head under his chin, and a new longing fills me. I want to feel his skin against mine, like I did in the dark closet when we first met.

He kisses my hair.

I look up to search his face.

His eyes close, and his lips glide from my hair, to my forehead, to my cheek.

My voice is the thinnest of whispers because I can hardly breathe. "Colt, I—"

Finally, his lips touch mine. My eyes flutter closed.

He kisses me with such intensity, I collapse further into him. I never want to leave the safety of his arms. I reach behind him to draw him closer, and our bodies fit perfectly, like a jigsaw puzzle that has found its lost piece.

He holds me until the streetlight flickers to darkness. In the distance, we hear the hum of the sewing machine, and the tiny pings of a small hammer on metal.

Colt loosens our embrace, and breaks the magic. "This is dangerous. Are you sure you can pull this off?"

I smile. "I know in my heart, like I know what I feel for you, that I can. Andy is waiting for me. I promised I'd take him out of this hellhole."

"But why this elaborate plan? We can just get Andy and leave and never come back."

I wrest myself away. "Well, for one thing, your best friend, Alder, and mine, Astoria. And what about Cheinstein, and St. Sally, and all the people counting on me to get rid of the rats? I won't go to the New World without trying to leave Metro City a better place. At least they won't need to battle the rats for food."

Colt's shoulders relax. "You're right. I just want to make sure you know what you're getting into. Okay. We continue as planned, but that doesn't mean I won't be worried about you."

"I'll be fine, especially *because* I know you'll be worrying about me." I jump back into his arms, and kiss him quickly. "We're wasting time. Once we get to Antarctica you can kiss me all day."

I take his hand, and lead him back down the dark staircase. When we enter the basement room, Cheinstein is modeling my new spectacles. His eyes are as big as quarters.

We all hear the whippoorwill call. Colt loosens the bolted door. He helps St. Sally and Mrs. Green through the secret passageway. Rafe follows.

"I told you I didn't need no Megamark uniform, but damn, you were right. The place is swarming with Guards."

"How did they not see you?" asks Alder.

"I used my boys to distract them. We started with all six, and then, one by one, they ran off, taking the stupid Megamarks with them."

I ask, "What if they get caught?"

"Don't be silly, girl." Rafe pulls a package of crackers from his pocket and throws them on the table for everyone to share. He munches on one. "I taught them. They're as slippery as river slime."

Colt turns back and embraces me one more time. Everyone turns away, pretending to be busy with something else. He slips a small plastic case into my palm. "The contacts."

"What about the ones you're supposed to trade to Hoffmann?"

"That plan is off the table now. The Megamarks are rounding up every street person they can find."

"But many are still hiding out somewhere."

"After tonight, we won't need to worry about it. We'll take Andy and the twins and all of your friends, and we're out of here. Culpepper thinks I'm coming in tomorrow with the exterminator they call The Viper. He has a special welcoming dinner planned for him at midnight. I'll pick you up tomorrow night at eleven."

Colt turns to the others. "I need to know everyone is ready. Once we start this, there's no turning back."

They all nod.

"Thanks, buddy," he says to Rafe. "We couldn't do this without you."

He slaps Alder on the back. "I need you to drive the shuttle if something goes wrong."

I scrunch my eyebrows together. "What would go wrong?"

Colt's mouth twists into a taut, pensive line. "If for some reason I can't get out, Alder will drive you all to the air caravan."

I search his serious eyes, in an attempt to find meaning I missed in his words.

"Don't worry." He grips my shoulder. His strong hand promises solid security. "We're all going to be together, but if something happens to me, I want you and Andy safe."

He kisses my forehead and turns. "Let's go, Alder. We're up."

Alder joins him.

"Let's do it." He hoists himself through the door to the alley.

"Okay." He raises his fist in defiance. As our eyes meet, Colt shouts, "Until tomorrow night."

He turns and follows Alder out.

My hearts rips when the doorway is empty. I watch the door, hoping he forgot something.

Colt's words shock everyone into silence. We stare at each other, as the importance of what we are planning sinks in. If we succeed, not only do we enjoy a better life, but everything changes for those who are left in Metro City.

Mrs. Green breaks the silence.

"Rafe told me to bring my old makeup." She holds up a small cosmetic bag. "It should still work."

"I had no idea you were an actress," I say taking the bag from her outstretched hand.

"She follows me closely. With downcast eyes, she whispers in my ear. "I worked on a stage, but it didn't involve much acting."

I wait for her to break the awkward silence.

Sheepishly, she wrings her ragged skirts. "I tell the boys I was an actress, but I was a burlesque dancer down at the docks."

She looks away, toward the high vaulted ceiling, as if some higher power would forgive her.

I touch her arm and smile. "Hey, we all do whatever it takes to survive."

"It was like being a nightwalker, but it wasn't. We stayed in the theater, and after our numbers, patrons paid extra to visit us."

"You don't need to explain, Mrs. Green, really you don't."

"Yes, I do. Seven years ago, I found myself pregnant after a regular patron's visit. I couldn't dance, and I couldn't afford an abortion. So William, God bless his soul, offered to marry me.

He was the bouncer at the club. He had a crush on me and was the best thing that ever happened in my life, and a wonderful father to the girls."

Suddenly, I realize the connection between Andy and the twins.

Chapter Seventeen

"That explains why Nyla and Nellie are with Andy. He bragged to me Andy was his son when he thought his words would be the last ones I'd hear. Andy and the twins are the only ones segregated from the rest. Tomorrow, you'll see them again."

A spark of hope shines in her puffy eyes. "I don't see how you can be so sure."

"Mrs. Bridgewater and Alder are keeping the children near the servants' door, within our reach. After the ruse is over and I collect the reward, Rafe and I will steal them back."

Though anxiety hides within my stubbornness, I meet Mrs. Green's gaze with confidence.

"I pray every day they'll return to me," she says. "As bad as this life is, it's even worse being apart from them."

I wrap my arm around her shoulder and nod, knowing her pain, and guide her back into the large room, now bustling like a busy hive. "Tell me about it."

As we pass Rafe, trying on pirate clothing for his part of the ruse, I hand him Mrs. Green's makeup. "Will this work?"

He pulls out white pancake makeup, black kohl eyeliner, colored eyeshadows, a sparkly glitter blush, and false eyelashes. Lastly, he studies a half-squeezed tube of gold glitter in glycerin. With a faraway look, he takes the makeup and disappears into Mr. Li's office.

St. Sally inspects Astoria's eye.

"It's healing nicely." She raises an eyebrow. "I must say, your eye patch is attractive."

For the first time since her accident, Astoria laughs. "Thank Blackbeard."

I whistle to get everyone's attention. "This is it. We're down to the wire. We all need to be clear about the implications if this doesn't work."

No one meets my gaze.

"Why wouldn't it work?" asks Rafe from the office doorway. "We've got it knocked! Let's go. I want to design your face. Hey, Cheinstein, paper, please."

"We've set a course, now follow it," says St. Sally. "If something should go wrong, we won't be any worse off. We're already hunted like the rats, and our children have been taken from us. If you fail, nothing changes."

Solemnly, we glance at each other and nod. *Failure is not an option.*

"So what can I do?" asks St. Sally.

"We've got the costume, the makeup, and the sound system. Daphne and Alder are taking care of getting the kids to an accessible place."

"And Colt better put on the acting performance of his life," says St. Sally.

My smile breaks into a grin. "Somehow I don't think that's a problem for him, but we still have one."

"What?"

"We haven't decided what to do with my hair."

"I thought you were going to cut it off," says Cheinstein.

"Yeah, you said something about shaving your head," said Rafe. "You know, if you shave your eyebrows, too, I can draw awesome fake ones that will change your whole appearance."

"Yes, that might work," says Mrs. Green. "I can show you how to do that. There should be a razor in my bag."

"You know, in the old days, the Mother Superior had me shave novitiates' heads before they took their vows," says St. Sally. "I can shave your scalp and Mrs. Green can do your eyebrows."

I note the hope in their eyes. They hurry to find the razor and select makeup. They believe in me more than I believe in myself. The question is whether I can fool Culpepper.

"Here we are," says St. Sally. "Now, this may feel funny, but it won't hurt a bit."

I close my eyes and think about our lives in the New World. *Andy will grow up with all of us, like a family in a fresh, wholesome atmosphere. Colt will stand by my side.* My heart flutters at that last thought. I open my eyes when a wispy, softness falls down across my arms to the floor. *It's too late to change my mind. I can do this.*

* * * * *

I lie next to Astoria's cot, on a tattered stage curtain from the museum's lecture hall. The concrete floor grinds into my hipbones when I move, and sleep evades me. I run my hands over my smooth, bald head as I toss, thick with worry. It feels like a part of me has been amputated.

I silently reach for my meager belongings to look for the disc player I'd found earlier. I take the player, my father's silver disc, and the tea light to the marble staircase. Leaving the candle on the lower step, my fingers shake as I slip the disc inside, then snap the top shut.

Cheinstein powered up the battery with a solar cell, and the dim flicker of the tea light catches the glint of the silver disc as it spins within the black case.

I jump when a voice blasts in my ear. I lower the volume until a powerful tenor sings. His voice fills me with emotion. A shiver shoots through me. Tears rush to my eyes. I wipe them on my sleeve. For the first time, I hear my father sing. *No wonder mother fell in love with him.* His rhythmic melody soothes me, and I sit on the marble steps to watch the sunset, playing the song over and over again, until I memorize the words and the melody. It's from an opera I've never heard, but the song parallels my life.

"If we succeed, tonight is our last night in Metro City." I take a deep breath, and say a silent prayer to my mother, asking her to lend me her strength.

Stirring noises in the basement alert me the others are rising. The aroma of strong coffee greets me as I enter. St. Sally, Cheinstein, and Mrs. Green work furiously, running from the back office to the worktable. Sounds of chopping and slicing mixed with tossing and scraping bewilder me.

Rafe taps me on the shoulder. "Are you ready, Jax?"

"Yes." I swallow hard, and I meet his warm brown eyes.

"Let's eat, then, I'll do your face. They're cooking up a storm in there with one Bunsen burner and a coffeepot."

Astoria joins us after setting the worktable with disposable plates and flatware. My gaze questions her, and she waves the plastic fork at me. "We need to celebrate with a feast for our last supper here, and you are our guest of honor."

Mrs. Green brings a plate of steaming fish and rice to the table.

Behind her, Cheinstein proudly carries a salad of greens.

And St. Sally fills each cup with coffee. "Take your places and dig in, everyone. Tonight is Jax's night."

* * * * *

I take an anxious breath before I place the magnifying spectacles on. The purple contacts are in my eyes, and my painted face feels taut under Rafe's artistry. The red and yellow striped cape Astoria sewed for me drapes over Romeo's red velvet costume, all the way down to my yellow legging-covered ankles. *This ruse will work. It must, for Andy's sake.*

I step to the museum door.

The whippoorwill whistle sounds outside, and I loosen the bolt. I'm about to step through, when Colt's voice touches my ear.

It's unusually loud. "No, it's fine officer. The Mayor is expecting me. I stopped to check my wing span disengagement mechanism. As I drove from the air caravan, parked at the old rail station, my warning light flashed."

"We can't take any chances, sir," says a voice heavy with Megamark Guard arrogance. "Our orders are to stop everyone. We're looking for that runaway Stone girl. The Mayor has placed a bounty on her head."

Colt's voice sounds strained, like it just raised an octave. "You may call Mr. Culpepper, if you like. I'm sure he'll confirm my presence in the street at this time."

"One moment, sir."

Tiny beads of perspiration break out on my upper lip. I hope the makeup won't run. My nerves rattle as I keep repeating the lyrics, and the plan in my head. *Colt is going to introduce me as the Viper. I'll bargain with the fat ass for the reward, then the rats will follow me to the river, where Rafe should be waiting with a boat. I'll sing. He'll row, and we'll lead the rats into the river. They should all be dead in a few hours.*

The Megamark's voice breaks my thoughts. "The Mayor says we should escort you to the City Council building. He's eager for you to arrive. Do you need any further assistance?"

Colt hesitates before he answers. A distinct hitch snags his voice.

"No-o, that'll be fine. Everything here is in order, just a loose wire connected to the electronic warning device." He slams the shuttle under-door that houses the expandable wing. "You needn't hold my door for me."

"It's not a problem sir."

I peek out the museum's camouflaged door.

Colt seems perturbed, as the Megamark closes the shuttle's door, and stands by its side.

"This is some vehicle you've got here," says the guard. "We don't drive anything like this in Metro City, just the PUV's and horse wagons. Of course, the Mayor has his personal SUV and the prison truck, but all other automobiles and hovercraft have been banned since the sun has become unbearable and gasoline is scarce."

He turns to board his PUV, parked at the front of the air shuttle.

I slip through the doorway, and softly open the shuttle's rear emergency door. The darkened windows hide me from the Megamark's view. When I sat in the driver's seat before, I'd no idea this thing was as big as one of those giant buses the schools used to have. I slip into a seat at the back.

"Well, what are you waiting for, Cowboy? Let's go. We've got a rat to roast."

Colt turns in the driver's seat. His mouth falls open. His incredulous stare, and the shock on his face, assures me Culpepper will never know me.

"What the hell?" He begins to rise.

"Just drive. Act normal. I'll sit back here."

"Geez, I knew you were coming up with a disguise, but you've outdone yourself. You won't have to sing to the rats. One look at you and they'll be scared to death."

"It doesn't matter what I look like, remember? It's my voice that hypnotizes them; besides, I had to make sure the biggest rat in Metro City wouldn't recognize me."

The sarcasm in Colt's voice rises. "Oh, there's no problem with that. Even I didn't know you."

Rafe must have done a great job. I squeeze my eyes tight at the sudden fear that sweeps through me. *That means Andy won't know me, either.* My eyes widen, unblinking, and then I remember he'll recognize the whippoorwill whistle. After a moment of rushed breathing, I calm down.

The Guard taps on Colt's door, and I jump in my seat, but he's only motioning for Colt to move out.

Within a few blocks, pairs of Megamark Guards on PUV's surround the shuttle, escorting it to the mansion. Others walk the beat like they used to when they were policemen. Metro City swarms with Culpepper's private army.

The contacts must affect my vision. I stare at one of the Guards. He appears older than the rest. His salt and pepper hair, long for a Megamark, sticks out from beneath his hat. He turns toward the shuttle as we pass. There's no mistaking his glare, but he's left far behind us, as Colt expertly maneuvers the shuttle down Main Street.

The City Council building is all lit up, as if they expect a dignitary to arrive. Street lights, sidewalk lamps, porch lights all glow brilliantly. The crystal ceiling chandeliers in the first-floor hallway sparkle through the heat-reflective windows.

Two rows of Megamarks line the front walk, from the street to the front door.

Colt jumps out of the pilot's door and briskly walks to the rear of the shuttle where he opens the back door for me.

I make one last check that the microphone-transmitter embedded in my geisha fan works. I slip on my red satin cap that Astoria made from the bodice of the lounge robe to match my cape. A vintage black ostrich plume she stole from the Victorian display is hand-sewn into the side seam.

Colt walks in front of me, briefly turning to guide me with his outstretched hand.

I project a stern face, as I stroll up the front walk, but inside I smirk, reveling in the peculiar stares from the Guard.

Colt stands aside to let me enter the mirrored foyer of the City Council building first.

I catch my own breath at my reflection on both sides of the hall. I understand why the reactions of the Guard and Colt were so intense. *Rafe did a fabulous job with my face. If I didn't know it was me beneath all that color and glitter, I wouldn't know myself.*

I lean toward the mirror, pretending to check my glitter gold lips, outlined in black, but I seriously inspect the rest of my appearance.

My entire head, neck, and face are white. Eddies of gold glitter cover my crown, swirling down in curls across my temples onto my cheeks.

Red makeup starts at the tip of my nose, straight up to my forehead where it arches three inches over both eyes. It trails down my temples and curves into the hollows of my cheeks, ending in small wispy tails, each dotted with a gold jewel. The red is outlined in black, both around my eyes and at the top, where black curlicues parade across my forehead in uneven design.

A sparkling mustache of gold paste jewels is glued to my skin under my nose, and across my lips. And my magnifying spectacles make my purple, otherworldly eyes look gigantic, much too big for my face.

Romeo's red velvet doublet and breeches with yellow leggings, match the red and gold swirls on my face perfectly, and the rhinestone button that held the vintage satin robe together now holds my red and yellow striped cape around my shoulders. *It's amazing how one can notice so many details in a moment, especially when they're so bizarre.*

As I disengage from my reflection, I glance back to see Colt turn.

He tosses his electronic key to one of the Megamarks. "Please park my vehicle in the back."

Again, I smile.

Alder's even keeled voice answers. "Will do, Mr. Conrad."

I turn the vocal processor to low, which will disguise my voice when I speak.

Colt guides my elbow, and ushers me through the double French doors at the entrance of the grand meeting room.

Surrounded by his City Council members, Culpepper paces as I enter.

"Bless us," he cries. His astonishment causes him to sit unexpectedly. The thud of his pompous fat ass almost drowns out his words. "What is that?"

His Council sits, too, their eyes, bulging. Whispers, hidden behind fingertips and meeting manifestos, circulate around the room.

"Come in," cries the Mayor, looking even heavier than the last time I saw him. "Welcome to Metro City."

The Council members simply nod their agreement.

I approach their meeting table.

Colt clears his throat. "Mr. Culpepper, honored Council members, may I present The Viper. Well known around the world, this exterminator has served sheiks, maharajahs, presidents, and queens."

I nod silently, affirming Colt's lies.

Culpepper begins. "Ah well, your reputation precedes you . . . er . . . sir."

Clearly, he is uncomfortable. He shifts his obese weight in his ostentatious chair. It squeaks, as he tugs at his ermine-collared jacket.

The Council members are also dressed in ridiculous riches. One woman wears a dress draped with pearls from her neck to her waist. The man with a tightened jaw sitting next to her sports a raw silk suit stained with perspiration.

Culpepper loosens his collar with a pudgy finger and blurts, "So, Viper, tell us how you purport to rid us of our vermin."

I stand tall, and speak into the microphone, fanning my face inconspicuously.

"If it pleases your honors, I am able by means of a mysterious talent, which I inherited from my father before me, to lure all small living creatures beneath the sun that creep or swim or fly or run. Your rats will follow me to their deaths."

"But how?" asks the pearl-draped woman.

"They will die in the river at the south side of the city."

The woman's hand flies to her chest, tangling with her pearls. "That river is toxic." She sits up straight and continues. "If one drop touches your skin, you shall be infected with a deadly bacteria."

"Exactly." I pirouette, coming to a stop, facing her again. "Will it not affect rat flesh, too?"

"How will you get them in the Elan?" asked Culpepper? "They live on the river bank. They know better than to enter the dangerous water."

"Quite simply. A colleague will row me to the island in the center of the river. The rats will follow, and die."

"How can you insure they will obey you?" asks the perspiring man.

"It's my enthralling voice. One note, and the hapless creatures will have no choice."

"How do we know you can do what you say?" asks Culpepper. "Thirty thousand dollars is quite a bit of money, especially now, and especially here."

I lift my chin, and cross my arms, as if to say I've no time for this nonsense. "You sought my references. Why, last June, I freed the shores of the Caspian Sea from an onslaught of gnats. More recently, I drove bloodthirsty vampire bats from

India. So, if I rid your city of the onerous rats, you will indeed pay me thirty thousand dollars. That is the bargain, as I understand it." I step closer to Culpepper, and give him a hard stare, almost daring him to recognize me.

He flinches as I approach.

"Thirty thousand?" he questions. "We shall give you fifty thousand if you also rid us of the vile, filthy street people."

If I had eyebrows, they'd rise to my hairline. "Ah, but I have not entered into this agreement to save you from humans. My call is to rid your city of rodents. That, I guarantee. I would be a fool to agree to a higher price for a commitment to murder."

I wait.

Culpepper stews. His shifty eyes flick back and forth, as he considers my answer.

"Very well, then, thirty thousand." Culpepper frowns. He speaks through his teeth with forced restraint.

I extend my gloved hand. "Payable in advance."

A smirk stretches across his face. He stares down his nose at me. He deliberately crosses his arms. "Payable when I've seen proof for myself that every rat is gone."

"It's not that I don't trust you, sir, but indeed, I must have one-half of the sum before I begin."

His cheek twitches. Again, Culpepper looks uncomfortable. He gazes at his Council members through narrowed eyes. After some unspoken agreement, his focus returns to me. "I don't believe that was part of our bargain."

"I don't believe we have a bargain yet, sir."

I glance at Colt, who stands stone cold still, and I'm strengthened by his presence.

His unwavering calm drifts over, and settles on me.

My eyes draw back, and I dart a defiant glance at Culpepper. "You sent for my services. Do you want me to rid your town of rats, or don't you?"

"Yes," he says. "Yes."

"Then we are agreed. Where shall I collect?" I turn toward the Council. "Your city treasurer, perhaps?"

"Come forward, Viper. I shall write you a check."

"I'm sorry, Mayor. I do not work for paper money, or check. The world is too volatile for that. Countries come, and countries go. I will take my earnings in gold, if you please."

Culpepper's mouth falls open. His fat fingers reach for his greasy lips.

"Do you have that much gold, sir?"

Off to the side, Colt stares at the floor. The vein in his temple throbs. He smirks at my masterful attempt to one-up Culpepper.

The materialistic mayor glances at his Elite Guard stationed behind him. He nods and then sweeps his gaze across the fifteen riveted Council members. Rising, he clutches his coat to his sides, then unlocks a safe behind a Picasso painting on the wall. He swings the safe door open to reveal an abundance of gold, lined up in uneven piles.

I nod, and extend my hand. "Very good, sir."

"One second, Viper. What guarantee do I have your scheme will work?"

"You have my word."

"And you have mine. Your gold shall be waiting for you here, when the rats are eliminated." He sneers.

My gaze darts to Colt.

He lifts his hat, scratches his head, and then nods to disguise his supportive look.

Clearly, it's up to me, now. Okay, Jax, do what you came here to do. Eliminate the rats, get Andy, and get the hell out of here. I take in a deep breath and direct my attention to Culpepper.

"Then it is time to begin." I exaggerate my motions in preparation to release my first *note*.

"Oh, no." He waves me toward the door. "Not here. There are no rats here. Out there, in the town."

I smile. "Are you sure you do not harbor rats among you?" *You are the biggest one.* "My agreement is to sing every rat to his or her death. I would be remiss not to start here."

Colt sucks in a breath. I nod toward him, and then to Culpepper. I'm careful to control my breathing. I let out a long, pitch-perfect note, the first of my song.

The Council sits awestruck by the tone's penetrating timbre, the same quality my father's voice possessed.

I surprise myself. It's apparent even to me I inherited not only his ability to sing, but also his harmonic richness.

I wait an extra bar before I begin. Rustling breaks the room's silence. I continue with my song, and a white and gray rat scuttles across the ceiling molding. Three black rats slither out of the air conditioning vent and leap over the Council's heads to the chandelier, which sways with their weight, tinkling the crystal prisms. But the most revolting of all is the large gray rat that pops out of the upholstered bottom of Culpepper's chair, and dashes across his feet, sending the fat ass falling backward as he tries to escape his rat-infested chair.

Ten more rats emerge from the woodwork. Altogether, fifteen rats encircle me.

I continue singing, and head for the door.

They all follow. Behind them, mesmerized, tiptoes the Council, with Culpepper at their lead.

I step out into the street and turn the digitech microphone processor on high. My voice is transmitted in every direction as I sing my father's opera song.

Softly, sweetly, my voice shall surround you . . .
Feel it, hear it, closing in around you . . .
To the river, to the sea, all you rats will follow me
in a dreaded trance you know you cannot fight,
just listen to my music of the night . . . .

Soon a conglomeration of chittering and muttering is heard underneath the melody of my song. The muttering turns to grumbles. The grumbles grow to a mighty rumble, and thousands of rats tumble out of the houses.

Great rats with long pink tails step over smaller rats eager to follow me. Lean rats run with brawny rats to join the rat exodus, as I march down the street, singing. Brown rats. Black rats. Tawny rats. White rats and silver, grave old plodders who hop on aged legs merge with young friskers, who run over each other's backs, raising their tails and sweeping their whiskers.

Rat families by tens of dozens. Rat brothers, sisters, husbands, and wives follow me to end their lives.

From street to street I sing, drawing every rat from everywhere. I can tell I'm getting closer to the Elan because its stench is impossible to avoid.

Step for step, the rats follow me, prancing, until we come to the toxic river. Though the danger is immense, seeing Rafe fills me with courage. I can't help but smile as I sing. He must have enjoyed painting my face, for white curlicues now adorn his dark skin and glitter swirls outline his jawline. He wears a brass-buttoned longcoat and a pirate captain's hat adorned with multi-colored ostrich plumes. His silver earring matches his costume. He's a perfect assistant for The Viper.

Rafe balances in Captain Whitman's rowboat. One foot on the dock, and arms crossed, a perfect picture of a long-ago pirate, but as I step onto to the dilapidated dock, I shiver. The pearl lady's warning echoes in my head. One false move by Rafe or me, and the rats will not be the only ones to die.

Chapter Eighteen

Rats stampede over each other. Fast movers crush old, slow ones in an effort to get closer to me.

They tumble on top of one another, some falling from the dock into the toxic river. Splashes mark where they sink, only to rise from the black oily waters and swim toward Rafe and me as he assists me into the boat. I glance back toward the city.

Culpepper, his City Council, and Colt watch my every move from shore.

My gaze settles briefly on Culpepper, his mouth open in disbelief, then flicks toward Colt. I send him a silent message. *I told you I could do it.*

Standing that close to Colt, Culpepper would never guess what they're feeling is totally different. He must think Colt's eyebrows are closely drawn together because he's squinting to get a better view of the Viper at work. But Colt is biting his lip, probably worried to see me on the dangerous river.

Culpepper lifts his chin, and rests his crossed arms on his bulging belly. He cocks his head to one side. He, too, is squinting, but he's closed his mouth, and his hard smile stretches into a sneer.

He won't be so smug tomorrow at this time. Andy and I will be reunited, and on our way to a new life. I can feel freedom.

The same stars that shine down upon Metro City every night twinkle above me, but tonight they witness the end of a scourge that will make everyone's life better. The homeless, the Guards, the children, Andy and me, even Culpepper will benefit from my performance.

My nostrils burn from the stench, and my throat is parched from so many repeated verses but I continue singing. The frenzied rats scurry.

Rafe pulls away from the dock with strong, even strokes, being careful not to splash the deadly water.

I scan the riverbank from the stern.

The audience has grown. Units of Megamark patrol guards join Culpepper, his Council members, and Colt to watch me lure the rats into the river.

Colt rests his hands on his hips.

I smirk, as the river's putrid air spurs me on to start a new verse, louder than before, just in case they can't hear me this far out. Tonight will be the last time I smell this odorous, disgusting river.

Hundreds of twitching rat noses, with oil-slicked whiskers, poke through the moonlit dark waters. They paddle furiously to catch the rowboat. Their ears perk up like tiny radar dishes listening for my voice to detect in which direction to swim. Behind them, their long tails act like rudders.

Rats kick, squirm, and paddle, filling the river until it looks like a living, breathing, furry animal, whose numerous muscles ripple under the ominous moonlight.

Each verse takes us farther away from the shore. Rats still jump off the dock. The entire river, between the shore and our boat, is covered with rat. I glance behind me at Rafe.

His brow beads with sweat, but he still rows. He stares up at me from beneath his fancy commodore hat.

"Are they dead yet?"

I shake my head, no. Should they be? How long does it take to die from the river's toxins? My mind wanders. Panic sweeps over me. At this rate, we'll hit Scrub Island and the sheer number of them will swarm over us. My voice shakes. My chest tightens. But I still sing.

Suddenly, the rats closest to the boat, the ones that entered the water first, begin to submerge. They don't return to the surface.

"They're starting to go under." I balance with the sway of the boat, and turn to get a better view. As if all of the rats were tied to the leader, and the first was an anchor, hundreds of rats disappear beneath the watery surface. The once furry river becomes a shiny, poisonous oil slick once again.

I relax my tense shoulders. Bursts of screams and shouts ring out from shore.

Culpepper raises his arms in victory, grabs Colt's hand in a powerful shake, and then jumps on the nearest PUV and leaves the riverside.

Colt hesitates. Even at this distance, I feel his eyes on me, but the Megamark guards misinterpret his admiration for sheer astonishment, as they urge him onto a PUV to follow Culpepper.

My smile twists into a confident grin. I'm already anticipating the next part of the plan, but the sound of Rafe's voice stops me cold.

"Fuck!"

I turn. Rafe's feet are poised in the air. He leans his weight backward to insure his boots don't touch the boat's deck.

"We're sinking!" he cries.

"What?" I can't catch my breath because I'm breathing too fast. My throat is already dry. "I thought"—I force a swallow—"I thought you said you checked for leaks."

"I did. It was fine. Holy shit!"

It's a slow leak, but dank water definitely fills the bottom of the boat. He thumps his right foot on the middle seat, and his left on my rear seat, to stand up partway.

He tries to balance the boat with his weight, but it begins to tip when he sways. We almost capsize.

"Squat on your seat," he screams. "At least your boots won't be touched when it gets to the back."

Anxiety squeezes my chest like a vice.

"How fast is it leaking?" *I've come too far to die like the dirty rats in this river of poison.* "Can't we row back?"

"We'll never make it." He looks behind the boat.

I follow his gaze to the middle of the river.

"We're going to have to head for Scrub Island." He's no longer rowing, but paddling with the oar. He leans over one side of the rowboat, as if it were a raft.

Cold fear grips my insides as I dart a gaze back to shore. They're all gone. Even if I scream for help, no one will hear me. The island is our only option.

Paddling on one side, Rafe turns the boat around. The contaminated water rises beneath the seats. It splashes just a few inches beneath our feet.

The shadow of the island looms dark ahead of us.

Carefully, I reach into my boot to retrieve my penlight. Its tiny glow leads Rafe to a small inlet that's relatively flat. The boat scrapes against the rocky shore and then lurches to a stop. The toxic water splashes at our boots.

I jump to the shale beach.

Rafe follows.

The noxious water hasn't touched us, but we have another problem. Not one tree exists on this shallow island, and there's no cave to shelter us from the sun.

My cleverness turns to hopelessness.

"We would have been better off to jump into the river. At least, it would have been quick."

Rafe grabs my quivering shoulders. He stares deeply into my eyes.

"Don't even think that. We've been in tougher situations before. We'll figure something out."

He pulls out his flashlight and starts to search the island.

All I can think about is Andy. I told him I'd come for him. If I die, he'll think I lied. He'll hate me for the rest of his life. And Colt? He'll think I was a fool, the smartass Ratgirl who thought she could sing the rats away.

Rafe clears his throat and breaks my melancholy.

I stumble after him. With each step, I scan our moonlit surroundings for shelter and survival food, even though I'm sure none exists.

"What do you think you're going to find? It's Scrub Island. Only bushes grow here."

I shine my light on the skeletal remains of scrub oak bushes.

"Correction. Grew here." The moon's angle over the horizon draws my attention from the bushes. "We have only hours before the sun comes up."

"Shh," says Rafe. "Stand still and be quiet. Do you hear that?"

I strain to listen. My eyes grow wide.

"It sounds like oars, back where we landed."

We charge toward the beach, shining our lights across the water. A single rower in another boat heads our way. My head falls back in thanks to whoever is protecting us, and I relish the glimmering stars. I wonder if it's Colt, but in the same thought I realize he has no idea we're in danger.

Immediately, Culpepper comes to mind. He must have sabotaged our boat. A horrifying compulsion flows through me. This is probably the clean-up crew to make sure we never get back, just in case we did survive the river.

I try to warn Rafe, but it's too late. When I glance back, he's helping the lone boater out at the rocky shoreline.

There's no struggle.

The pair exchange brief words, then walk toward me. My mouth falls open. The rescuer is a Megamark Guard. *Alder? How could he know the boat would spring a leak – unless he fixed it so it would.*

Emotions I don't want to deal with begin to surface. Distrust. Anger. *No, it couldn't be. Rafe is too welcoming for it to be Alder.* I question my judgment in the brief time it takes for Rafe and the Megamark to walk to where I stand.

It's not Alder, but I can't believe who it is.

Chapter Nineteen

"So you had a close call out here, did you? Seems to me you've got no other way to get back to your precious little brother, *Viper!*"

There's no mistaking the callous gray eyes that pierce mine from beneath the Megamark cap. An overgrowth of salt and pepper hair curling at his neck confirm what I'd seen earlier. He's too old to be a real Guard. Somehow, Otto Hoffmann has traded something for a Guard uniform, and he's infiltrated Culpepper's men.

"Now, we finish our bargain. Here, where there's no nightwalker to influence your decision, nor a smooth-talking religious penguin to manipulate mine."

I glare at him. "What are you talking about?"

"You tell me. What happened to Colt bringing me those purple eyes you're wearing?" His cold stare fixes upon my face. "Colt cut me out of the deal, but maybe I was always out and didn't know it."

The sting of his flinty eyes sends shivers down my spine. St. Sally's words return like beacons in the night. *Hoffmann can be a vindictive son of a bitch.*

I suck in the foul air, trying to stay calm. "No. Culpepper stepped up his patrols, in case you haven't noticed. It was impossible for Colt to make the trade with you at the station. And as for the plan—there were always nine spots, but if we don't get back to the Council Hall before the sun rises so I can claim the reward, no one is going anywhere."

Rafe lunges forward, a sneer plastered on his face. "Are you telling me you sabotaged our boat to blackmail Jax into taking you to Antarctica?"

"Ah, yes, and no. Yes, I *am* blackmailing her to insure I'm onboard that air caravan when it pulls out in the morning. But, I also want passage for my niece, nephew, and sister."

"What?" I step so close to him I smell his sour breath. My face feels like it's blazing, but I'm sure he can't tell how red it is beneath the makeup and the dim moonlight. "If there was no room for one, I can tell you there is definitely no room for four. Who would I leave behind?"

Hoffman pulls a revolver from his back waistband and aims it at Rafe.

"We could start with him."

Rafe freezes where he stands. He darts his wary gaze my way, and in one swift move charges Hoffmann. But the pawnbroker is quicker.

Before Rafe reaches him, Hoffmann has wrapped his free arm around my neck. He hauls me into his chest in a chokehold.

Come on, Jax. Talk to him Tell him what he wants to hear.

The cold tip of the revolver presses against my temple.

Hoffmann brazenly tightens his grip. His oily whiskers touch my face.

"That was a stupid move, boy."

Rafe backs away, his hands raised above his head. "Take it easy, old man. You kill her and no one's going anywhere."

Hoffmann's hot, uneven breath on my neck increases my determination to outwit him, even as my muscles tense beneath his grasp.

"Who will remain behind? I already told you there's no room."

"Well, then, make room. Simple as that."

Rafe inches toward us.

I keep Hoffmann engaged, but he raises the gun, and squeezes the trigger. A bullet digs into the sand two inches from Rafe's boots.

"Don't fuck with me, kid. I was a sharpshooter in the Army before the world went to hell, and I never miss. Now, where were we? Oh, yes. That no good Megamark. He gets plenty of food and lives in a climate-controlled facility. He doesn't have it bad like the rest of us. So he's number one to strike from the list. I'm sure Rafe, here, would agree."

He looks to Rafe for approval.

Rafe nods.

"Now, Viper, do you agree?"

"How can I barter with a gun to my head?"

"Point taken. I'll ease away, but one false move, and your sidekick here will be as dead as the rats." Hoffmann releases me.

I jerk away, massaging my neck.

"I'll take the Megamark's place. My sister and her children will take the three spots that Green hussy and her twins would have had."

"Even if you dislike the woman why would you deny freedom and a better life to her children?"

"They're just the scum offspring of a no-good whore."

"Be careful what you say, old man. Your freedom rests on the decision made by the daughter of a no-good whore!"

Rafe pulls me aside.

"Jax, we're wasting time." He whispers in my ear. "I agree with what he says about Alder."

"You would. You want Astoria all to yourself."

"Then, I'll stay. If Alder and I stay, that's two spots for Hoffmann's niece and nephew."

"No. I won't leave you behind."

"You can't make me go." He's steadfast, as he crosses his arms.

He's right. *I can't force him to do anything. Never could.*

"Are you sure?" A weighted sigh escapes my lips, but heaviness still rests on my shoulders.

Rafe's face tightens.

"It doesn't matter." His tone is sharp. "What does matter is that Hoffmann's our only way off this island, and if we're going to save Andy, we have to meet his demands."

"Damn him!" I stomp away, digging my boots into the dry beach sand, but I don't get far. *Rafe is right.* I throw my hands up in surrender. *Andy is what's important here.*

"I can manage two spots for the children, and if you'll allow Mrs. Green's children to go, I'm sure she'll give her place to your sister."

I hate how Hoffmann drives such a hard bargain. I trudge back to Rafe, waving my hand in the air. "He always finagles a higher price for himself, but even if I agree we still need one more spot."

"St. Sally will stay," says Rafe. "She always puts the welfare of others before her own. Hell, she wouldn't be putting up with me if she didn't. Do it."

He pushes me toward the loathsome pawnbroker.

Determined strides take me the rest of the way, my mind clicking with each step. By the time I reach Hoffmann, I have another idea to help make up for lost time. I extend my hand to the crafty pawnbroker. "I agree to your terms, but I have my own to add."

His eyebrow twitches. "And what would that be?"

"I want that Megamark uniform, and your gun. Now that you've cost us critical time, we might need another ploy to enter Culpepper's Council meeting."

"That's not going to happen."

"It will, if you want to be free of this hellish life."

"I've got nothing on under here. I'd have to run the streets naked."

"Not my problem, old man. You want out of here for yourself and your family. I want safe passage to the city's shoreline for Rafe and myself, and I want that gun and uniform, now."

"But it's cold on the river at night."

"You should have thought of that when you sabotaged our boat."

"It wasn't me who took the crowbar to your boat. I only stood by and witnessed it. It was Culpepper's Captain."

233

"Why would he send his captain to sabotage the task he hired me for?"

Rafe answers. "He must have timed it out. He ordered it to be a slow leak, so we couldn't get back."

"That asshole thinks he hit the daily double," spit Hoffmann. "Two for one. He got rid of the rats and doesn't have to pay."

That might explain his overzealous hoot on the shoreline; he couldn't know I am Viper. My temper flares. I kick rocks down the beach, visualizing Culpepper's disgusting face on each one.

"Well, thanks to you, he didn't succeed. I'm not happy you wheedled me into taking you, but I'm grateful you were keen enough to trade your information and for being selfish enough to come after me to guarantee passage for your family. Now, strip."

"All I have is your word. It's not good enough!"

"Do you have paper? I'll write it down and sign it."

Hoffmann pulls a pen and paper from the front pocket of the uniform. Before I write anything, I hold out my hand to accept his revolver and uniform.

As we climb into his boat, he tucks his guarantee between his chattering teeth.

* * * * *

The oil-slicked sand on Metro City's shore seems eerie without long-tailed rats scurrying over the granite rocks or peeking out from scrub bushes near the water.

I pass the revolver to Rafe, and yell to Hoffmann over my shoulder as we leave. "Wait with your family in the shadows of the courthouse, in approximately one hour. I've got final details to confirm. Don't come out until you hear the sound of a whippoorwill call."

"I could use the gun for our escape, but what are you going to do with the uniform?" asks Rafe as we head straight to the museum.

"You're going to wear it."

"I am?" His brow furrows. "Why?"

"If what Hoffmann says is true, then someone tipped off Culpepper to our plan. Maybe he even saw through my disguise."

"If he knew it was you, he'd have been all over you like flies on shit. There's no way he'd let you out of his sight. He would have made a spectacle of killing you in front of his Council."

"Yes, but this way, he'd be assured I died in the river, and he wouldn't have to pay the money he promised."

"No one could recognize you in that get-up. I must say, I did an excellent job disguising your pretty face."

"Why, Rafe, in all the years I've known you, you've never even hinted you thought I was pretty."

I laugh as Rafe holds the secret door for me, a mischievous sparkle in his eye. He whistles three times.

Cheinstein barely has the door unlocked and I'm through, pacing the floor of the museum like an expectant father.

"Slow down," says St. Sally. "Did something go wrong with the rats?"

"It depends on what rats you're talking about. All the furry ones are dead." I slam my fist into my open palm. "It's those human rats that still run the town and row the rivers we need to be wary of."

Astoria brings me a cup of warm coffee, but I push it aside. My gaze comes to rest on Squeakers, sleeping peacefully through my rants. I look to Cheinstein.

"What's wrong with him? Why isn't he jumping all over the place like he usually does?"

Cheinstein drops his eyes to the floor, as if he did something wrong.

"Jax, I, ah, I . . . ."

Astoria rushes to Cheinstein's defense. "Desperate to get out, Squeakers threw himself into the glass. It must have been when you were singing."

"I thought he was going to give himself a concussion, so I placed a few drops of my mother's anesthesia in his water. When he got tired of knocking himself silly, he took a sip of water, and the next thing we knew he was motionless."

My eyes bulge. "Is he dead?"

"No, his eyes were open. Just like what happened to the fish," said Cheinstein. "The anesthesia wore off, and he fell asleep."

Cheinstein finishes his explanation, and a new plan enters—no--*explodes* in my mind.

"That's it!" I hug Cheinstein until his face is as red as my eye makeup. "We're going to use your mother's formula to get Andy back."

Everyone looks as confused as Cheinstein. "How?"

Chapter Twenty

"Okay, now that everyone is on board with the plan, make sure you're packed and ready to go." I try to sound confident. "Because once we start this, it can end two ways, and one is better than the other."

Rafe changes into the uniform. "Hey, maybe Hoffmann was right. The life of a Megamark isn't so bad. At least it's three squares and a nice place to sleep."

"What are you talking about?" asks Astoria, stuffing her abuela's pillow into a cloth sack.

Rafe takes her into his arms, and in front of everyone, gives her a long, passionate kiss. He seems more surprised than we are.

"I just had to do that before you're gone and I never see you again."

Astoria blinks. Her cheeks blush red.

"B-but you're coming with us." She glances toward me for an explanation.

I shake my head. "Unfortunately, he's decided to stay."

Astoria and St. Sally flank Rafe.

"Why?" Astoria's voice reveals more concern than I expected.

"I won't allow you to stay, Rafe," says St. Sally. "If something has come up and you need a volunteer to stay behind, it shall be me."

Rafe winks at me. "Told ya."

I clear my throat, which brings everyone's attention to me. "There's been a slight change in the freedom list. It seems Culpepper sabotaged our rowboat in the hopes I'd drown, and he wouldn't have to pay me the thirty thousand dollars. He'd be rid of me and the rats at the same time."

"Then how is it you are standing here?" asks Mrs. Green.

"Your friend." I nod at St. Sally. "You were right, Hoffmann is vindictive, and it turns out he also has no conscience. When Culpepper left us to die, Hoffmann rowed out to Scrub Island and saved us, for a price."

Sudden comprehension dawns on St. Sally's face.

"Ah, so he's weaseled his way back on the list. Very well. I shall stay. There's no need for Rafe to."

"Oh, but there is." Rafe hides the gun beneath the buttoned uniform jacket. "He also bartered our lives for the freedom of his niece, nephew, and sister."

Mrs. Green and Cheinstein's stares cut straight to me from gathering their meager belongings. Astoria's face turns as white as mine.

St. Sally stands, reserved and determined, not surprised by Hoffmann's greed.

"Even if Rafe and I stay, you're still short one spot."

I look to Astoria for forgiveness at what I am about to say. "The other part of his demand is that Alder stay as well."

"No," shouts Astoria. "If Alder stays, I stay." Her brown eye is ablaze with loyalty and love.

Rafe winces at her words.

"Let's not panic, people. There's enough space that he can trade his better items to make up the cost of the other ticket. For now, let's assume we're all going. We'll deal with Hoffmann when the time comes. If need be, we have two volunteers to stay behind."

"Three," says Astoria.

"No, two. I'm not leaving without you. You can't take care of yourself, like Rafe."

"But Alder—"

"Will come with us, and so will Rafe and St. Sally. I told Hoffmann to meet us in an hour. If we move fast, we'll be gone before he gets there."

They gather around the worktable.

I diagram my plan.

"I'll sneak back to the Council Hall. Rafe will escort all of you there, as if you're his prisoners. That way, you'll draw no suspicions from the other Megamark guards patrolling the street. When you get within two blocks of City Hall, you're going to break up into pairs.

"Cheinstein, with St. Sally. Mrs. Green with Rafe. Mrs. Green will still pretend to be Rafe's prisoner, until he's close enough to hear my whistle.

"I'll pick the lock at the delivery gate so St. Sally and Cheinstein can approach the servants' door on the side of Culpepper's mansion.

"Colt told Mrs. Bridgewater to secure the children in the servants' kitchen to wait for the whippoorwill call. Once she lets you in, Cheinstein goes to work, and St. Sally escorts the children out the door to Rafe and Mrs. Green, waiting nearby.

"Tori, you man the walkie-talkies to coordinate the rendezvous point. Each group has a communicator.""

I turn to Mrs. Green. "I'm counting on you to keep Andy as safe as if he were your own."

She presses her hands against her heart. "I swear on my life, I will."

"Everybody understand their part?"

Astoria shoots me a wide-eyed stare. She starts to speak, but closes her mouth, with a guilty glance at Rafe.

I know what she's thinking.

"Astoria, Colt threw Adler the keys to his shuttle. My guess is he'll be waiting with Colt somewhere, and they'll pick you all up, but you need to stay together."

"Where will *you* be?" Astoria's forehead wrinkles over her eye patch.

"I'll be right under Culpepper's nose, and if the anesthesia doesn't work, I'm afraid I won't be going with you."

"I'm so scared." Astoria rushes to hug me.

"If everybody does their part, my plan can work. If anything goes wrong, we need to get Andy and the girls out. Honestly, I'd rather die, and know he's safe. Let's move forward. Keep our eyes open. It's tricky, but hey — all the rats are gone. Some plans do work."

Astoria looks at me like we'll never see each other again.

"Astoria, you must believe me. This is for Andy. If he's safe, I'll be happy no matter what happens to me. Now, we have to go. Before it's too late."

"But—"

I flutter my eyelids and hold my hand up in her face.

"There's no time. That's the plan. Come on. It's your choice. Either you're coming, or you're not." I rush to the door and turn. "Rafe, you're first."

He climbs up, followed by St. Sally, Mrs. Green, and Cheinstein, who carries Squeakers in a small cage. Astoria stops to hug me once more.

"I love you," she says.

* * * * *

The Council meeting starts as scheduled, at midnight when Colt introduces me as the Viper.

I glance at Nonna's watch for the millionth time. The hands point to 4:30 a.m. Lights still shine from the mansion windows and the Council Hall.

The power show of Megamark Guards is gone. Only four walk the grounds, more at ease than when I came earlier. *Of course they're at ease. The rats are dead, and as far as they know, so is the Viper.*

When the Megamarks turn away, I scramble from behind a thick tree to the stone wall and then to the well-watered rosebushes in front of the Council's main door. The blossoms are yellow, Nonna's favorite. I pluck one and inhale its sweet fragrance. It reminds me of her rose garden. Somehow, I feel Nonna watches over me. The feeling boosts my confidence.

I peer through the transition windows that change from clear to dark when exposed to the sun's ultraviolet rays. Inside, the mood is festive.

Three children, dressed in flowery organza dresses, and big bows in their hair, dance in front of the pearl lady. Two are brunettes. One has honey-colored hair.

The man in the perspiration-stained suit holds a little boy on his knee.

Six more children chase each other around the adults.

I search for Andy among them, and that's when Culpepper claps his hands.

I can't hear his words, but I see him point toward the doorway connecting the Council Hall to his mansion.

In walks Mrs. Bridgewater, followed by Nyla, Nellie, and lastly, Andy, cradling Nonna's book in his arms. A frown envelops his face.

Damn. Now what? St. Sally and Cheinstein are waiting at the servants' door. How am I going to get them from here? Colt! Where's Colt? No way anyone can miss that cowboy hat of his. I squint to scan the room. I realize I've found him when my heart skips a beat, but he's not wearing his hat. He sits on a couch talking with another Council member. *He wears his duplicity well. Culpepper would never guess he's an Eco.*

Everyone stands at Culpepper's request. His four personal chefs march in from the kitchen, escorted by a Megamark guard. Each chef, carrying a crystal punch bowl, wears a formal white chef jacket and a tall pleated hat. The last chef has a decisive limp. I glance from his feet to his face, and gasp.

Cheinstein was just supposed to spike the punch. I study his movements as he doles out goblets of the claret to the Council members, guests, and the higher echelon of the Guard. Culpepper boasts a goblet in each hand.

The Megamark guard who escorts the chefs looks first at Cheinstein, and then at Colt. He nods, and Colt nods back. A closer look reveals it's Alder. The subtle motion implies they're ready.

I take it as my signal to move in. I'm confident I'm right; when I burst through the front doors, Cheinstein's somber face stretches into a grin.

I stand in the doorway. Shoulders back, chin held high, and hands on my hips, I stare long and hard at Culpepper, challenging him to acknowledge his thwarted scheme. I've no need for the microphone now.

I shout, "Mr. Mayor."

My voice cuts through the celebratory din.

All eyes dart to me.

"I see you are celebrating the satisfactory completion of my work. I've honored my end of our contract. Not one furry scoundrel exists in the whole of Metro City." *Well, maybe one. He needn't know about Squeakers.*

My gaze flashes to Andy's face, his eyes wide with wonder. He must think he's seeing a creature from Nonna's book come to life. Or maybe he recognizes my voice and can't understand why it's coming from such a bizarre being.

"I've come to claim my reward. Passage out of Metro City and my thirty thousand dollars in gold."

"Ha!" Culpepper stops his toast midway to his lips. "Thirty thousand dollars?" He smirks. "I don't think so."

The Council members nod in absolute agreement.

"Besides," says the Mayor, taking one step closer. "Our business concluded at the edge of the Elan."

His gaze settles briefly on my painted face, then flicks away toward his Council members in a dismissive nod. "We saw the vermin sink with our own eyes. What's dead cannot come back to life, but I fear there was one loophole in the death of our decrepit rats. You see, by my eyes, *you* did *not* kill the rats."

Sleaze drips off this man. He just admitted they died.

My muscles tense, but I muster calm and continue my charade, forcing the shock of instant anger to dissipate. *I can't blow it now.*

"How dare you call me a liar and say it was not I who killed the rats? I bid them follow me to their deaths. If I did not kill them, who, then, do you propose caused their demise?"

He cocks his head, and raises an emphatic eyebrow.

"Why, the bloody, toxic river passed her poison into the rats. The river killed them, not you,

Viper." He leans toward me in an aggressive stance, daring me to challenge his decision.

My eyes bulge. I gasp. *All this for nothing! I should have known. He's a damn liar.*

I search for Colt. He leaps to his feet, making his way through the Megamarks and the mingling guests, toward Culpepper. I struggle to keep my jittery voice from betraying me.

"Had I not coerced them into the river, they would still nest in your chair, waiting to feast on the tender flesh of your children." I strike at the recent death of his newborn son.

His over-stuffed face turns as red as the wine in his goblets. "I *said* you'd not be getting the thirty thousand dollars."

At that moment, Colt reaches his side.

"Syl, had I known you intended to swindle this character, I would never have borne him away from his other obligations in the rainforests of Brazil. He was scheduled to be there, instead of here, and I promised him the payment, as you advised me to."

Culpepper waves Colt away. "Rest easy, Colt, my boy. We'll pay the Viper something."

His raucous laughter echoes throughout the hall. He turns his attention back to me.

"Some of us had a wager you wouldn't make it back from the toxic river. But seeing you have returned in one piece, friend, we won't shirk our duty of offering you something to drink."

He waves to the chefs to offer me a goblet of wine punch.

Cheinstein hurries with a full goblet and reaches me first. His eyes widen as he hands it to me.

"Don't drink," he whispers.

I throw the wine to the floor. "I do not want spirits or drink. I've come to collect the gold you promised me."

Culpepper hesitates. "That's imported wine you're wasting, Viper. I would think you'd have better manners."

"I would think you'd have better scruples, sir."

"Well, perhaps we can spare fifty dollars from the city's treasury to fill your purse."

He reopens his safe to remove a bill.

"But as for the thirty thousand dollars we spoke of, well, that was in jest." His self-satisfied smirk becomes a sneer, and then he continues, "You see, it was pure entertainment on our part, wagering whether one rat, or two, would be left. And seeing that none are, it's a boon to my city, and will help clear the way for the new underground housing development scheduled for this spring."

He steps back to reveal a scale model of an underground city. "I plan to return Metro City to its former glory. Those who fled will return. We'll attract new, younger, richer citizens who want to partake in a luxurious lifestyle."

I spit at his feet. "Do not trifle with me, sir. I have no time to spare. I must be on the next air caravan that leaves your bizarre city, for I am expected in the Sahara to rid an oasis of scorpions."

Holding two goblets of wine, he raises one in a brusque salute. "Be that as it may, Viper, you'll not get more than fifty dollars for your work here."

"Then you leave me no choice, but to use my voice again."

"You're too peculiar for me to take your threats seriously. What say you all?" He turns to his Council and Megamark Guards scattered throughout the room. "Is fifty perhaps too much to pay this odd fellow?"

They respond by raising their glasses. "To Sylvanis, Mayor of Metro City, the *new* destination city."

Culpepper raises a glass to his lips, but speaks before sipping. "So you see, Viper, you may sing until you burst, but you'll not see us again. Do your worst."

Confusion blends with anger on Colt's face. He questions Culpepper's actions. "Syl, this is wrong."

"Stop whining, Colt, and drink. Here, take one of mine. I'll get another." He motions to the first chef, who promptly slips another wine-filled goblet in his hand.

Colt's gaze darts from me to Culpepper to Mrs. Bridgewater.

Culpepper notices. "Is there something going on here?" He stares into Colt's eyes.

"No, sir." Rather than give anything away, Colt chugs the wine.

Culpepper chortles as he downs his own. His followers do the same, and in less than one minute, they stand immobile, except for their eyes.

Their chittering din ceases. The silence is obvious. Even the hum of the air-conditioning has stopped. I smile. *Rafe's Altar Boys are on the roof.*

Alder lifts Colt's arm over his shoulder and makes his way toward the front door. Colt's alligator boots leave black streaks across the marble floor. Rafe charges in and slips Colt's other arm around his shoulders. The two of them struggle to get Colt outside.

Mrs. Bridgewater and St. Sally stand behind Andy and the twins. Nyla wraps her arms around both Andy and Nellie.

I must act. I don't know how fast the anesthesia will wear off. I breathe deeply and start to sing one of Nonna's songs.

*"When whippoorwills call, and evening is nigh,
I hurry to my Blue Heaven."*

I whistle the whippoorwill call three times. Andy quickly looks up. He separates from Nyla, grabs her hand, then pulls her toward me. But when he gets close, he freezes at the sight of my face. His eyes widen in terror. Once again, he turns to Nyla for comfort.

"It's me, Andy. It's Jax."

Tentatively, he peeks from Nyla's shoulder.

Only one way he'll recognize me. I connect the microphone to the geisha fan and sing.

"Close your sleepy eyes. Come rest your weary head.

*You will be safe in your comfy, cozy bed.
I will protect you. Sleep without a care
and know by my love that I always will be there
. . . ."*

Andy runs into my arms. The children of the Council members gather around us. It's happening again. It was no coincidence when the alley children followed the rats. My songs mesmerize them, too, but they come only when I sing children's songs.

I guide the children toward the door, and come face to face with Hoffmann.

He bursts into the Council Hall, not aware of what has happened.

"I heard the call. Is it time?" His sister and her family wait at the door.

"Yes. We're leaving now," says Cheinstein. He hobbles next to me.

"Ah, not before I take my share of what this bastard owes me." He rushes past me, oblivious to the motionless adults, and darts around the Council room stealing gold candlesticks and sterling silver trays.

"These will bring a good price in the New World," he snickers.

Ignoring Hoffmann, I turn toward the door and grasp Andy's hand, but he breaks free to run to his chair.

"I'll be right back, Jax."

Anxiously, I keep singing. As I wait for Andy, my gaze is drawn to Hoffmann. Blinded by his own greed, he makes his way past the stock-still Council members. He doesn't even notice Culpepper is motionless.

"I'll take this too, if you don't mind." He pulls the second goblet from Culpepper's hand, and gulps down the drugged claret.

At the same time, Andy grabs Nonna's book, then dashes back to me.

Nyla pulls Nellie to follow us, and the ten Council children come, too.

The booty in Hoffmann's stiffened arms crashes to the floor, as the children and I reach the front door. I switch to a more lively children's song

"The farmer's dog lay in the barn and Bingo was his name-o.

B-I-N-G-O, B-I-N-G-O, B-I-N-G-O and Bingo was his name-o."

The two street children, waiting at the door with their mother, join Andy, the twins, and the Council children. We march down the Council's front sidewalk.

Their mother screams, "Otto, they're taking the children." Panic contorts her face, as she scans the room. "All of them."

Children clap, sing, and skip after me.

If Culpepper won't pay me so I can buy passage on the Air Caravan for Andy and my friends, I'll take the children with me. I hope Colt isn't mad when he sees me coming with thirteen children instead of three.

"The farmer's dog lay in the barn and Bingo was his name-o.

B-I-N, clap, clap. B-I-N, clap, clap. B-I-N, clap, clap and Bingo was his name-o."

Suddenly, the doors of the city climate-controlled homes burst open. It sounds like a bustling, and then merry cries. Shoes click, and clatter as children run out into the street to join my parade. Ten-year-olds carry babies. Toddlers march hand in hand.

Homeless children climb up from their hidey-holes beneath the church, the library, and who knows where else, followed by frantic adults desperately trying to stop them.

I recognize the little girl who used to sleep on our doorstep and her brother behind her. She smiles. *Can she recognize my voice, too?*

Boys and girls with rosy cheeks and flaxen curls mix with lice-infested children wrapped in rags. All of them, with sparkling eyes, skip down Main Street following me.

Culpepper and his cronies can only watch as I steal their children right out from under their noses.

Marching backward, I break into a new song, one as lively as the first. By the time we travel two more blocks, I lose track of how many children follow me. *It's got to be all of the children in Metro City. I hope they fit in Colt's shuttle. He'll probably get fired for this, but it's too late to stop now.*

As we head toward the Elan, a ruckus erupts far behind us, down Main Street. Sirens blare, drowning out the children's glee. Flashing lights rush toward us. The anesthesia has worn off.

Chapter Twenty-One

I switch to a repetitive silly song and the children squeal with delight, but beneath their laughter, I hear Hoffmann's sister scream, "Bring back my children."

She chases after us, but I can't stop, not even for the street people to take their children.

The Megamark Guards drive their PUV's through the homeless crowd, making way for the horse-drawn collection wagons and Culpepper's own white, high-speed SUV.

Some of the street people ignore the Megamark. They're in no danger of being arrested, now. The Guard's sole assignment is to apprehend me. But others, having been conditioned to fear them, cringe close to buildings, and let them pass.

My heartbeat races as fast as my feet. I keep glancing back in amazement. One of the homeless men jumps on a Megamark Guard riding a PUV, and they both tumble into the street, sending the PUV crashing into a brick building near those who cower. Whether it's in an effort to save his children, or a chance to attack the Guard, I can't tell, but soon his actions are imitated.

A riot spreads like the threatening heat of the sun.

The homeless purposely assault the PUV's with stones and debris. Both men and women jump on the riders, sending them crashing into the street.

The street people swarm Culpepper's SUV, and though his driver tries to ram through them, they hinder his acceleration. The vehicle can't get any closer, and then I see why. St. Sally and Mrs. Bridgewater lead them. The man with the blond ponytail, who was shackled next to me at the meters, marches beside them. He spurs the crowd on.

"It's Jax Stone," he yells.

I slow to a jog when I hear my name. I can't believe what's happening behind me.

"She saved us from the sun. Now, she's saving our children."

Culpepper leans out of the open SUV window. Perspiration streams down his face, so red it looks like it will burst. His eyes grow wide with wild fury.

If the hate in them were daggers, I'd be dead.

The homeless pound on his back and try to drag him from the vehicle. His weight saves him. He pulls his revolver and shoots one the people hanging on his side of the car, but immediately, another replaces the fallen body.

One of the Altar boys karate chops Culpepper's arm. His gun falls to the street.

A homeless man retrieves it, and repeatedly shoots at the SUV until the weapon runs out of bullets.

Culpepper shrieks. "She's taking them to the river to drown them like the rats. Stop her. I'll pay good money to whoever brings her down."

Mrs. Bridgewater said he didn't like to be double-crossed.

Still singing, I pick up the pace once more, striving to get away. I'm so involved in what is happening behind me I don't notice Andy's strides getting slower until I feel the tug on my arm. *It's a good thing I'm holding his hand.*

I look down.

He struggles to hold onto Nonna's book.

I stop to pick him up. As the children gather around me, the older ones sense my urgency. They lift the younger ones, and we continue.

No one from the crowd heeds Culpepper's plea.

The time it takes for the children to regroup allows me to hear the volley of accusations between Culpepper and the people of Metro City.

"Let them, go," shouts St. Sally. "She's saving their lives. She's taking them to the New World. Let them go."

"Stop them," counters Culpepper. "Don't believe this absurdity. She can't take one hundred children with her. She doesn't even have money for her own passage."

"He's a liar," shouts Mrs. Bridgewater. "He wants the children to be slave laborers for his new city. He can't stand looking at our children, because they remind him of himself. He was once a homeless orphan like them."

"Now, who is lying?" he shouts. "Don't believe the old bag. Her brain is addled from age."

Mrs. Bridgewater waves her clenched fists and her pace picks up speed.

"My brain is quite well, thank you, and so is my memory. I remember the young boy who was the courier for the worst drug lord in Metro City, the homeless boy who lived in the sewers before any of you were driven there by him." She points an accusing finger at Culpepper, and the street people attack his SUV, pulling him from the vehicle.

Two homeless men seize him.

"You lie, woman," Culpepper shouts, "after everything I've done for you."

Mrs. Bridgewater laughs. "What you've done for me? You mean closing the library so I couldn't help children? Leaving me destitute with no place to live?"

"I gave you a place to live," he shouts. He struggles to free himself from the men.

Most of the Megamarks stand with gaping mouths. They listen as Culpepper's tale unfolds.

I still sing. More children gather around me, as the verbal duel between Culpepper and Daphne, his elderly house servant, continues.

"That you did, in exchange for me keeping silent about your past, and how I cared for your wounds when that vile gangster beat you. And how I fed you, when you were starving. You'd sneak into the library just before closing time and I'd find you in the stacks, hiding in the dark, your spirit as broken as your body, new bruises on old ones.

"It's not surprising you've raped so many women, trying to erase your own repeated sexual abuse by the drug lords. And when one woman tried to stand up to you, you took everything away from her, her livelihood, her home, her mother, and finally, her life.

"It was just another piece of business for you and those vile drug dealers you associate with. But she kept your most prized treasure from you. She took her secret to her grave. No one knew, until now, when her brave daughter dares to steal it back from you."

I clasp Andy tighter, resting my chin on his shoulder. Sudden coldness strikes my core. *He not only raped my mother, he killed her. And he wants to kill me, too.*

Daphne continues her rant. "For forty years, I've kept your secrets, but no more. You've become a tyrant and we've lived in fear long enough. Now, you're making our children relive your horrors."

"Oh, God," I whisper into Andy's shoulder. My eyes blur with tears. I don't know if I cry because I saved Andy from a terrible fate, or because of the horrendous fate Culpepper endured as an orphan child.

"Jax." Andy winces. "You're squeezing me too tight."

"I'm sorry, Andy," I whisper. "I've missed you."

"Me, too," he says, and hugs my neck.

Down the street, Culpepper's voice grows louder.

"Shut the old bag up," he yells, "and then go for the clown-faced girl."

"I will not be shut up. I saved you when you were a helpless boy, and now she is saving these helpless children from you."

Finally, the Megamark Guards ignore Mrs. Bridgewater, and ambush the men holding Culpepper. He hops into the SUV, and it lurches in our direction.

"Stop *him*," shouts St. Sally. "Let Jax take the children to freedom."

The crowd surges after Culpepper, blocking the vehicle's movement again.

I can't watch any longer. They'll be on us in a minute. Panic increases my stamina. My pace quickens, forcing the children to move faster. Time is of the essence, and Andy's weight makes my breathing labored, but I push ahead.

"Faster!" I scream. I sing, as I spring, briefly glancing over my shoulder.

The children run, too. As we approach the river, the shuttle pulls out into the intersection, one block away, as prearranged.

Rafe throws open the shuttle's front door.

Cheinstein opens the back.

I jump in, still singing.

The children pour through both doors.

I hand Andy to Cheinstein, and run to the front of the shuttle.

Colt, in the copilot's seat, squeezes my hand. He's still woozy from the anesthesia.

My mind churns, even as I sing another rendition of *This Old Man*. The Elite Guard is gaining ground. My heart races. I whisper, "If you can't drive, we're trapped."

"Don't worry," says Colt, running his hands through his black curls. "My man has it under control."

He nods toward the pilot's seat.

Alder starts the shuttle's engines.

Astoria, Cheinstein, and Mrs. Green calm the children.

Rafe stands at the back, calling out coordinates of the approaching Megamark Guards.

"They're going to surround us. You won't be able to take off," he yells.

I dash to the back to see for myself.

Hoffmann runs after the shuttle, cursing. "Come back, Jax. We had a deal."

The street people witness Hoffmann's futile attempts to board the shuttle. They pull him back into the crowd. A loud cheer goes up from the docks. The people, who before cowered in fear, join the others and converge on the Megamark Guards, toppling their PUV's and poking the horses with sharp sticks.

Horse whinnies echo through the chaos. They rear up against the carts they're harnessed to, refusing to advance.

The only vehicle to get through is Culpepper's SUV. He's running over the people who jump in his way, and he follows us out of Metro City, into the country.

I return to the front.

Mrs. Green takes over singing.

Cheinstein tells corny jokes to keep the children occupied.

"Where am I going?" shouts Alder. "This isn't the way to the station. We'll never get back to join the main caravan."

"Then we need to do something else." I look to Colt for an answer.

The rotating lights on Culpepper's SUV flashes through the windows. He's too close. His men will soon be climbing all over the shuttle.

"Doesn't this thing fly, too?" Panic chokes me. I try to catch my breath. "I overheard you say it has wings."

Colt has regained his abilities. "It does, but where will we fly?"

"Anywhere to get away from Culpepper. On land, he's catching up to us. The air is our only escape. If he shoots our tires, we're finished."

"I need a coordinate." Colt sets the air controls. "We can't go far. This is only a commuter vehicle. It needs to be attached to the air caravan for full power. And it will be daylight in an hour. Even though the shuttle is climate controlled, when the power cells run out of energy, everything shuts down."

The retractable wings unfold from the sides, up and out, like a bird getting ready to soar.

"So where are we going?"

"To the mountain near my grandmother's cottage. It's got a cave. My mother took me there the day we buried Nonna. Couldn't we park the shuttle in the cave until the air caravan can pick us up?"

Colt pushes levers and pulls back the co-pilot's steering wheel. "Do you know the coordinates?"

I shake my head. "I just know where it is. It used to be covered in pine and oak trees, and a lake pooled at the bottom of the mountain. My grandmother's cottage was near the lake."

"That sounds like Beacon Mountain," says Alder. "Huge pines and oaks covered the mountainside, and a beacon, at the top, guided the planes to the old airport."

"I-I guess." I never went to the top. I glance over my shoulder. Megamarks bang on the back door, trying to pry it open, and Rafe pulls desperately with all his weight to keep it closed. "But we have to go, now."

"Beacon Mountain?" Colt's question brings my attention back to the conversation. "I know where that is. That's where my grandfather had his log cabin."

"Then go. Now," I shriek. "Rafe's having a hard time keeping the door closed. They're on us."

"Okay, I can guesstimate the coordinates. Hold on."

A laser shot blows the back wheel, just as Colt and Alder simultaneously push the throttles back.

The shuttle tilts to one side as we lift off.

The Megamark struggling at the back door drops to the ground.

Rafe clings to the doorway, and Culpepper fades from sight, on the road beneath us.

* * * * *

The first traces of light brighten the sky as we approach the mountain. From high in the air, I cannot distinguish the cave entrance from the mountain face.

"There." I point to a gap in the mountainside. "Do you see it?"

"That's not the cave I remember," says Colt, "but it will do. We'll be there in a few seconds. Radio my co-pilot. Tell him where to pick us up."

He shoves the radio in my hand. His fingers touch mine. A tiny shock pulses through me. He must have felt it, too, because he briefly looks into my eyes and then returns to the controls.

"I don't know the coordinates."

"I'll try," says Alder, grabbing the transmitter.

The children must think they're on an adventure. Most of them have never been off the ground. The sights below mesmerize them, as wide-eyed, they point out sights to each other.

Nonna's cottage is below me. The roof has caved in, and a yellow rosebush, near the pond, still blossoms in a field of weeds that was once her garden.

Tears fill my eyes. Headed toward the mouth of the cave, we pass over Nonna's resting place.

All at once, Culpepper's high-speed SUV darts over the hill below us. Colt pulls back on the throttle, and the pitch of the shuttle's engines change to a lower frequency.

Beads of perspiration line Colt's brow.

"This is going to be like threading a needle. I can't put the wheels down because there's no smooth landing strip, and I can't fly full speed into the cave. Tell the children to bend forward. Brace for impact."

I give the whippoorwill call.

All eyes turn toward me in the front of the shuttle.

"Boys and girls, we're going to have a tough landing, so I want you to do what I do."

"Like Simon Says?" asks Andy.

"Yes, like Simon Says. Everyone bend forward, grab your ankles, and don't look up until I tell you to. We're going on an adventure in a mountain cave, so once we land I want everyone to come to the front door, toward me, please."

After the children are in place, I strap myself in the seat next to Andy.

Astoria and Cheinstein sit in the middle of the shuttle; Mrs. Green and Rafe sit in the back.

As the mountain looms in front of us, Colt cuts the power, forcing the shuttle into a slow glide toward the mouth of the cave.

"Dump the fuel," he yells.

Alder releases whatever fuel we have left.

I squeeze my eyes shut and protect Andy's body with mine.

"Pull, Alder, pull," Colt yells.

The shuttle vibrates.

Chapter Twenty-Two

Colt guides the shuttle into the mouth of the cave. Glass splinters, and sounds of the wings ripping from the underbelly is deafening. The hard jolt of the impact sends us forward into the seats in front of us. A shower of pebbles and dirt spray the shuttle's windows. The thud of rocks beating on shuttle's roof sound like the mountain is falling in on us.

I desperately clutch Andy. I need to protect him to my last breath.

The shuttle screeches to a stop. The only sound is the trickle of pebbles that slide down the shuttle's titanium side.

I open my eyes. The damaged shuttle is almost completely inside the cave, but the back door swings open, allowing shafts of morning sun to illuminate dust particles that swirl above the children's heads like mini-ash clouds. Pine limbs protrude through the broken windows, their wispy needles covering some of the children like a mossy umbrella.

"That was fun," squeals Andy. "Can we do it again?"

I swallow hard. We may have eluded Culpepper, but the hard part is still ahead of us.

"No, sweetie. We're going to explore the cave now." I hope I made the right call; otherwise, I'll have led these children to their deaths.

Rafe staggers to the back door.

"Crap," he yells. "He's right on top of us."

My senses jump to attention. No time for second-guessing.

"Andy, you're going to go with Cheinstein. I'll meet you in the cave. Cheinstein," I yell. I dash past him, forcing Andy's hand in his. "Get the front door open, and lead the kids into the cave. I don't think Culpepper can get to us in there. The only way in is through the back of the shuttle, and in moments he'll have it blocked."

I continue to the back to help Rafe and Mrs. Green.

"The door's jammed, Jax," Cheinstein shouts. "My leg's still not strong enough to kick it open."

"I've got it," yells Colt. He supports his weight on the front seats and kicks. He smashes the door open against the cave wall, with his alligator boots, the gap large enough for the children to flee in a single file.

"Here, take this." Colt shoves a duffle bag from the pilot's quarters into Cheinstein's hand, then heads toward the back of the shuttle.

The children follow Cheinstein.

The rest of us turn our attention to Culpepper's SUV. It comes to a stop on the rocky bluff, fifty feet from the shuttle.

Culpepper's Elite Guards dash from the SUV, and surround him.

He struggles, huffing and puffing, out of the vehicle. They all have guns, including Culpepper.

"We've got you now, you sewer bitch. You've nowhere to hide. The sun will be in full force within the hour and you'll all die. I don't care if you and your vermin kind fry. I thought I insured your death by the sun before, but you're a sly devil, you are. Give me my children, and I'll let you live. Maybe you can survive. Maybe not, but I won't have you leading my children to their deaths."

I answer him from the shuttle's rear doorway, hands on my hips. Hate darts from my bulging eyes. I don't break visual contact with the scum bastard.

"You'll never set eyes on Andy again."

"Ha!" He waves his soldiers forward. "You're a fool, Jax Stone. We've got you outnumbered. I'll just kill you, and take Andy. You can't stop me."

I clench the doorway so tightly, I feel like I can crush the metal within my fists. My nostrils flare. I narrow my glaring eyes to answer his challenge.

"I'll die trying."

Just then, a child wiggles between my legs, jumps to the ground, falls, and rolls down the mountain face screaming, "D-a-d-d-y! Save me."

The flash of auburn hair bobbing through the brush, and her wails for Culpepper, make it impossible not to recognize Nellie and her high-pitched whine.

Mrs. Green shoves me out of the way, and jumps out after her.

"Nellie." She screams. She runs full force after her tumbling daughter. Her legs tangle in her long skirt, and she falls, sliding to a stop just short of Nellie, who clings to Culpepper's leg.

Another child's voice echoes from the shuttle.

"Nellie, come back." Nyla struggles, as Astoria, and Colt stop her from following her mother and sister. She's so busy fighting them she doesn't stop until a blast from a gun explodes.

Nyla's face turns white. Her eyes grow wide.

"Get her out of here," I shout.

Colt carries her, huddled in a fearful ball, to Cheinstein at the front, then returns.

Mrs. Green, bleeding from the gunshot wound in her stomach, pleads for her daughter.

"Don't take her away from me, please."

"Why? You kept her hidden from me for seven years. You and the Stone whore. They're my children. They belong to me!"

Culpepper hands Nellie over to one of his Guards, storms up to Mrs. Green, and kicks her.

"Kill her." He turns to attend to Nellie. "Then, kill the rest of them. The children will eventually get hungry. We'll come back for them tomorrow."

But before the captain can raise his gun, Alder jumps from the shuttle. He races toward Mrs. Green.

Rafe covers him with Hoffmann's gun.

Culpepper stops cold. "There's nothing worse than a traitor. Kill him first."

Next to me, Astoria gasps. She bolts forward to stop him before I can prevent her, but Mrs. Green, lying on the ground in front of the Megamark Guard, is closer.

She reaches up and pulls his ankle as he shoots.

The bullet hits Alder in the shoulder, hurling him to the ground.

Culpepper turns and aims his gun at Mrs. Green. He holds the revolver so tightly his arm quivers. Immediately, he cups his left hand around the butt of the gun, and clasps his fingers over his right hand to steady it.

Mrs. Green makes the sign of the cross.

He squeezes the trigger.

The ear-splitting explosive sound rips through me, and I'm helpless to do anything.

Astoria tries to jump from the caravan to help Alder.

Rafe pulls her back.

"I'll get him. Cover me." He hands me the gun, then jumps from the shuttle, rolling combat-style to where Alder lies, aiming his gun at Culpepper.

Wide-eyed, Culpepper heads for cover, but before he can dash behind the SUV, Alder's shot knocks him to the ground.

Rafe dives over Alder, protecting him with his body. They roll behind a large boulder.

The anguished expression on Alder's face speaks volumes. Grasping his shoulder, he cradles his arm to his belly and hands Rafe his pistol.

As the armed guards close ranks around a screaming Culpepper, Rafe gets off a shot that blasts into the stomach of the closest one. Then he slips Alder's good arm over his shoulder.

Rafe runs Alder back to the shuttle, and heaves his body at Colt, leaning out the shuttle's back doorway.

I jerk my head from Colt and haul Alder into the safety of the shuttle, as another bullet rings out across the rocky bluff. My gaze follows the sound to Culpepper, lying on the ground, his right arm propped by his left, his gun aimed at the shuttle.

Blood erupts from Rafe's mouth. His knees buckle. His eyes bulge, and he falls, as he focuses on Astoria.

Crawling to the shuttle, hindered by gasping breaths, unstoppable determination burns in his eyes. He slips his hand into his pocket, then pulls it out, reaching forward to Astoria.

On her knees in the doorway, she stretches to touch his hand.

His fingers grasp hers.

"Tori," he whispers with his last breath. He collapses to the ground.

She's left with a filigree heart in her outstretched hand.

I shake my head. *This can't be happening.* Without thinking, I pull Astoria back into the shuttle, as if my grief can pull Rafe to safety with her. But, it's too late for him. My pain bottles itself in my heart; my only concern, here and now, is Astoria.

Once she's inside, I rise to see blood dripping from Culpepper's wounded arm as he assists Nellie into his SUV. He squirms into the driver's seat to watch the Megamark Guards from the horse-drawn carriage advance with guns drawn.

"Everyone get back," shouts Colt. "Leave the way the kids did. I'll be right behind you."

Astoria helps Alder through the front door, but I stay with Colt.

"What are you going to do?"

Colt sucks in his cheeks. "I told you to leave," he says from the side of his mouth. He keeps his eyes on Culpepper.

I square my shoulders, refusing to listen. "Not without you," I yell.

"Go," he shouts, pushing me through the aisle to the front of the shuttle. "I'll be right behind you."

"You didn't answer me." I spin around. "What are you going to do?"

Colt shoves me through the front door. He pushes several buttons on the dash. He grabs a communicator, squeezes through the door, and grabs my hand. We barely have enough time to ease our way between the cave's rock wall and the charred, crumbled frame of the shuttle before the shuttle explodes.

Just as we clear its nose, we're thrown forward into the cavern. Rocks from the mountaintop tumble down the cliff face to bury the opening in a landslide.

Colt lands on top of me, shielding me from rock projectiles.

I raise my head. We're sealed in the cave. It's totally black.

* * * * *

"Are you okay?" whispers Colt. His warm breath, so close to my ear, sends a quiver through me.

"I'm fine." I push myself up to a sitting position.

Pinpricks of light glow farther into the darkness. In the stillness, Cheinstein's voice echoes through the vast cavern ahead of us. His voice clearly reflects off the rock walls.

"Open Sesame." He reads a fairy tale to the children from Nonna's book.

I smile. Leave it to him to find a story about a cave.

Colt and I make our way toward Cheinstein's voice and the tiny glowing lights. First one. Then, two. And then a dozen. As we approach, it's obvious the sewer children are prepared for the darkness. The Council's children shiver as they huddle, wide-eyed, at Cheinstein's knee. Some of the street children comfort them. Others gather around Andy and Squeakers, as he shows off his rat's tricks. Even Andy does his part to distract the children from realizing they're trapped in a mountain.

Astoria bends over Alder, lying on a flat granite slab protruding from the rocky wall. She's trying desperately to inspect his wound with a flashlight.

"I'll help her," says Colt. "I've got a first aid kit in the duffle."

"Good idea." I follow him.

He turns and grips my shoulders. "Why don't you go wash that stuff off your face? It freaks me out. And now that you're not singing, it might scare the kids."

I brush my fingertips across my cheek. Dirt granules cling to the face paint. The paste jewels from my upper lip are missing and now that the adrenaline has subsided, I feel like my face is suffocating.

"I think there's a stream in here, somewhere. At least there was six years ago, when I stayed here with my mother."

"Here." Colt shoves an emergency candle and a few stick matches in my hand. "Go find Jax. Get rid of the Viper."

The candle's flickering flame reveals his bright smile in the murky darkness. He rushes off to help Astoria and Alder.

I make my way through the cave's rocky path.

Even though the sun blasts the mountain outside, inside, the dampness of the ancient cavern is unmistakable. *The sun's warmth must never touch this cave.*

The pathway narrows as the rock face falls off to the left. I run my fingers along the moist, earthen wall to guide me.

The path runs up, and then down, sloping gently to a rock floor, where a small opening appears to be a tunnel. I remember following my mother into this tunnel. *This must be the way to the underground spring.* As a child, I thought nothing about crawling through a narrow tunnel, burrowing deep within a mountain, but as an adult, the thought of the weight of the earth above me only adds to my worry about the children and Alder.

My face feels taut, but it's more than caked, white makeup. My sweaty hands tighten into fists, and then loosen. I creep through the tight passageway.

Colt warned me I was impulsive. I thought I could take all these kids to Antarctica to start a new life. Now, they're doomed to die in a cold mountain.

My thoughts nudge me on; I secretly hope I'll find an escape route. The narrow tunnel widens into a cavern. I remember this is where mother and I drank from the spring. But as I bring the candle forward, an emotional tidal wave crashes over me. Shivering starts. It won't stop. *I must have made a wrong turn in the dark.*

No stream meanders through the mountain here. I hold the candle high above my head; the dim light reflects on the water of a massive underground lake. I scan the endless cavern that surrounds it, and the vast space steals my breath. Stalactites hang from the cavern's ceiling, reaching down over the lake like sharp teeth, while stalagmites rise up from the water to meet them. *I feel so small, like I'm in the mouth of an ancient monster, a mouth that will swallow the remnants of this horrible night.*

I tip my candle to let dripping wax form a base on a nearby rock that holds the candle upright, while I remove the striped cape, Romeo's clothing, and Nonna's watch. I toss the purple contacts to the ground. I lost the magnifying spectacles and my geisha fan somewhere. A melancholy ache tightens my chest. I realize I lost the only thing my father gave me. *That's not true. He gave me his talent to sing. What's done is done.*

I step into the cold water and wince. Shivers rise from my toes to my scalp. I run my hand over my shaved head. Tiny stubbly hairs already grow back.

I throw myself forward in a shallow dive, and lose myself in the frigid water. Submerged, I wonder if I should stay under, and allow the mountain to take me. Tears for Rafe mingle with the lake's cold water. *He sacrificed himself for Astoria. No, for all of us. He knew the danger. He was never one to stand down.*

My lungs hurt, waiting to breathe in the moist air above the surface. I scour my face, trying to wash away my guilt along with the makeup. As I burst from the water, I gasp, only to realize my wheezing breaths are not from trying to fill my lungs with much needed air, but because I'm still crying. Tears of joy, at again holding Andy in my arms.

Tears of sadness, at the loss of Rafe.

"I'm so sorry, Rafe." I sob. I talk to him, hoping his spirit can hear me. "You protected us. You always put us first. I used to think it was only because you loved Astoria, but I was wrong. You didn't have to risk your life to save me from the meters. You didn't have to break into Culpepper's air ducts so I could find Andy. You were a true friend, always there for us. What will we do without you?"

"You'll go on, for Rafe. He'll always be with us."

I'm numb, either from the cold water, or my grief, or both. But I recognize Colt's voice, and turn.

He stands, holding a candle, at the edge of the lake near my discarded clothes.

The snaps of his shirt pop as he strips it off. "I thought you might want company."

My voice catches in my achy throat. I'm so choked up I don't answer. Before I can find my voice, he removes the rest of his clothes and dives beneath the frigid water.

I tremble as his head submerges, thinking of how the rats' heads went under in the river, and never came back up.

"No," I whisper, torn by memories of dying rats, and yet longing for Colt's comfort. But he's already underwater, and can't hear me. I wrap my arms around myself to quell my uncontrollable shaking. It's not until Colt rises from the water, pulls me to a rock island ledge, and takes me in his arms, that I stop.

The warmth of his dark eyes burns through my self-doubt and the frigid water. "Colt, I—"

He places his finger on my mouth. "Not now," he whispers.

The sensual shock that pulses through me when his fingers caress my lips is powerful.

They slip from my lips to my chin, and lift it slightly.

I close my eyes and wrap my legs around him, allowing myself to get lost in his closeness.

Colt's lips melt mine. His kiss is gentle and perfect; everything I dreamed it would be. And for once, my sorrow turns into joy.

"Come on," he says. "This water is too damn cold. You're freezing."

He pulls me as he backstrokes toward shore. When we get to where my clothes are, I see that he spread a blanket on a large rock. My eyes find his in the candlelight, and the spark is not from the flickering flame.

"I've dreamed about running my fingers through your beautiful blonde hair as we lay together, but I guess I'll have to keep that a dream."

I tilt my head. My mouth falls open. I try not to show disappointment, but my shoulders fall. My face must show it.

Colt chuckles. He pulls me into his arms.

"I meant I'll have to wait to run my fingers through your hair."

He gently lays me on the blanket, and the cold droplets of lake water quickly warm in the heat rising from my body.

A golden sun charm on a leather rawhide strip around his neck glints in the candlelight. Something about it jostles my memory, but I'm overcome with emotion.

I've dreamed of feeling Colt's body next to mine, from the moment he held me in Culpepper's closet. *I can't believe my dream is coming true.* I feel Colt's hard muscles, all of them, against my body, and I close my eyes, running my fingers through his dark curls.

His next kiss transports me to a world of light, far away from the darkness I've known all my life.

Chapter Twenty-Three

I wake up to a cavern filled with eerie blue light. The candle is nothing more than a puddle of wax. I bolt upright and find myself alone. My first thought is that lying with Colt was all a dream, but I'm on the blanket, and then, the sound of his boots scraping on the wet rocks echoes throughout the cave.

Colt's shadowy, muscular figure, like a perfectly sculpted statue, is a silhouette against the blue reflection that lights the water.

I glance around the cavern. *Why are the black waters now a beautiful, soft azure?* The color reminds me of the sky.

"Colt, where is the light coming from?"

He runs back, throwing on his clothes, and answers. "I think it's the sun."

"Inside the mountain?" I scramble to dress, stretching the holey, yellow leggings up my legs.

"Yes, and I think I've been here before." He secures the big Western buckle on his belt.

I pull on Romeo's doublet and breeches, leaving the puffy sleeves laying across a rock. "We're inside a freakin' mountain. Are you saying you've been in this mountain before?"

I study how intensely he searches the cavern for clues.

"No, I've not been inside this massive cavern, but I think I've thrown stones down into this water. I remember hiking with my father and grandfather. I told you he had a cabin in the mountains."

"Yes, when I told you my grandmother had a cottage near the lake below the mountain."

"I think this is the mountain." He starts toward the shaft of sunlight that penetrates the lake, at the far side of the cavern.

I follow. "That would explain why they met every weekend for tea."

"And Daphne and St. Sally lived out here, too."

"They all did. The Ecos left Metro City to get closer to the earth."

"So, there was a shallow cave, with a tunnel at the back, where a female fox raised her kits, about a mile from my grandfather's cabin. I used to crawl through it while my father and grandfather discussed Eco politics over the campfire. At the end of the tunnel, there was a hole that came straight down from the top, as if a meteor from space once fell through the mountain.

"At noon, when the sun was directly overhead, it shined down that shaft, and I saw blue water far beneath me. I used to fantasize a prehistoric world existed down here, and I was the only one who knew the secret entrance. I used to drop stones through the hole, and count to see how long it took to hear the splash."

For the second time, a warm glow spreads through my body. My heart drums in my chest. My hope rejuvenates.

"That explains why we can breathe, but it also means there's a way out."

We break into a run, climbing up and over the rocks that line the lake's shore until we come to the sunlight pouring down like a shaft of honey.

"I never thought I'd be thankful to see the midday sun. This means we can bring the children up to your grandfather's fox's cave, and wait for the air caravan to pick us up at night."

"Wait here." Colt climbs the rock ledge. He eases himself up, and then meanders back and forth across the cliff face.

"How hard is it to make the climb?" I yell.

"It's narrow," he yells back, "but solid. I think we can transport the kids up here in small groups. There's a gap near the top, but I can lift them up if one of you hoists them from beneath. I'm going to find out how high it is. I'll be right back."

His feet disappear into the opening above his head as he lifts himself through.

It seems like an eternity, but he's gone only several minutes. Impatiently, I shift my weight from foot to foot, unable to stand still. I yell, "Colt?"

"Colt, Colt, Colt," echoes back from the deep cavern. Still no response. I try again.

"Colt?"

"Colt, Colt, Colt."

I start for the path, when I finally hear my name echo back from the hole in the cavernous ceiling.

"Jax, Jax, Jax. Come here, here, here. You've got to see this, see this, see this!"

I climb the ledge, reaching higher with each turn. When at last Colt is in sight, I shout, "Have you found the way out?"

He jumps back through the opening to the rocky path, and hugs me. Then he practically lifts me into the opening above my head.

The rock wall on either side of the opening is warm, but not hot. I find myself lying on a smooth, rocky grotto floor, but it's not the fox's cave. It appears to be carved from the mountain in levels, like an amphitheater, and at the front stands a rock ledge that serves as a table.

Colt lifts my elbow on his way to that ledge. I can barely keep up with him.

"Look at this. I had no idea anything like this existed. Did you?"

It takes me a moment to realize what he's talking about. I stare at the wall behind the ledge.

We're in an ancient meeting place. The paintings on the wall do not lie. Sunlight from the shaft that passes through the grotto reflects off four symbols: a droplet, either rain or tear, a sun, a heart, and finally, an oak leaf. Inscriptions are carved into the stone beneath each. *Earth's blood. Earth's light. Earth's love. Earth's bounty.*

"Do you know what this is?" He doesn't even give me a chance to answer. "It's the Eco's congregation chamber."

"They must have met here in secret. That would explain why they all moved out to the country."

He points to the symbols. "These were their philosophical beliefs. The sun for the Earth's light." He pulls his golden charm from beneath his shirt. "My grandfather gave me this when I was twelve. It was his."

"All of the Eco leaders must have had one." I pull Nonna's watch from beneath Romeo's doublet to show Colt the oak leaf hanging on the chain. "Daphne gave me this at Culpepper's mansion that first night. She said something about failing my mother, but she said she would not fail me."

I hold it next to Colt's sun. It's made of the same metal.

"She also said my grandmother bestowed her charm on me, something about my watch."

Nonna's watch rattles as I hold it up. *I always thought it was a loose mechanism inside.*

Colt pries off the back, and a golden filigree droplet falls to the ground. I pluck it between my fingers, and place it next to the other two.

"It must be the Earth's elements, those needed to preserve life. Growth. Sun. Water."

"But what about the heart?" asks Colt. "The love of Earth?"

"I'm not sure, but I think Astoria has it. Didn't Rafe drop a golden heart in her hand just before he died? I thought it was his way of telling her he would always love her."

"It was," said Colt. "And it makes perfect sense. St. Sally raised him. He was the closest thing she had to a grandson. She probably passed hers on to him."

"So now we have all of them, but what are these notches in the rock wall under each symbol?"

Colt leans close to inspect the tiny indentations. "They look like minute impressions of the large symbol above it."

I join him in his examination. "They're fine and delicate, like the charms."

Our eyes meet with a certainty.

Colt pulls his sun charm from his neck, and places it into the small sun impression.

Suddenly, the sound of sliding granite alarms us. We bolt straight up and turn around.

A small section of the stone table in the center of the amphitheater rises.

I run to examine a three-dimensional oblong rock in the shape of a rectangle. A thin seam near the top indicates it's a box, but I can't open it.

"Let me try." Colt forces the top, until his fingertips turn white. It won't budge.

I raise Nonna's gold droplet. "These are more than pretty charms. They're keys to something the Ecos held most dear."

"Try yours."

I place Nonna's droplet into its similar impression. Again, the granite behind me slides, but it sounds louder.

"Look at this," yells Colt. Another box is rising, but the first one has receded.

I dart to where Colt stands and run my hand along the granite's smooth surface.

"Colt, this isn't a table. It's an altar."

He checks his charm. It came back from the impression when the first box returned into the altar.

"Maybe they need to be pressed simultaneously?"

"Good idea." I return. Nonna's droplet is still in the wall, but I remove Daphne's oak leaf from Romeo's doublet, and insert it under its corresponding symbol.

The droplet box recedes, but none other stands above the altar.

"This is strange."

We try each charm individually again, and all three corresponding boxes rise in conjunction with its charm, but we can't open any of them.

Colt shakes his head and he strokes his chin. "This doesn't make sense."

"Unless each charm needs to be used in conjunction with the other. We only have three. Astoria has the other one." Heaviness settles in my chest thinking of Rafe's sacrifice, but Colt's excitement chases it away.

"Then let's get the kids and Astoria up here."

* * * * *

We make our way back down the steep, rocky path and stop at the rock where I left Romeo's sleeves.

I use the laces to tie one sleeve around my bald head, as a hat

"Oh, that reminds me." Colt reaches into his duffle, still on the rock. "Astoria said you might want this."

He holds out Juliet's wig. "At least, you'll look pretty normal when we get to Antarctica."

I playfully punch his shoulder again. I flip the wig on my head, and tie the sleeve over it. "Yeah, now the kids won't be afraid of me."

"What about your cape?" He pulls it up from the rock.

A grin spreads across my face. I wrap the cape around the waistband of the breeches, then fasten it at the back.

We enter the main cave. Most of the children sleep snuggled next to each other, heads on laps and bellies. Nyla and the little girl from our doorstep nestle on either side of Andy, and Squeakers sleeps in his cage near Andy's head.

A little girl with a bedraggled bow in her honey-wheat hair sleeps between Alder and Astoria.

I smile. "I'll wake them. You get Cheinstein."

"Astoria." I nudge her shoulder.

She wakes immediately.

"Is something wrong?" She squints her good eye with concern.

"No." I beam. "Actually, everything is fine. It couldn't be better."

Alder wakes at our conversation, and carrying the little girl with him, joins Cheinstein and Colt waking up the children.

"Is that his sister?" I ask.

"Yes," says Astoria. "I think she looks just like him."

"I'm happy for him, and you, and me." I twirl away to wake Andy, Nyla, and the little girl from our doorstep. "Wait a minute." Astoria jumps up, and spins me back toward her. Her gaze lands on the cape, then the turned skirt, and her mouth falls open.

My eyebrows rise. "It's not what you think."

"Oh, yes, it is. Welcome to the joy of womanhood, Jax." She hugs me.

I return her embrace.

The men have all of the children up and waiting in a group as I approach.

"Listen, boys and girls. We're going on another adventure." I motion with my hands as I explain. "Through a tunnel, and into a beautiful fairyland cave with a shining blue lake. Then, we're going to climb up a rocky path to a smaller cave where the sun shines to show us the way. I need you to divide into three groups. I want the younger children in the first group, and the older ones in the second, so they can help lift the little and the middle ones." I nod. "Can you do that for me?"

The children arrange themselves, but we need to make some changes.

"I'll take the youngest children and Miss Astoria first. The rest of you wait here for me."

Andy runs to my side. "Why can't I come with you, Jax?"

"You will Andy, but you'll be in the last group with Alder. You know why?"

He pouts as he shakes his head.

"Because you're not a baby anymore. I want you to stay close to Nyla. You'll be in her group."

"But she's seven." His eyes brighten. He straightens his shoulders. "You're right. I am bigger. I even share."

He hands Nonna's book to Nyla, wraps his arms around Squeaker's cage and sits back down to wait for his group's turn.

"Okay, boys and girls, are you ready to sing?"

"Yes," is their overwhelming response.

Colt leads the way, Astoria is in the back, and the children follow behind me.

I sing.

"The children go marching one by one, hurrah, hurrah.

The children go marching one by one, hurrah, hurrah.

The children go marching one by one, the little one stops to look for the sun,

and they all go marching up through the earth to a new, happy home, Boom! Boom! Boom!"

After the youngest group is situated in the amphitheater with Astoria, Cheinstein leads the oldest, gathered near the opening to help hoist the middle-aged group.

Andy's group, led by Alder, brings up the rear.

Chapter Twenty-Four

The children gather on the stone benches. Some stretch out to sleep more. Others continue to sing, as I persuade Astoria away from Alder and his sister.

"Colt and I discovered something extraordinary. We want you to help us solve a mystery."

"How can I help?"

"We need you to use the charm Rafe gave you. It turns out it's more than an expression of his love for you."

In the sunlit cave, it's easy to see Astoria's cheeks flush. She pulls the charm from one of the patch pockets on her gown.

I grasp her hand and lead her to the rock wall with the symbols. "You stand here, in front of the heart. Colt and I will stand in front of the rest.

When I say push, insert the heart charm into the small indentation beneath the painted symbol. Okay?"

"Got it." She stands poised, waiting.

I hand Nonna's droplet charm to Colt, since it's to the right of his grandfather's sun symbol. He stretches to reach both. Astoria stands before the heart with St. Sally's charm. I use Daphne's oak leaf.

"Now!"

Colt, Astoria, and I insert the four charms. Nothing happens.

"This is absurd. There's got to be a reason."

Cheinstein wanders over to witness our efforts. "Perhaps they need to be pressed in sequence? Earth, Water, Sun, Leaf."

"It's worth a try. You go first, Astoria."

She pushes, then Colt, then I push mine. Still nothing.

"The secret is in the order," says Cheinstein.

"We did that already."

Cheinstein strokes his chin. His eyes have a faraway look. "Maybe the answer lies in who is inserting the key. Maybe a code scans it from the fingertip, like a recognized print or a DNA reading."

Realization hits. "So only an Eco can open the boxes! That sounds typical of the Eco philosophy. Only those who believe they can save the Earth, will. Let me try something. We got two boxes up before. Let's try out Cheinstein's theory. You go first."

Colt inserts the sun and the second box rises.

Then I insert the droplet. The third box rises and the second one recedes.

"Now you, Astoria."

She inserts the heart and nothing happens.

"Damn, you're right, Cheinstein. Whatever mechanism they incorporated into this rock is high tech. It would have taken a genius to develop it, and hide it so well in such a massive rock."

Before my words leave my mouth, Cheinstein and I exchange knowing glances. As I stare into his eyes, I feel a tug at my clothes.

"What are you doing, Jax? Can I play, too?" Andy pokes his tiny finger into the heart impression in front of Astoria. The rock grinds behind us, and the first Earth box rises.

"Well, that pretty much proves Cheinstein's theory." I place my hands on Andy's shoulders. "Stay here, Andy. We need your help."

"I can help?" His eyes grow wide.

"Yes. I told you, you're a big boy now." I ruffle his hair. "We're going to need your help in many ways."

Astoria's interest focuses on Alder, trying to settle a few rambunctious children who have decided to play tag in the amphitheater instead of sleeping. "If you don't need me anymore, I know someone who does."

She leaves, and we turn to Cheinstein, who studies the rising and falling stone boxes. "These four boxes should rise when the keys are pushed simultaneously. The electromagnetic configuration of the mechanism is armed with the DNA recognition stimulus, which, when triggered at the same time, allows access to the rising action of the—

"Thanks, Cheinstein." I smile and turn to Colt. "We got it."

He nods. "Ready when you are, Jax."

"Andy, I need you to push Astoria's charm into the small picture of a heart when Cheinstein tells you to. Okay?"

"I'm ready, Jax." He beams as he stands tall, so sure of himself, his tiny finger pointing toward the rock wall.

Cheinstein stands in front of the granite altar. "Now."

Colt, Andy, and I push at the same time.

My grin spreads, as multiple grindings of rock on granite sound behind me.

We leave the wall to join Cheinstein.

Colt presses the lid of the first box, and it releases, popping open a half-inch. He lifts the top, and we peer inside. A green journal, filled with research, tops waterproof-sealed packages of dirt: red clay, black topsoil, brown dirt with white specks, volcanic ash, pink sand, and on and on.

Cheinstein lifts two of the packages. "These are dirt samples from across the entire world."

While Cheinstein lectures us on different soils of the Earth, Colt presses the three other tops. Each contains a journal of research and samples of that element. Water samples, artificial light sources for indoor growing, and lastly, super-calibrated, genetically altered seeds. Packets for vegetables, flowers, bushes and trees, all hermetically sealed.

Cheinstein acts like a child on an old-fashioned Christmas morning. Each stone box brings him joy, but as he pulls out the seed packets, his slow smile grows into a wide, satisfied grin. His face grows bright.

His mouth drops open as he inspects the seed packages. He reads the label aloud, almost dazed by the words: *Super-Genetic Seeds: Species altered for multi-climate control. Dr. Xiao Mei Li.*

I pull a packet from his hand. "We'll take these with us."

Cheinstein finds his voice. "Oh, yes, most definitely. I can continue my mother's study and—"

"Someday," I say, "we can bring these to the areas of the world most desperate to survive Earth's changing atmosphere."

Colt adds, "It's up to us to carry out the Ecos' plan for the world. We're their legacy. Whatever we do to cure Earth's ills will benefit mankind everywhere, despite assholes like Culpepper."

"We'll start with the children, and teach them all we know about nature and how to preserve the Earth."

I hold on tight, as Colt swings me around.

"You did it," he yells. "You got rid of the rats, and you took the kids. You got over on that bastard."

"No, *we* did it. We all did. I couldn't have gotten Andy back without every one of you helping me." My eyes drop. My happiness evaporates, as I whisper, "Especially Rafe and Mrs. Green."

"They knew the danger. They were willing to take the risk. Look, we took every child in Metro City except the one who wanted to stay with

Culpepper. That counts for something. We're going to help save the world, one child at a time."

"But St. Sally and Daphne are still there."

"That's a good thing. They're two of the original Ecos. The people of Metro City are going to need them, to demonstrate how to survive."

"Well, they do have Mrs. Li's aquaponic fishery in the museum's basement."

"And her stash of super-pollinated seeds," adds Cheinstein.

Colt leans back against the stone altar. "Now that Culpepper is no longer an Air Care-a-Van customer, he's going to be hard pressed to feed his Megamark Guards and scientists. His power is going to hell, just like his city."

I feel lines form between my sparsely bristled brows, as I squint. "What do you mean? How can you be so sure the air caravan won't still make its scheduled rounds, and bring him his fuel, steak, and wine?"

Colt doesn't hear me. He's so wrapped up in our discovery he darts across the amphitheater to an arched wooden door at the back of the cave, lifts the bolt, and then flings wide the door.

"Colt," I yell, following him to the open door. "What are you doing?"

The hot midday sun pours into the cool chamber, mixing with the shaft of light from above. Beyond the brilliant light is a mountain meadow that once bloomed with wildflowers. In their place stands burned grass, surrounded by dead trees.

He rushes to the middle of the meadow before I can stop him.

"Come back!" I yell from the safety of the cave's entrance.

Colt pivots, a radio controller he pulls from his belt in one hand. After signaling in every direction, he darts back. The few minutes' exposure to the hot sun blisters his skin.

I pull him into the cool safety of the amphitheater.

"Well, that's it." He rubs his hands together, excited to get started. "Now, all we have to do is wait. I just radioed my copilot. After he delivers the rest of the food and supplies to the barren, rocky desert in Egypt, he should be back to pick us up. The children will have no trouble filling the empty caravan."

Colt chuckles, even though his red skin looks painful.

"I heard you." Colt's expression suggests he's the only one who knows he has a secret. "To answer your question—because I crossed him off the client list."

He throws his arm around my neck.

I push off his shoulder and leap back. "You mean *you*—"

"Not me. It's my father's company. He didn't want me to go back to Metro City. He hates Culpepper, but my grandfather convinced me, when I was a boy, never to abandon the things that mean the most to me. And though Culpepper thought I was under his employ, it was the best way to bring fresh food and water to the Ecos still in the area. Didn't you ever wonder why St. Sally and Daphne knew me so well?"

"It crossed my mind, but I had other things more important to consider at the time! How did you get the supplies to them without everyone knowing?"

"Hoffmann played his part well. He had no idea I used him as a front. I actually bartered with him for some of the vegetables. He sold them to the vendors for exorbitant prices, but the Altar Boys picked up crates of sun-dried vegetables and a few fresh meats at sunrise, when everyone else retreated underground. Rafe was my chief contact."

I gasp, pressing my hand to my chest. "I had no idea."

"Why would you?" Colt shakes his head. "That's the whole point of a covert operation."

"Well, that would explain the meat he'd bring for me to cook. He cut it up so small, I always thought it was squirrel or groundhog. I never questioned what kind of animal it was."

As we approach the center of the amphitheater, Astoria rocks Alder's little sister. He kneels at her side.

Cheinstein fills Colt's duffle with the contents of the stone boxes, and Andy sits at his feet, pouting. He holds his cheeks in his hands, while Nyla tries to read to him.

It's a perfect time for us to snuggle. I sit cross-legged next to him, and pull him close in a hug. His face scrunches.

"Why is Tori with that little girl and soldier instead of us?"

"That's Alder and his little sister. Astoria is going to live with them when we get to the New Continent."

"Why?" His platinum eyebrows furrow. "Doesn't she love us anymore?"

"Of course she does." I tighten my embrace. "But we have Nyla. She's going to be your new sister-friend."

Nyla smiles and hugs Andy.

He crinkles his nose.

"What about Cheinstein?" He looks up with admiration. "Is he going to live with us, too?"

"No. Cheinstein will attend the University in Antarctica. He's going to become a very famous doctor or scientist one day."

"Well, what about that big man over there with the red face? Why is he staring at us?"

"That's Colt. He's a friend of mine, and yours, too. I think it would be nice if he came and lived with us."

Andy frowns. "He's so big, he'll eat all of our food."

"Not where we're going. There'll be plenty of food."

"Where are we going, Jax?" asks Nyla.

"That's a good question. Boys and girls, could you come gather around me so I can tell you about the next part of our adventure?"

Nyla and Andy squeeze closer to me.

The other children sit or kneel behind them.

"Nyla has asked where we're going. I'd like to share the answer with all of you. We're going to a joyous land, where waterfalls gush over mountaintops, and trees grow sweet fruit. Flowers, the colors of the rainbow, blossom in every garden, and each of you can play in the sun."

Some of the children balk. It's clear they cannot comprehend standing in the midday sun.

"The skies are blue, and birds sing all day long. Puppies will play with you, and spotted, baby deer will run with you. Bees make sweet honey from the flowers for your taste buds' delight, and you can ride horses that gallop like the wind."

"It sounds wonderful," says Andy.

"It is, buddy." Colt offers Andy his hand, man to man, and they shake.

Andy studies his new family and smiles.

I continue. "Tomorrow is July 22, 2511. It's the first day of our new lives."

Andy and Nyla get to know Colt, and I contemplate what tomorrow may bring. As our new lives start, I can't help but think Culpepper will also be starting a new life, one he never envisioned for himself—stinking and dowsed in darkness, scratching through the alleys to sniff out morsels of food—the life of a rat!

* * * * *

"We are orphans. We use our brains and our bodies to make this a better world. We thrive in Eden Springs. Our futures are as bright as the sun."
Jax Stone

Made in the USA
Charleston, SC
08 April 2013